# Paparazzi Princesses

**BRIA WILLIAMS & REGINAE CARTER**

WITH *KARYN FOLAN*

CASH MONEY CONTENT

PAPARAZZI PRINCESSES

First Trade Hardcover Edition: June 2013

Book Layout: Jacquelynne Hudson

Cover Design: J. Marison

For further information log onto www.CashMoneyContent.com

Library of Congress Control Number: 2012953938

ISBN: 978-1-936399-35-2 Hardcover
ISBN: 978-1-936399-36-9 ebook

2   4   6   8   10   9   7   5   3   1

Printed in the United States

# Paparazzi Princesses

# Chapter One

## KAYLA

"Where are they?" I was running like a crazy person between the suite at the Beverly Hills Hotel that my mom and I were sharing and the one that my so-called sister, Promise, and her mom, Bella, were in, wearing nothing but one of those nice plush bathrobes they always have at the nicer places. I had just taken my shower and was waiting for the lady to come and do my hair. I found my pants and top in the closet where we'd put them, but my shoes—my beautiful fuchsia Christian Louboutins in the exact same shade as the little ties along the side of my perfectly ripped T-shirt—were gone. Gone!

"Where are my shoes?" I bellowed in a panic. "Mom! The shoes are gone!"

"They can't be!" Mom came running in from the adjoining room, where she'd been helping Bella decide between the two possible outfit options she'd laid out for the night: an orange micro-mini-dress with cold shoulder sleeves or a purple tunic with a rhinestone-studded leather belt. Bella can wear colors like that really well, because her skin is the most flawless shade of amber brown you've ever seen.

We were all going to the Mickies—the Music Choice Awards—and we were going to get our pictures taken. Or at least, most of us were. My mom (her name is Mara) avoids that kind of thing and usually just stands back, holding our purses while the cameras are flashing. She says she prefers to remain anonymous, which I think sounds very exotic and mysterious. She's not a singer or a dancer and really doesn't have any interest in being in any part of the entertainment industry, but she'll sit with all of us and enjoy the ceremony. She just doesn't want to get her picture taken. But this time, for the first time, I—Kayla Jones—was going to walk the red carpet with my dad, head of the Big Dollar music empire, Lullabye Jones. Promise's dad, Terry Walker—you know him by his stage name, IDK—was up for just about every award they give at the Mickies, and we were all there to support him.

But for me, it was more than the excitement of attending the awards show. Tonight would be my first time on the red carpet, and I knew I had to look great.

See, unlike the awards for acting, where the stars always dress up in fancy party dresses, the music awards are edgier. People dress both more casually and more daringly. For example, one of IDK's artists—Lilly Day—dressed up like a sexy nun. One year, another artist wore a bikini. I'm not trying to go that far (and my parents wouldn't let me if I wanted to), so I spent a lot of time trying to come up with something that said "hip" and "youthful" but also made it clear to everyone that Kayla Jones wasn't a baby anymore.

So, after spending hours going through my "Look Book"

(a notebook I started about a year ago of pictures and drawings and things that I like), even more hours on the Internet checking out styles from stores all over the world, and even *more* hours thinking about how to make a fresh twist on them that would be appropriate for an almost-teen girl attending the Mickies with her dad and mom, I settled on a pair of white skinny jeans with silver-sequined cuffs.

On top, I picked a silver camisole covered by a white T-shirt that had been strategically slit along the top and the sides to show my left shoulder and then tied with fuchsia ribbons along the side seams. I knew I would wear my hair in a sleek side ponytail over the front of the bare left shoulder. I'm usually not allowed to wear makeup, but since this was a special event and there would be photographers everywhere snapping pictures, I'd chosen a pink lip and a neutral eye.

And the fuchsia flats . . . only now, less than two hours from the start of the show, the shoes were gone.

Mom looked in the closet and then started moving the few items of clothing hanging in there around as if the shoes might have magically jumped into one of the pockets.

"But—I don't understand. They were right *here*!" She gave me a suspicious look. "You haven't been wearing them, have you?"

"No!" I said, probably a little too quickly, because her eyebrow went up. "OK, I slipped them on yesterday when we were unpacking—but just for a second. I put them right back!"

My mom was crawling around on the floor. She reached out as if they might be under the bed, but the bed was on a platform, and there was no way anything could be under it. She picked up my suitcase and dumped everything inside it out onto the thick white comforter. I had unpacked everything but a couple of pairs of underwear, an old T-shirt, and an extra pair of pajamas, and it all spilled out in a messy hodgepodge.

But no shoes.

"I could have sworn . . ." she muttered, unzipping the special shoe caddy in the front of my Louis Vuitton. You could tell just by looking at it that it was empty, but she felt all inside it anyway. Then she grabbed her own suitcase and gave it the same treatment, while Bella—that's Promise's mom—looked around the room as if the shoes might have put their feet up in the side chair or decided to sit down at the writing desk.

No shoes.

"Are you sure you brought them?" Bella asked. She padded through the open door to the adjoining room and started going through her things. "The girls were bouncing back and forth between rooms. Maybe they got mixed in with mine . . ." She pulled out one sky-high pair of shoes after another. One pair was even the exact same shade of fuchsia as my missing pair, and I could tell from the red soles that they were the same brand as mine. But mine were flats, and there was no way my mom was going to let me borrow Bella's six-inch spikes and go clomping down the red carpet . . . even though I know I would have been *fierce*!

"Promise?" Deidre, Bella's assistant, headed for the corner of the bedroom, where Promise had stowed her bright pink peace-sign-covered luggage. "Do you think they might have gotten mixed in with your stuff?"

Promise was lying on the sofa in their suite, flipping channels as if there wasn't a problem—or, since the problem wasn't *hers*, as if she didn't care. It was starting to make me mad.

"No," she murmured in a bored voice. "Her stuff's been in her room, not in mine."

"Promise!" Bella said sharply. "Help Kayla look for her shoes!" She cut her eyes at Deidre, and Deidre hurried to Promise's luggage and started searching.

"Go ahead and look. They aren't here, Mom," Promise said. "You all have been looking for the past twenty minutes, and you haven't found them. They aren't here. She must have left them at home—"

"I didn't!" I was sure I hadn't left them. I remembered zipping them into my suitcase. I remembered seeing them in the closet—and I remembered seeing them on my feet—and so did Promise, since putting them on in the first place had been her idea. We'd modeled our outfits for each other last night after we'd checked in while our moms were hanging out together in the other suite. We weren't supposed to, of course—they were afraid we'd get them messy. Promise was just covering her butt by saying that I'd left them. "I had those shoes yesterday, and you know it, Promise Walker."

Normally, if you back Promise into a corner, she'll come out swinging. I braced myself for her to say something crazy to keep her mom from finding out about our little game of dress-up, but instead, she just shrugged her shoulders and pressed the button on the remote again, as if she was too bored to get involved with anything.

That didn't make any sense. We were about to go to the Mickies! We were about to walk the red carpet! And if there's anyone alive who loves to get her picture taken more than Promise, well, I haven't met her. Lately, though, whenever we were together, that's how she acted: as if I was the most boring person alive and she'd rather watch her toenails grow than spend another second with me.

"No. We definitely brought them," Mom said, opening the closet again. "I put them in here yesterday when we arrived. The whole outfit was hanging here. The clothes in the garment bag and the shoes on the floor."

"Maybe the maid stole them." Promise offered without looking up from the television. I knew that she'd been to things like this before—much more than I had—but come on. There's no way the TV was more interesting than what we were about to do.

"We've stayed here lots of times and never had a problem with anything like that," Bella said.

"Until now, Mom." Promise rolled her eyes as if she was worldlier than all of us put together. "Some people steal."

"That is true," Deidre agreed. She has her hair cut really short—almost as short as a dude's—but she always wears some kind of big dangling earrings to keep it feminine. Today she had some long blue peacock feathers that brushed her shoulders. I usually see her in jeans, but she had dressed up some today, in black slacks and top with a portrait neckline. "Sad but very, very true."

Promise pretended none of us existed. I was about two seconds from crossing the room and smacking her when my mom said, "Well, whatever happened to them, we've got to do something."

She dropped the suitcase she was holding and grabbed her purse. "She can't wear any of our shoes. I'm going to run out and buy another pair before it's too late."

"Oh, I can do that for you, Mara," Deidre volunteered.

She's like that—always the first to jump in and help. I've always sort of wished she worked for us because she really likes kids and makes things fun. But Mom says she doesn't need an assistant because her life isn't like Bella's. Bella has had several reality shows—the last one was called *Being Bella*, and it was all about her family—and just recently, she started getting movie roles. Nothing big yet, but I think it's just a matter of time. She's really busy and sometimes has to travel, so they need Deidre to get Promise back and forth to school and keep their schedules and stuff. My mom's just a mom. Raising me and my brother, JJ, is her only career.

"Thanks, Deidre. That's sweet of you, but I think I've got a good idea of what Kayla had in mind," Mom said.

"Do you want me to come?" I asked.

"No, Kayla. I know your size, and it will be better if you stay here. Stephanie will be over in a little bit to do your hair."

"But what about you? Don't you need to get ready?"

Mom laid her hand on my head. "This one is about you, sweetheart. Tonight your dad wants to show you off. That's why you get to walk the red carpet: your dad thinks it's time people learned more about you. He's so excited for you to start your own career. It's almost like those things they used to have in the old days. A coming-out party."

Promise's head swiveled away from the TV. "Coming out?" she wisecracked, her lips twisted with mischief. "Is Kayla gay?"

Bella swatted Promise on the bottom. "Not like that. Like a debutante. You know what that is?"

Promise shook her head. To be honest, I had never heard of it, either.

"Google it," Bella said. "In the old days, girls used to wear a pretty white dress and be presented to society. Even black girls used do it, some of them. Tonight Kayla's wearing her white jeans and T-shirt, and she's gonna step out as the next generation of the Big Dollar empire."

"I'm going, too," Promise whined. "Am I stepping out as the next generation of Young Dollar?"

Young Dollar is Terry's label, but it's a part of Big Dollar, too. Since Terry/IDK is my dad's adopted son—and my adopted brother—you could say that with us, everything is all in the family.

Bella hesitated. I saw her take a quick glance at my mom, and I thought the look meant something like "See what I have to deal with?" but she didn't say that. "Of course," she said soothingly. "But you've been to these things before. This is Kayla's first time. It's supposed to be special." She smiled. "Besides, you'll be stepping out for real *for real* when you perform with the LOL Girls at the Georgia Stars of Stage and Screen event next month, right?"

"Oh, yeah." Promise shot me a look that said, "Ha! I'm going to be performing, and you're not!" then smiled a smile that was all challenge. She was daring me to come for her. Daring me!

It was a low blow, and she knew it. I've been working with a vocal coach for the past six months, trying to become as good a singer as she is without any lessons at all. It's hard for me. No matter how hard I work, I can't seem to keep on key, and my voice teacher was so frustrated with me that every lesson was like a trip to a torture chamber. I had told Promise that one night when I just needed someone to listen to me, someone to be on my side for a second. And now here she was, throwing it back at me?

"What are you trying to say, Promise?" I demanded. "What. Are. You. Trying. To. Say?"

"Nothing!" Promise said innocently. "I really don't know what you're getting so mad about, Kayla."

"You know exactly what I'm mad about, Promise!" I screamed, stepping into her face. "You can make all the snide remarks you want, but you and I both know you took my shoes—"

Deidre stepped between us. "Hey, now, hey, now. It's just a pair of shoes. Nothing to fight over, right? You have dozens and dozens of pairs of shoes. Now, don't worry, honey," she said kindly. "I know you're going to look perfect. You'll make your daddy proud."

I was still pretty mad, but I let it go. I really didn't want my mom to start yelling at me for knocking Promise into next week, so I turned away from Promise without saying another word to her.

That's how it is between us a lot of the time. We're practically sisters, but sometimes we act like competitors. I'm not sure why. We're supposed to be family. Maybe that's the reason right there. Promise is a little less than a year younger than I am—she turns thirteen in November—but we've been hanging out since we were in diapers. When we all lived in New Orleans, we had fun together . . . but of course, we were little then. Now she lives in Atlanta, and I live in Miami, and when we get together, all we do is argue.

"I'd better get going. It'll be fine. I'll be back in no time, OK?" Mom said.

I nodded. "OK. Thanks, Mom. Oh, wait . . ." I hurried into the bedroom and pulled my Look Book from my suitcase, flipping the pages carefully until I found the right one. "Don't even try to match the pink. The wrong shade will ruin it. Go for something silver. Silver's less likely to clash." I pointed to a picture. "Something like this will work."

Mom shot Bella her own "Look what I have to deal with" look.

"OK, Kayla," she said, sticking her card key into her pocket as she headed for the door.

An image came to my mind like a flash.

"Mom? Did you bring your little Marc Jacobs sundress? The black one?"

Mom frowned in confusion. "Yes, but why?"

"You should wear it." My mom doesn't step out as often as Promise's mom, but she's got a perfect figure, with a tiny waist and big hips and thighs. That dress always made her look like a superstar. I took her long, straight black hair and piled it up in a messy pony. "And your hair like this. Big gold hoops. Black patent wedges." I nodded in satisfaction. "You'll have everyone saying, 'Who's that?' and it'll only take a few minutes to pull together."

Mom laughed. "Thank you, Kayla. I think that's exactly what I'll do."

"You got any suggestions for me?" Bella asked.

"The purple dress," I said immediately. "It's your color. Gold shoes and jewelry. Big curly hair."

Bella nodded. "I was thinking that, too." She shook her head. "You've got a gift, Kayla Jones. No doubt about it."

I loved hearing that. And I loved it even more when Promise rolled her eyes and glared at me. She can't stand it when I get more attention than she does.

My mom left, and I went back to my room. Even though the connecting door was still open, I didn't hear anything from Promise's suite. Even the TV had gone silent. It didn't matter to me; I was done with her. Yeah, in another couple of hours, we'd probably pose together on the red carpet, getting our pictures taken as the next generation of our fathers' music dynasty. But that was for the paparazzi and the fans. For real, I was just done with that shoe-stealing heifer.

And when Khrissy, one of the biggest stars in the music industry—so big she doesn't even need to use her last name— walked up to me right after the awards show was over and said, "Kayla Jones, you look fabulous!" all I wanted to do was make sure that Promise knew that despite her best efforts, I'd won.

I'm normally not starstruck at all. We were at the Mickies, after all; there were famous people everywhere. You couldn't turn around without bumping into someone whose latest hit you just downloaded onto your iPod or whose video you just saw on VH1. Because of who my dad is, I've met so many famous people that most of the time, I'm not even impressed. Some of the people you listen to on the radio come over to my house for dinner, kick off their shoes, and burp and scratch themselves like an annoying cousin who works your last nerve. And of course, I grew up with Terry—IDK—and he's probably the hottest rapper in the world right now. Lots of people are in awe of him, not just because of his talent but because of the tattoos all over his face and body. But to me, he's just Terry, his actress ex-wife is just Bella, and their daughter, Promise, is like my sister.

I'm telling you all that just so you know: I'm no stranger to celebrities. But meeting Khrissy? That was different.

I've heard her voice on the radio like three million times. I know the dance for "Lock It" so well that I can do it in my sleep, and I've seen her movie *Glamorous* so many times that I can recite whole sections of it. I know one of the other actors won an Oscar, but if you ask me, Khrissy deserved one, too.

My dad also likes her . . . but more because she *sells*. She sells a *lot*.

"That's the kind of artist I want you to be . . . only better," my dad whispered to me when Khrissy and her husband took their seats on the other side of the Kodak Theatre in Los Angeles.

"She sings, she dances, she acts, and she's got a crossover kind of look," he continued. "The look is the easy part, but you gotta keep up with your lessons, Kayla. Yeah, I got all kinds of software that can help a singer get the notes right. But Auto-Tune can only cover so much, you understand? You're my daughter, and the public's gonna expect more than that."

"Yes, Dad," I said, nodding. But even though he was talking about the singing and dancing classes I take every day after school, all I could think about was the *look*. Dad thinks it's easy to put clothes together, but I know it's not. I mean, you have to think about everything: hair, jewelry, shoes, makeup, even underwear. If you step out with panty lines showing, it's not going to matter how well you sing. You're going to be labeled as "ratchet," and that's going to be the end of it.

That's why I love Khrissy so much. Even more than because of her talent, I love her because she's totally beautiful and has an incredible sense of style. She's got long hair the color of cinnamon, and her skin is the same shade as brown sugar. For the Mickies, she was wearing her hair in big, fluffy curls that cascaded away from her face and down her back like a mane. Her dress was this sheer-looking tunic that reminded me of a peacock: greens and blues and blacks and golds all dancing around in a pattern with a keyhole neckline. I hadn't seen anything like it in any of the fashion magazines yet; I'm guessing it was made just for her. And it looked perfect on her, too, not just because it worked her skin tone but also because she's got just the right amount of junk in her trunk to make a dress like that do what it's supposed to. You have to have curves to wear dresses like that—and I don't have curves in any places yet.

"You're only twelve," my mom always says when I start talking about how I don't have any kind of figure at all: no boobs yet and no "badunkadonk." Most of the girls my age have one or the other; some of them have both.

"Don't worry about it." Easy for her to say; my mom has curves, too. No one is going to call her a "pirate's dream." (Sunken chest—get it?) She's not that big on top, but at least you can tell she's a woman. And my mom has all kinds of curves on the bottom.

"Wow! I had no idea you were such a fashionista," Khrissy said. "Can we get a picture together?"

"Really?" I was so excited I could have done a back flip over the first three rows of chairs in the slowly emptying auditorium. Someone—one of Khrissy's assistants, I guessed—immediately stepped up to take a shot. "Mom!" I said urgently, but she was already pulling my iPhone out of her purse to take the picture for me. Khrissy dropped an arm around me, and I was glad for the hours I'd spent standing in front of the mirror in my room, practicing smiling. This picture *had* to be cute. It just had to be.

"Very nice," my mom said as she handed me back my phone, but I didn't look at the photo right then.

"She's really something," Khrissy said to my mother.

"Fashion is her one true love." Mom laughed. "I only wish she worked as hard on other things."

"And what are you ladies talking about?"

My dad had been taping some kind of interview with Terry. I'd seen the camera and the lights on them several feet away, but I guessed they were done now, because he stepped over to us and put his hand on my shoulder. Dad was wearing his Versace sunglasses with diamonds in the temples and a bright sparkling diamond the size of an ice cube in each of his ears. Other than that bling, he was dressed simply: a custom-made Armani black T-shirt that hugged the muscles in his chest and revealed the sleeves of tattoos on his strong brown arms and a pair of dark jeans above a pair of Jordans.

"How are you, Khrissy?"

"Congratulations, Lullabye," Khrissy said. "IDK did really well tonight. I was just talking to your lovely daughter about her outfit. She wears clothes wonderfully."

"Oh." Dad didn't sound happy. "Did she tell you she sings?"

"Really?"

Dad nodded. His eyes were invisible behind his dark glasses, but his soft, laid-back voice had just the smallest edge to it. "We hope to be putting out her first album in another year or so. Watch. She'll be performing at the Mickies next year. Believe it."

*Never.*

That was the word that popped into my mind, but I held my face still, with that stupid smile as if it had been painted there. Inside, though, my stomach flipped a little. The thought of performing in a space as large as the Kodak made me want to throw up. The thought of performing in front of *anyone* made me want to throw up.

"That's wonderful! Then she's multitalented." Khrissy must have heard the edge in my dad's voice, because she suddenly looked nervous. "Well . . . I don't know if Kayla would be interested in this, but I'm starting a clothing line, and I think she would be a perfect model for the brand."

Modeling?

"Oh, my God!" I couldn't stop myself. I grabbed my mom's arm in excitement, practically bouncing on the toes of my replacement silver flats. "Oh, wow! Can I? Please?"

If I could have smiled any wider, I think my face would have cracked down the middle. The image of me on a giant billboard, with a cool metal-free smile on my face, in the cutest outfit I could imagine, filled my mind. Maybe I could be like Tyra Banks or—gulp—Mary-Kate and Ashley Olsen! In seconds, I'd move past modeling to create "KJ by Kayla Jones," a whole label for girls my age distributed in stores nationwide to record-breaking sales. And finally, people would know that even though I'm recording industry legend Lullabye Jones's daughter, my passion is fashion, not—

My dad shook his head. "No. Kayla's focus is on music right now," he said simply. "If she takes any pictures, it's going to be for the CD jacket—and that's all."

"But Dad, I'd be great at it! I'm always practicing poses, and people tell me I have an interesting face and the right body type. Please! Couldn't I at least try it?"

As I said, he was wearing his sunglasses, so I couldn't see his eyes, but his jaw tightened, and his lips clamped down tight over his platinum-lined teeth.

He was angry.

I closed my mouth and stared back down at those dumb shoes. My dad doesn't get angry a lot, but it's not something you want to be the cause of.

"When she's a Mickie-winning artist, she can model all she wants," he said gruffly. "Endorsement deals will be rolling in the door. Music first, modeling second."

I felt tears stinging my eyes. I wanted to say something. I wanted to beg him to let me model. I wanted to tell him how much I hated singing lessons and how much I loved fashion. I wanted to tell him that Promise was the one who wanted to dance and act, not me. But I didn't. I know how much it means to him that his children are successful performers—like him.

Khrissy didn't know all that. "But Lullabye, it could all work together!" she began. "It would be terrific exposure—"

My dad's arm tightened around my shoulder, but it didn't feel as if he was particularly happy or proud of me just then. It felt as if he was reminding me of all the expectations I needed to live up to—and just how far I still had to go.

"Nice to see you, Khrissy," he said, turning away from her. And that was that.

"'Bye," I said, somehow finding a way to smile so that Khrissy wouldn't think I was rude or that I didn't appreciate the phenomenal opportunity my dad had just turned down. "Thank you." I heard my mom mutter something quiet and gracious, and then she fell into place behind us.

In the limo back to the hotel, I finally got to look at the picture my mom had taken of us with my iPhone. Khrissy looked as if she had stepped out of the pages of a magazine . . . and to my surprise, so did I.

"Kayla, are you crying?" Mom asked. "Is something wrong?"

I shook my head, but I couldn't stop the tears that were rolling down my face.

Dad squeezed my shoulder. "Aww, don't cry, Queen. I know how hard it is going to these things, watching other people win. But don't worry. One day, you'll be walking away from the Mickies with an armload of awards—Best New Vocalist, Best Song. Everything they got. Just keep working hard on your singing, and you'll see."

"Yes, Dad." I sniffed, blinking back my tears. I'd do anything for my dad, and all I've ever wanted is for him to be proud of me, but at the same time, I felt he'd kind of put me into a big, golden trap—and I wasn't sure I'd ever be free.

# Chapter Two

## PROMISE

"And don't forget, rehearsal this afternoon," Mom said.

"Mom!" I practically screamed in aggravation. Don't get me wrong, I love my mom. She's really pretty, and she's really talented . . . but she's also a nag. She keeps forgetting that I'm not a baby anymore. I can tell time, and I can keep a schedule. So by the time she reminded me for the hundredth time about the LOL Girls rehearsal this afternoon, I was about ready to scream.

"I know!" I'd missed the last two rehearsals—one because they changed it at the last minute and another one because I was out of town with my mom. Michaela and Daria were pretty pissed off, and their parents were grumbling about me thinking I was "special." I needed to be at rehearsal, and I needed to be on my game. Our next gig was in three weeks, and I had to kill it. "I know better than you do!" I grumbled.

Normally, that tone would get me in trouble, but I guessed she was pretty preoccupied, because she kept talking as if she didn't even hear me. Her eyes stayed focused on the road ahead of us. "Well, I don't like hearing this stuff about you acting like a diva."

"Oh, please," I grumbled. "Diva? Me?"

My mom rolled her eyes. "Just be sure you get there and don't be late. And don't forget you have a hair appointment Friday, and we're going to Miami on Saturday. If you want to reach your dad, text him after three o'clock—"

"Mom!"

This time, she looked at me. "I'm sorry. I guess I just want to make sure you're going to be OK, since I'm going to be on location and gone for a while. This is our last day together."

On location. It sounded so Hollywood, and I was having a hard time connecting that phrase to my mom. Yes, she'd been a TV star for a few years now, and I'd had to get used to having cameras in my face, following my every move. But doing a movie? I was proud of her, jealous of her, annoyed with her, and excited for her—all at the same time. I mean, having a mom who's a reality star and a dad who's a rock star is bad enough. Having a mom who's a *movie* star? That was bound to be a whole 'nother level of stuff to deal with.

"Mom, you'll be back in two weeks," I told her, sliding down deeper in the bucket seat of her black Escalade. "And it's not like I'm going to be alone. Deidre will be here."

Deidre's been my mom's assistant since her first reality show, *Rapper Wives*, back when I was little and she was still married to my dad. Deidre does the shopping and answers the phone, manages our schedules, arranges our travel, and keeps up with the money. Deidre usually takes me to school, but today, since it was her last day in Atlanta before she headed to New York, Mom wanted to take me.

The only problem was, the more she talked about all the things I needed to do, the more I wished she'd stayed home and packed her suitcases and let Deidre take me as usual. I was already stressed out about things with the LOL Girls. And if I were going to be honest, I wasn't crazy about my mom going to New York without me, especially while my dad was on tour. Dad doesn't live in Atlanta, anyway, but at least when he's in Miami, I get to see him when I go down there to hang out with Kayla.

And speaking of Kayla . . . I'm a little stressed out about her, too. She's got some crazy idea that I've got her pink shoes locked up in my suitcase from the Mickie awards, and she's not speaking to me. Like, why would I do that? Really, Kayla?

Whatever. Everyone thinks Kayla's so perfect because she's a cheerleader and gets good grades and does what everyone expects her to do. As if that's a good thing. OK, so she looks great all the time and knows how to smile just right and doesn't put her foot in her mouth all the time the way I do— but she's not perfect, I don't care what anyone says.

Just as we were pulling into the parking lot of Riverside Christian Academy—where I'd been in school since first grade—Mom said, "I'm going to run in and talk to the headmistress for a minute," completely ruining what had already started out as a kind of crappy day.

See, my mom is beautiful. Even when she doesn't do anything to herself, she's hot. This morning, she had her long black hair pulled into a ponytail and no makeup. She wore a light pink tank top and a pair of black yoga pants, finished off with a pair of flip-flops on her feet. Even in that, she managed to look glamorous—like Hollywood.

And if there's anything I hate about my mom, it's that. She's so pretty that I always feel . . . well, not pretty. Even though people tell me how much I look like her all the time.

"The headmistress? About what?"

"What do you think? I just need to let them know I'm going to be away." Mom shut off the engine and scooped her purse up off the floor. I grabbed my backpack and sighed, bracing myself for what I knew was coming.

See, my school goes from preschool all the way to twelfth grade. There's always a group of the high school boys hanging out on the front steps of the building, hitting on the girls as we go inside and cracking on one another. Usually, I'm one of their favorites. They call me "baby," compliment me on how I look in my boring old school uniform, and flirt and stuff.

But when my mom comes to school, it's totally different. My mom is young, only twenty-seven; she had me when she was only a little older than I am now. And some of those boys are eighteen. You do the math. They aren't just playing around. They really think they have a chance with her.

They spied us from the parking lot and were shouting out her name before we even reached the steps.

"Morning, Miss Bella!" one of them called out. "You look beautiful today!"

Someone whistled. I shot Darius—a tall senior with his massive Afro pulled into a tail at the nape of his neck—a dirty look, but he was too busy staring at my mother's behind to notice.

"Cut it out!" Mom was trying to sound annoyed, but there was a big smile on her face. "I'm not even trying to look good this morning."

"That's just it, Miss Bella. You don't even have to try. You always look good."

"You boys behave," Mom said, waving the compliment away.

The boys practically fell over themselves trying to be the first to get the door for her. She thanked them all with another big smile, while I gritted my teeth and tried to act as if I was OK with the role of the Invisible Daughter. On any other morning, every one of those boys would have been yelling my name—"Promise! Promise!"—and all that attention would have been mine. They're just OK—if I was old enough to date, I wouldn't date any of them—but that's not the important thing. What's important is the attention.

I mean, this is *my* school. All the boys want to be *with* me, and all the girls want to *be* me. If you want drama, I can bring it. That probably sounds conceited, but what can I do? It's the truth. I'm not the only celebrity kid at this school, but my parents are the most well known. For example, the only other kid who was at the Mickies last weekend was Bass D's son, Jamal. Actress Michaela Kyle's daughters were in kindergarten here, but she hadn't had a show in years. There were a couple of other kids whose parents were something in the entertainment business—after all, there were a lot of black performers living in the ATL—but compared with me and my parents?

Sorry, wrong number.

"'Bye, sweetheart." Mom leaned over to kiss my cheek. "See you tonight. Don't forget—"

"I know. Rehearsal this afternoon."

I left her at the front office door and headed down the hall toward my first class, Mr. Barker's social studies class.

"Hey!" Tia bumped my shoulder in greeting. "What's the matter? How were the Mickies? I looked for you on TV, but I didn't see you."

Tia's my girl. We hang out together almost every weekend. She's not famous—her parents are just regular people—but she's really pretty and smart. She's got smooth nut-brown skin—a bit lighter than mine, which I would personally describe as the exact shade of brown as the monogram of a Louis Vuitton bag—and long hair that had been lightened just slightly to a color that reminds me of hot sauce. She's twelve like me, but she's allowed to wear makeup. Today she had on pink lip gloss, mascara, and a little eyeliner.

"It was OK." I didn't want to talk about the Mickies. "My dad won a bunch of awards, and I got to walk the red carpet and have my picture taken . . . but after that, it was pretty boring sitting in that auditorium listening to a bunch of speeches. None of my favorite artists performed, so for me, it was a bit of a snore fest. But I've been going to the Mickies with my mom for at least four years, so I guess I wasn't 'coming out' or whatever it was Kayla was doing. You should have seen her head whipping around every time someone even slightly famous came down the aisle. When Khrissy walked up, I told my mom I had to go to the bathroom. I just didn't want to watch Kayla embarrass herself. What did you do this weekend?"

Tia laughed. "Nothing as interesting as *that*. Homework." She paused. "Did you ask your mom if you can sleep over at my house this weekend?"

I shook my head. "There's no point. She's going to say no like she always does. Besides, I'm supposed to be in Miami this weekend."

"Why doesn't she like me?"

"It's not you. It's all the usual stuff about my not being able to do what normal girls do. She thinks if I'm out of the sight of an adult for a second, I'll post sexy pictures of myself on Instagram."

"Does she think my pictures are sexy?" Tia sounded unsure about whether that might be a compliment or an insult.

"I guess. All I know is, she said if I were to do something like that, it would bad. Bad for my image, bad for my career. And hers. And Dad's. And there's all this stuff about safety and the usual blah blah about not being as grown as I think I am." Just thinking about it made me feel too weighted down to do anything but breathe. "They're so overprotective of me, it makes me want to scream." I sighed. "So what's the news around here today?"

"Nothing you don't already know. The big flash is that your mom is in the building."

I rolled my eyes just as the bell rang.

"See you at lunch," Tia muttered, and scurried away to her seat across the room.

I hate social studies. I hate history. Seems to me it's the most boring subject you can take, and Mr. Barker is the sort of teacher who can take something that's dull to start with and stretch it into such incredible boringness that death seems a better choice than wasting another minute listening to another lecture about feudalism in medieval Europe. As if that has a thing to do with anything I'll ever have to deal with in real life.

So is it my fault that I sometimes have to slip my phone out of the front flap of my backpack to check my Instagram? Isn't it more important to know whether the "good morning" picture I posted as soon as I woke up had made the Most Popular list?

"Miss Walker!"

My head shot up.

Mr. Barker stared at me over his dirty glasses. "Is that a cell phone in your lap? Don't you know the school rules about electronic devices?"

I probably could have lied and said it was a calculator. Seriously, that old man can't see three feet without his glasses, and I know because he dropped them once and couldn't see that they were right on the floor beside his foot until he stepped on them. One of the other teachers had to drive him to the mall for a replacement pair.

I would have done it, only I used that one the last time I got caught. Instead, I sat up straight and fixed my eyes right on the old man's face.

"Yes, it's my iPhone, and yes, I know the rule." Then I gave him my best "What you gonna do about it?" look. And waited.

Mr. Barker approached my desk with his hand outstretched. "I'm sorry, Miss Walker," he said firmly. "This is your third violation. Give it to me. I'm afraid I'm going to have to speak to your parents before you can have it back."

"Knock yourself out. If you run, you'll find my mother in the office talking to the headmistress. I'm guessing your running days are probably over, though."

I don't know why I said it, but when the class burst into laughter, I felt better than I'd felt in days.

"And if you call my dad, you're just going to get one of his assistants. He's on tour. I think he's still in the United States, though, so at least you won't have to pay international rates."

"Quiet," Mr. Barker said angrily.

"Of course, you can use my phone. I can afford international rates," I couldn't stop myself from adding, and once again, the class went wild.

"That's enough, Miss Walker." Mr. Barker snatched my phone out of my hand. "Not only will I be discussing this incident with your parents, but I will see you this afternoon for an hour's detention."

Oops. I remembered all my mom's reminders about rehearsals. I pictured Michaela and Daria working on the steps to our dance routine without me. Again.

"Today? But Mr. Barker, I have a rehearsal with my group—"

"You should have thought of that before you broke the rules and then spoke out of turn to your elders, Miss Walker. Now, as I was saying . . ."

Mr. Barker is a jerk . . . and I'm an even bigger one. After all the reminders about rehearsal, there was no way I'd be able to do the detention and make it on time. The girls would be mad, and I'd be in big trouble with my mom for missing it when she had reminded me over and over again. I glanced at the clock with a sigh. It wasn't even ten in the morning yet, and I could tell it was going to be a very, very long day.

"Well, it's about time!"

Michaela spat the words at me as I hurried into the little practice room. It looks like most dance studios—wood floors, lots of mirrors, ballet bars built into the walls—just a little smaller for private lessons. The room was on loan from one of the music producers who lived and worked in Atlanta, and I could tell from the way the other girls looked that they'd been getting grief for being there longer than their usual allotted time, waiting for me to show up.

"Did you get my message?" I threw my books and clothes into a corner and took my place in front of the mirror. I'd changed in the car while Deidre drove as fast as she dared from Riverside to the studio. Gone was the blue school skirt and white blouse that I had to wear to school every day, exchanged for a white T-shirt knotted over my hip, with my bright green sports bra straps showing just enough to look good, a pair of black bicycle shorts, and my favorite Jordans. I stared at myself as I pulled my hair into a ponytail with a bright green scrunchie. The look said "casual R&B goddess," just what I was going for.

"Yeah, we got it." Daria rolled her eyes. "But we were here already by then. You can't just change the plan at the last minute, Promise."

"I'm sorry, but it's like I told you: I didn't have a phone. He didn't give it back until after the detention was over, so I couldn't—"

"You couldn't borrow someone else's phone?" Daria had the highest singing voice of the three girls, and sometimes when she wasn't singing, she sounded as if she was squeaking. Right now, she sounded like angry Minnie Mouse. "Or call Deidre and ask her to call our moms?"

"I'm so sorry. I just didn't think of that."

"Yeah." Daria turned away from me and paced to the center of the floor. "That's the problem. You don't think."

"Look, I know you guys are angry, and I'm really sorry. It

won't happen again. Let's just get started, OK? Where's Derrick?" Derrick is our choreographer.

"Gone, Promise. He couldn't wait around for you all night. He has other clients," Daria said icily.

"Oh." I knew by the way Daria said it that Derrick was as angry with me as they were. He'd probably even taken his annoyance with me out on them with a particularly demanding rehearsal. "I'm sorry. Should I call him or something?"

Michaela bent over and picked up her bag and her water bottle. "I don't know. I've got to go. I have a test tomorrow."

"But . . ." I turned to Daria, but she was grabbing her stuff, too.

"Do us a favor, and be on time next time," she said.

"Look, it wasn't my fault. The teacher—well, I'm going to tell my mom to transfer me out of that jerk's class. He's jealous because my dad's a big success, and he has nothing to show for his own miserable life. He's taking it out on me, but it's not my fault old homey is a failure."

Daria and Michaela left the studio. Their moms were both waiting in the little reception area at the front of the studio, sitting in the nice, cushy chairs and flipping through gossip magazines. Deidre wasn't there.

Daria's mom frowned at me. I always get the feeling she doesn't like me very much, but she sounded concerned when she asked, "Who's here for you, Promise?"

"Deidre. She had some errands to run, so I'll just wait here for her." I nodded toward the door. "You have to have a key or know the code to get in, so I'm sure I'll be fine."

Daria's mom nodded. "Well, I hope she won't be too long. It's dark already, and I'm sure you have homework."

"Yeah. I'll just sit here and work on it," I said. "I'm really sorry about being late."

Daria's mom sighed. "Well, Promise, it's not just you. When one of you is missing, the whole group suffers. You understand?"

I nodded. The woman tried to smile at me, but she couldn't quite bring herself to do it. No. She doesn't like me. She doesn't like me because I'm better than Daria, and we all know it.

Alone in the waiting room, I could have done my homework, but instead, I found myself back on Instagram, staring at a picture of Kayla and Khrissy. I thought Kayla had posted it, but it turned out Khrissy had. "A young lady with real style," she'd written.

I hated to admit it, but Kayla did look great. She's taller and thinner than I am and has the kind of body that designers like for showing clothes. I've taken some pretty good pictures in my life, too—trust it—but next to Kayla, I always look too big.

I wanted to write a comment on Khrissy's picture, like the thousand or so others who'd written something. I'd been racking my brain ever since I got my phone back, trying to think of something sweetly snarky to say. But I hadn't come up with anything yet. I'd come up with something, though, before I saw her on Saturday. I'd come up with something if I had to hire a team of writers and make them work twenty-four hours a day.

A whole hour went by before Deidre burst into the room, looking around as if she was expecting a bustling dance class and not just me, sitting alone in one of those chairs, flipping through my pictures on Instagram.

"Where is everybody?"

Deidre is as different from my mother as any woman alive can be. She's short to my mom's tall, round compared with my mom's curves. She's far from glamorous, but I think she's pretty in her own way. She has copper-colored skin that never seems to need any makeup and light brown eyes that always seem to be laughing. She wears her hair natural and cropped short so that it makes these cute little twists around her ears. Today she had on huge gold hoop earrings, the size of CDs. I hardly ever see her in anything fancier than a T-shirt, and today she had on a bright blue one and a pair of faded jeans that looked as if they couldn't have withstood even another inch of her behind. I know, I sound mean, but there's nothing as wonderful as one of Deidre's soft, warm hugs.

"Oh," she said after I told her the story. "Well, I'm sorry about that, Promise. But maybe you don't need those girls, anyway. Maybe you should start thinking about being on your own. You could talk to your dad about it next time you have some time with him."

"Yeah, maybe." Deidre always knows just what to say to cheer me up.

"And you could have texted me. I would have swung back around for you," she said breathlessly, shaking her head so hard her earrings swung and showing the slight gap between her front teeth when she smiled. "Your mother had a long list for me this morning, and she keeps texting to add to it! We've got one more stop, but it's on the way. She wants something out of her storage unit, and then we're done. Someone from the school called, and your mom said she wants to talk to you as soon as you get home."

"Yeah, I know." All the good feelings I had had just a second ago at the thought of being a solo artist drained away. I was in big trouble, and this definitely wasn't going to be the night to make a case for my moment in the spotlight.

"I won't be a second," Deidre said, parking the SUV in front of U-Store-It.

It was a series of low buildings with brightly painted doors, connected by wide walkways covered with awnings. The entire complex was circled by a fence, and here and there were a few lampposts. There was a security gate at the front, which Deidre had accessed by entering a code. It creaked slowly open in front of us and slowly closed behind us as Deirdre navigated the Escalade toward the closest parking space to Mom's unit.

"She says she needs a couple of her coats for this trip to New York. It's a lot colder there in March than it is here. If I get lucky, they'll be right in front." She shut off the engine. "I'll lock you in. Just sit tight."

I didn't answer. Tia had just sent me a text: "Did you see the picture of Kayla and Khrissy yet?"

Ugh.

Deidre slid out of the car, turned back quickly to lock me in with a touch of the key fob, and headed down a corridor that was lined with small storage units. Even if I had been paying any attention, she would have been invisible to me. The lights in the place must have been motion-sensitive, because all of a sudden, the street lamp near the car flashed off.

I was about to answer Tia when my phone blooped with another incoming text. From my dad.

I swallowed hard, but my throat was so dry it hurt. The

message wasn't so bad . . . but I knew what was coming, and I dreaded it.

"Wat u doin'?" was all it said.

"Waitin' 4 D," I replied, hoping against hope that Mr. Barker hadn't followed through on his threat. "Where r u? Show 2nite?"

Dad didn't answer the questions. Instead, the next text let me know how busted I was: "School called 2 day. Well?"

My shoulders sagged. I don't see my dad that much—the Mickie awards was the first time I'd seen him since I toured with him for a week or two at the end of last summer, about six months ago. But it seemed that whenever I did something wrong, he was always the first to know about it. Somehow Dad's lectures always made me feel worse than any yelling and screaming my mom could ever do.

Something crashed against my window, startling me so bad my phone slipped out of my hand. I looked toward the sound—and started screaming.

There was a man standing at my window. He was dressed in black clothes and wore a black ski mask pulled down over his face. In his hand was a big black gun, and it was pointed directly at my head.

"Open up! Gimme your money!" he shouted.

There was something about his size and his voice—he was really slim, and his voice was kind of high—that made me think he wasn't that much older than me, but he held that gun as if he knew exactly what to do with it.

I didn't know what to do, but I knew I wasn't going to open that door, no matter what.

"Open up!" another voice shouted, and then I saw the second guy, taller and maybe a little older than the first one but also dressed in black, standing on the driver's side. "Open up, or I'll blow a hole in your fancy ride—and you, too!"

"I—I—can't," I stammered.

"You heard the man!" he shouted, cocking his pistol. "Get out, or I'll blow your damned head off!"

"I—I—can't!" I screamed. "It's locked! I don't have the keys—"

One of the guns barked so loudly that I threw myself into the little well between the dash and my seat, my hands over my ears, screaming. I heard the glass in the rear passenger door shatter. Another shot landed in the driver's-side door with a sickening thud.

"Can you get out now?"

I was so scared I didn't know what to do. They were going to kill me, I was sure of it. Sobbing, I fumbled for the lock and popped the door open. No sooner had it clicked open than the boy grabbed the door and pulled me out of the car, practically throwing me onto the sidewalk.

"Come on, let's go," he said to the other guy, who had pried open the steering column and was busily fussing with the wiring.

"I'm tryin', I'm tryin'." He cursed. "It's got that antitheft stuff. We can't take it. What else we got?" He grabbed my iPhone and then dumped my backpack out as if it was a garbage bag. They found my wallet and pulled out all the cash I had—probably a few hundred dollars—then threw it on the floor.

"Nothing else here but clothes," the taller one said about the duffel bag.

"Take it anyway. She's wearing Jordans, and those earrings are probably real. Take 'em off! Now! Hurry up! Hurry up!"

My hands were shaking, and I was crying so hard I could hardly see. I couldn't breathe, either—I was too scared. Even though I'm a good dancer and normally I can really move, I couldn't get my shoes off. It was as if they were suddenly stuck on my feet and I couldn't remember how to make them come off, even with a gun pointed in my face. And it was even harder to to get my little diamond studs out of my ears. My fingers were sweaty and trembling so bad I couldn't grasp the tiny posts. My ears ached because I kept pinching them and trying and pinching until my whole face was wet with tears and sweat and the only sound I could hear was my own breath as I gulped for air.

"I-I'm s-sorry," I sobbed. "I-I can't"

We all heard them at the same time: sirens, coming closer and closer to us. I guess the car alarm or the gunshot had signaled them, but sirens screamed toward us. The robbers looked at each other, and I could tell they were panicking.

"You just had to fire that thing," the short one said to the tall one.

"You fired, too."

"Gimme those damn earrings!" the short one screamed at me.

"I'm trying, I'm trying . . . please don't hurt me, please don't hurt me." I closed my eyes and prayed: *Please, God . . . please let me get these earrings off. Please let me get them off so they'll go away and leave me alone.*

I pinched at the post as if my life depended on it, and the second earring slipped free.

The tall one snatched them out of my hands, and they took off running, scaling the security fence as if it was a kids' jungle gym, and then disappeared into the darkness on the other side.

"Why isn't the thing you need ever in the front?" Deidre was saying when she turned the corner. "I had to dig way back into all that stuff and nearly empty the entire—"

She stopped short when she saw the car with its shattered windows and me sitting on the ground with tears rolling down my face.

―✦―

"Why did you leave her in the car alone, Deidre?" my mom repeated for the thousandth time. "Why didn't you take her with you?"

I don't really remember how we got back home; I was so upset it took me a while to calm down. But it turned out that those sirens weren't for me. The cops never showed—that much I remember.

Now, sitting in our living room and listening to my mother freak out, I just wanted to go to my room. Normally, I love the living room, because we have this huge L- shaped sofa that's made of a really soft suede. It's so comfortable and soft and welcoming—usually. Tonight, though, it felt too big and empty. I wanted my bed. I wanted to pull the covers over my head, bury my face in my pillow, and cry.

"I really didn't think—" Deidre began, looking ready to cry.

"You're right, you didn't think!" Mom was positively furious, as mad as I've ever seen her. I guess she was still pretty scared, too. Every so often, she kept coming over and putting her arms around me, as if she was as glad as I was that things hadn't been worse. "What if they had hurt her? What if they had kidnapped her? What if—"

"She's all right, Bella. Let's not scare the girl to death with what could have happened," my dad said over the speaker phone. "Deidre, did you call the police?"

"No," Deidre said. "I called your security people first, then Bella. I didn't think you'd want the authorities involved."

"You did good, Deidre," Dad said. "You're right. Those little thugs didn't know who they were robbing, and much as I don't like letting them get away with it, I don't need this kinda stuff in the press. The last thing I need is for people to know we don't have our act together on the security front. Let's keep this outta the blogs and off TMZ, know what I mean?"

Deidre nodded as if Terry was in the room and could see her. "I understand," she said at last. "That's why I called your people first. They came and got us and took the car."

"Tell me again. Just what were you doing in that part of the city at nine-thirty at night?"

Deidre explained about the trip to the storage unit after the LOL Girls rehearsal. It felt like something that had happened years ago until Deidre said, "And Promise had to stay late at school because that detention—"

"I had almost forgotten about that!" Mom swung her anger toward me. "I got a call from Mr. Barker today. Something about using your phone during class and then mouthing off when he told you to put it away. Is that right?"

"I'm sorry, Mom," I said softly.

I must have looked and sounded pretty pathetic at that

point, because instead of yelling at me, she just said, "All right, Promise. She's exhausted, Terry," she told the phone. "It's been a tough day for her. I think she should go to bed while we figure this out." She cut her eyes at Deidre, and I knew that Deidre was in far more trouble than I was, whether she deserved it or not.

"You're right." Dad sounded far away and tired. "Go to bed, Promise. And Promise? Don't tell anyone about this, OK? For your safety, I think we ought to keep this close and focus on making sure it never happens again, all right?"

"Yes, Dad." I don't know if it was because I was tired or still shaky or just glad to alive, but I started crying all over again. "But please . . . don't fire Deidre!" I begged. "It's not her fault she left me. I didn't want to go with her. I wanted to stay in the car. It's *my* fault, not hers."

"Deidre's the adult. You're the child. She shouldn't have left you alone, and we're going to have to talk about what should happen next." My dad sounded very determined, and I was scared all over again—this time for Deidre. "Now, go to bed," he continued, more gently. "It's all gonna be OK."

I pulled myself up off the sofa like a little old lady. My legs felt like Jell-O, and my shoulder hurt from where I had hit the ground when the robber threw me out of the car. I hadn't had anything to eat since lunch, but the thought of food made me want to throw up.

Somehow I made it to my room. The second the door closed behind me, I dropped to my knees. My mom taught me long ago to thank God for everything, and I don't think I'd ever felt more thankful than I did at that moment.

"Thank you, God. Thank you, Jesus," I prayed. "Thank

you for not letting those boys shoot me. I'm sorry I haven't been very nice lately, and I promise to be better. I'll be respectful to my elders and nicer to my friends. I'll apologize to Mr. Barker, and I'll make it right with Kayla. I'm going to be a better person, I promise. You'll see, God. But please protect Deidre, and don't let my parents fire her. She's always been good to me, and she doesn't deserve to be let go. Please protect her, God. In Jesus's name. Amen."

Before I fell onto the bed, I made a quick purchase on my phone, and then, with my conscience clear, I fell into a deep, exhausted sleep.

# Chapter Three

## KAYLA

Clear your desks of everything but a pencil or pen," Mrs. Hinckley told the class. "Pop quiz! Let's see how well you understand *Romeo and Juliet.*"

Mrs. Hinckley looks young enough to be a student, but don't let that fool you. Not only is her class hard, but she's as mean as she is young. If you're looking for a break in her class, forget about it. Behind her back, we call her the Bloody Red Queen, because she loves to cover papers with red ink.

Everyone groaned, but my heart sank to the pit of my stomach. We'd gotten back from the Mickies in the middle of the afternoon yesterday, and I'd had a voice class that evening. I was supposed to do my homework on the airplane, and I'd opened the book, but all that "dost" and "docst" stuff gave me such a headache that I'd closed it after only one page and took out my Look Book and the latest issue of *Teen Vogue* instead. Before too long, I was happily ripping out some pictures of spring looks that I liked and sketching my own ideas around others. Before I knew it, the flight was over, and we were on the ground.

I guess I could have read some of it after my voice lesson, but after *that* disaster, I hadn't wanted to do anything more than watch *Pretty Little Liars* and go to bed. I should have known the Bloody Red Queen would pull something like this. But I don't think it would have mattered. I felt so crappy after that voice lesson that I couldn't have studied if I'd wanted to.

You know what happened? My voice teacher fired me. That's what happened.

See, my vocal coach may not be famous, but she's worked with all kinds of really famous and successful singers. Her name is Aurora Tyson. You name the star, and the chances are she's worked with him or her. She helps R&B powerhouses get every ounce of soul out of their voices. She helps pop princesses hit those little teasing high notes. She helps screamo rock stars keep the edge in their voices so they can sing without damaging themselves. And she's been trying to help me find—and then carry—a tune.

Only it's not that easy, because I suck.

"Kayla!" she said impatiently, banging a single note on the piano over and over and over. "This is the note. Here!"

She sighed and paced the room, showing me the back of the long sweater she almost always wore over whatever else she had on. It was brown and old and didn't really do anything for her, since it was almost the same color brown as she was, but twice a week, when I visited her, she had it wrapped around her shoulders or over her arms, no matter what the temperature was outside. Her studio was often just a little cold, and I guess it was comfortable. I actually once gave her a pretty shawl that was a whole lot more dramatic and suited her personality. It was black, with silvery threads running through it and a deep fringe on the hem. It was something I put in my Look Book, but I couldn't imagine myself ever really wearing it—not without some modifications, anyway—and it seemed to suit Aurora really well. I guess it's in a drawer somewhere in her house, because I've never seen her wear it.

She circled the room, exhaling her frustration, then returned to the piano and struck the note again.

"Aaaahhhh." She sang it in a clear soprano that is as good as the voices of lots of people who have hit songs on the radio. "It's here, Kayla. Sing it with me: aaaahhhh."

"Eeeerrr," I sang, doing my best to match her note. "Eeeer-rr."

"Aaaahhhh!" Aurora plinked the piano over and over again. "Aaaahhhh!"

"Arrr! Aarr!"

"No, no." She stopped abruptly and closed the piano, shaking her head. "This is not working. This . . . this just isn't working, Kayla."

"I'm trying, Aurora!" I insisted, and it was true. I *was* trying. I tried every lesson, and I practiced at home with the tapes Aurora gave me. I practiced every day, Mom made sure of it. I don't know if you've ever tried your hardest at something, only to fail over and over and over again, but it's a rotten feeling. I really wanted to get better, but it just seemed that the harder I tried, the worse I got.

"I know, baby." Aurora crossed the room and pulled me into a hug. She's not very tall, but she's kind of heavy, and being hugged by her always makes me feel as if I'm holding on to a human-sized teddy bear. "I don't think I've ever had a student who worked as hard as you do. And that's the truth." She kissed me on the top of my head. "Now, where's your dad? Did he bring you today?"

You know that feeling you get when you know something funky is about to go down and you're not sure you can do anything to stop it? I got a funny feeling as soon as she mentioned my dad. And after the way he'd shot Khrissy down without even listening to her, I had a bad feeling about how he might react to anything Aurora said that didn't fit with his idea of how my career should unfold.

"I think he's out in the car," I answered slowly. "Usually, he waits and then drops me off at home before he goes to the studio."

Aurora nodded briskly. She peeled off her ugly old brown sweater in a way that made me think of someone getting ready to do battle. Beneath it, she wore a pretty floral sleeveless top in a bright lemon color that made her brown eyes pop. It made me hate the brown sweater even more.

She reached out for my hand. "Let's go do this, baby," she said firmly.

Dad's cars are like his offices. He has a bunch of them—eight in all right now, I think—but usually, when he's driving around Miami with me or my brother, he takes one of the Maybachs. He rarely drives any of his cars himself; he has a driver, so he can sit in the back and talk business. That's what he was doing when Aurora and I stepped out of the studio. It was late afternoon, and the sun was already starting to sink, making the black Maybach look kind of orange around the edges.

Aurora took a deep breath, marched up, and knocked on the rear passenger window. She was still holding my hand tightly, and I felt like a bad little kid being escorted to her daddy for stealing a candy bar from the drugstore.

The window slid down with a mechanical buzz, and my dad's face appeared where the glass had been. He looked the way he usually did when he wasn't going out somewhere or getting interviewed, wearing a pair of sweatpants and a white T-shirt, the ball cap on his head covering the tattoos on his head. He had taken off his sunglasses, and his dark brown eyes had shadows beneath them. After he'd dropped Mom and me at the Beverly Hills Hotel, he'd gone out to a bunch of after-Mickie parties and then jumped on the plane back to Miami without going to bed at all. I was sort of tired from it all; he had to be exhausted.

He looked first at Aurora and then at me with question marks in his eyes. "Hey, what's up?" he muttered warily.

"Tell that driver to get out an' open the door for a lady," Aurora said, as if she was talking to a little kid. I don't think she's old enough to be my dad's mom, but that's just Aurora. She has this way of seeming like *everyone's* mama.

For a second, Dad just stared at her. You didn't have to know him really well to know what he was thinking; it was written on his face in capital letters: *Who does this B think she's talking to?*

He looked at me again, and this time, I hung my head. I didn't know what Aurora was going to say, but I was pretty sure I was in trouble.

He sighed and rubbed his forehead with his index finger, showing us a flash of the diamond there. "Hey, man," he muttered to Tony, the driver-bodyguard who went with him almost everywhere. "Open the door."

A moment later, I slid into the Maybach beside my father. It's a huge car in the back, almost as wide as a limousine but much nicer. There are television monitors, a refrigerator, and the most amazing sound system. You can pop up a little table so you can eat or work—like those little trays on airplanes but better. The seats are made of white leather, and they can recline almost flat if you want to sleep. We weren't going to be sleeping today, though.

Aurora slid in next to me, and Tony closed the door. He was about to get behind the wheel, but Aurora said in a firm voice, "Why don't you let this young man go inside the studio and get a bottle of water, Lullabye?"

Tony looked from Aurora to Dad, waiting.

"Go 'head, man."

Tony closed the car door and disappeared inside the studio.

Dad turned to Aurora with his mouth open, but she didn't give him a chance to say a word.

"This is a sin and a shame, William."

*William?*

That's my father's real name, but no one—and I mean no one—calls him that. Even my mom calls him either Lullabye or Will. Never William. Aurora was talking to my dad as if he was the naughty boy in the classroom, and I couldn't believe Dad would let that go on for very long.

I glanced at his face, expecting to see storm clouds gathering between his eyebrows. But to my surprise, he was smiling. The platinum around his front teeth gleamed in the darkening car.

"What sin did I commit this time, Aurora?" he said, laughing.

"Trying to make a singer out of this girl, to satisfy your own ego, that's the sin," Aurora said indignantly. "I'm sorry, Lullabye, but singing isn't Kayla's talent. She's a lovely girl, and I know she'll find her place in this world, but—"

The smile on Dad's face faded as quickly as it had appeared. If I could have scrambled into the front seat right at that moment, I probably would have. But I was sandwiched between two forceful, determined people who were about to have a knock-down, drag-out fight—over me. There was no escape. I slid down in the seat and made myself as small as I could, staring through the front windshield at the setting sun.

"What are you talking about, Aurora?" Dad demanded. He didn't raise his voice—it was soft and even—but the friendliness that had been in it before was all gone. "Kayla has a pretty voice."

"Her vocal quality is fine, but her ear isn't. She couldn't carry a tune if it came with a handle, Lullabye! Surely you know that. She can't help it. Not everyone's—"

"I've worked with plenty of artists who couldn't—"

Aurora waved a plump brown hand at him. "Yeah, yeah. I've heard that crap a thousand times. And you're right, plenty of successful recording artists can't sing. And maybe you can make Kayla into one of them. But you need Auto-Tune for that, not me. Sending this girl in here twice a week is torture for her and a waste of time for me."

"A waste of time, huh?" Dad growled. "If that's how you feel about it . . ." He shrugged as if he didn't care, but I could tell he was furious by how tight his jaw was. "We won't be back. You're good, Aurora, but you ain't the only vocal coach in the world. With an attitude like yours, it's no wonder Kayla isn't doing good with you. Maybe she needs someone else. Someone who can inspire her to work hard—"

"Oh, leave the girl alone, Lullabye!" Aurora sounded as mad as my dad looked. "She's working as hard as she can right now! She just doesn't have any talent! She's a sweet girl, and she's knocking herself out trying to please you, but it just isn't there."

"It's there. We're gonna put it there. She's my daughter. She's part of me. Music's in her blood."

Aurora shook her head. "It doesn't work like that, Lullabye. And you know it," she said gently, patting me on the arm while she spoke. "Kayla is a lot like you, that's true. She's smart and determined, and I know she'll make a big splash in this world." Tears came to my eyes, because I knew what she was going to say next. "Just not in music, Lullabye. Not in music."

"Get out the car, Aurora!" Dad shouted, interrupting her. "Get out!"

I covered my ears. I'd never heard my dad yell like that before, and I'm not ashamed to say that it scared me.

Aurora didn't seem fazed in the least.

"You think about what I've said." She cocked her index finger at him, but she also popped the door handle. She slid out of the car, and when I glanced up, I could see her backside one last time before she disappeared inside the studio.

"Forget her," Dad said angrily, covering my hand with his. "We'll find you someone else. Someone who believes in you as much as I do, Kayla."

That got me. I'd just felt a little misty before, but when he said that, I started bawling like a lost five-year-old.

Dad believed in me. He believed I could be as big a star as

Khrissy, and he was willing to go to the ends of the earth to help me get there. The problem was, I knew deep in my heart that everything Aurora had said about me was true.

What was I supposed to do? How could I tell him that when all he wanted was to see me follow in his footsteps?

I couldn't.

After all that, *Romeo and Juliet* was the last thing on my mind. Even though I know my dad pays a lot of money for me to go to one of the best schools in Miami, and even though I know he's counting on me to get good grades, I hadn't bent the spine of the book again. And now here was Mrs. Hinckley, talking about a pop quiz?

*I can't win.*

"Ugh . . . I hate this play! I—hate—this—play!" The new kid in the seat next to me grabbed his hair as if he was about to rip it out of his head.

His name was David, and we had most of the same classes. My school, Gatewood Academy, isn't that big, so pretty much everyone knows everyone, but David had only been a student here for a month or so. English was the only class where he sat anywhere near me, and so far, other than "hi," we hadn't said much to each other.

Until now. Now he had my attention, because he was saying exactly what I was thinking.

"You can say that again," I agreed, looking at him, really looking at him for the first time. I'm not boy-crazy—although a lot of my friends seem to do nothing all day but talk about who's cute and who's not and waiting for this one or that one to notice they're alive—but he actually *was* kind of cute for a white boy. He had curly dark hair, brown eyes, and nice teeth.

Even in his khaki school uniform, you could tell that he was an athlete. He'd joined the basketball team, and I'd seen him at a few of the games. He was pretty good. Someone had told me where his family had moved from, but I couldn't remember. It was out West, Arizona or Nevada or Montana. Somewhere like that.

"I *hate* this play!" David repeated, gritting his teeth. "Why couldn't we just watch *Gnomeo and Juliet* in class and be done with it?"

I rolled my eyes at him. "You know they aren't going to let us do that," I said as Mrs. Hinckley began handing out quizzes at the front of the classroom.

"But why not?" David asked. "I mean, that was a decent movie. And it was based on the same sort of story but with cute little lawn ornaments as characters. And at least I understood it. This play . . ." He shook his head. "Makes me want to kill myself, too, you know? 'Cause that's what happens in the end. They kill themselves."

I was laughing so hard that Mrs. Hinckley glared at us. David shot me one last grin, just as Mrs. Hinckley put the quiz facedown on his desk and then moved on to put one down in front of me.

I stared at the paper, dreading the moment when I'd have to turn it over and face my doom.

Mrs. Hinckley handed out the last few papers and then paced back to the front of the room. She noted the time on the big black clock on the wall behind her.

"You may begin," she said.

I took a deep breath, turned the paper over, and scanned the ten questions.

*Question 1: Whom does Romeo forget about when he beholds Juliet?*

*Question 2: Why is Tybalt called the prince of cats?*

I didn't have a clue. Not one clue. David was hunched over his paper with his pen in hand, his face scrunched in concentration. He wrote something and then lifted his head as if he was thinking. I didn't realize I was staring at him until he turned and looked at me.

It was embarrassing. I dropped my eyes back to my quiz as if I'd been caught peeking into someone's underwear drawer.

*Question 3: What adult is the first to know of Juliet's feelings for Romeo?*

*Question 4: Who is Queen Mab?*

I don't know if you've ever had a moment like that, a moment when you just knew that you were like those people sailing on the *Titanic* and that since there wasn't anything you could do to keep yourself from drowning, you might as well just jump into the water.

I curled my fingers over the quiz paper, crumpling it silently into a fist-sized ball. Somehow it seemed better to destroy the test and get a zero than to turn it in and get the same grade.

"Time!" Mrs. Hinckley called out, just as the bell tolled the end of the period. "Pass your tests forward!"

There was a flurry of passing. When Christine, the girl who sat in front of me, turned back for my paper, I said, "I gave it to him," and pointed to David. David blinked at me, but I stuffed the crumpled test paper into my backpack, gathered up my books, and left the classroom before he could say anything.

Gatewood Academy is a private school. It has classes from kindergarten up to the eighth grade, but that's it. For high school, you go to another school. JJ, my brother, graduated last year, and now he's a freshman at Amsterdam Preparatory High School. I'm in the seventh grade, but in two years, I'll probably go to Amsterdam, too.

Gatewood is actually pretty small, six buildings arranged around a central lawn. The Lower School is kindergarten through fifth grade—the elementary school, I guess you would call it—and it's located in the two buildings closest to the main office. The Upper School—the middle school—is grades six through eight. It's in its own building on the other side of the lawn. The Upper and Lower Schools share the gym, the auditorium, and the art and music buildings. The whole school probably has about four hundred students; in the whole Upper School, there are only about one hundred of us, and in my seventh grade class, there are thirty-five of us, which means everyone knows everyone.

Which means that if there's drama, everybody takes a side.

I get along by maintaining a strict "drama-free zone" around me. I bend over backward to get along with everyone, no matter what.

One of the coolest things about Gatewood is that it doesn't have a cafeteria like other schools. Every day, we get lunch delivered from a different local restaurant: one day we might get Chinese and the next a burger and fries from McDonald's. I love that. And we don't have a lunchroom, either. We eat outdoors, at tables set up under a covered gazebo. Since it hardly ever gets really cold in Miami, it works out fine. When it rains, you might get a little wet—but only if you run across the grass instead of walking on the covered walkways that lead straight to the tables.

One of my favorite parts of the day is strolling along those walkways—catwalks, we call them—to my lunch table. I always imagine I'm on a runway in Paris or Milan or New York. I never really stomp it out the way I do sometimes at home, but I hold myself a little straighter and concentrate on walking from my hipbones, not just with my legs.

"Kayla! Wait up!"

Courtney came running up to me with a big smile on her face . . . and I was immediately a little nervous.

"I feel like I haven't seen you all year!" she said, throwing her arms around my neck. It wasn't true, because I'd just seen her in social studies. "Since you quit cheerleading, well. . . ." She pulled her lips into an exaggerated sad face. "It's just not the same." She frowned. "Why did you quit cheerleading? You were so good at it!"

I hoped I didn't wince. That was kind of a sore subject. I really loved cheerleading, and I hadn't wanted to quit. But Dad said it took too much time, time I should be spending on my music career.

"Well, I have some other stuff I have to do after school now," I answered, and prayed that Courtney wouldn't ask "Like what?" so I wouldn't have to explain. When you tell people you're taking voice lessons, the first thing they say is

"Sing something!" And I really, really didn't want to have to deal with *that* right now.

I was thankful that Courtney didn't ask. "We don't even sit together at lunch anymore. This year, you always sit with . . ." Courtney's frown flickered like a bad light bulb. "Well, you know." She lowered her voice as though she were afraid someone would hear. "You sit with all the *black* kids."

I just stared at her for a long moment. Like me, Courtney has long hair—hers is light brown—and we were wearing the identical school uniform: khaki shorts with white blouses. When I first started going to Gatewood—when we moved to Miami right after Hurricane Katrina—I noticed that most of the kids at this school didn't look like me. Most of them were Jewish, and I sometimes felt really different from them. But after the last couple of years, because of a scholarship program that helps minority kids afford a school like Gatewood, there are more black students.

At first, even though they were brown-skinned like me, I wasn't sure of them. I had gotten used to being at Gatewood, and even though the kids are white, we're similar in other ways. Our parents have money, for one. And we all live near the school, for two. The new kids live in parts of Miami I'd never even been to before I got to know them. And they all hung together as if they didn't want to talk to the rest of us.

"Don't you talk to those kids?" Mom asked me after I'd finished cheering at a volleyball game last fall, nodding at the other black kids.

"I don't really know them."

Mom frowned. "I know you're shy. And I know those kids don't have what you have in terms of material things, Kayla.

Sometimes that can make things strange with friends, when they can't afford the things you can. But those kids share a heritage with you, and it seems to me that's enough for you to overcome your shyness and try to get to know some of them." She patted me on the shoulder. "One day, just walk up and say hello, OK?"

I did. That's how I met Shanita, Darryl, Kelvin and Chemine. We had so much fun together; this year, I sat with them all the time.

"Well, if you come sit with us, then it won't be all black kids." I said. I thought it was a pretty decent solution if Courtney really wanted to hang out with me.

"What?" She giggled nervously, the pink undertone in her skin rising to the surface. "I mean, wouldn't I be out of place?"

That bugged me. All those years when JJ and I had been the only black kids in the entire school, we'd just dealt with it. But now Courtney didn't want to be the only white kid sitting a table?

*Puh-lease.*

But I knew I couldn't say all that without bringing on more drama than I wanted to start. As I said, it's a small school. I save my drama for the clothes I wear on weekends.

"Of course not," I said slowly. "Unless you don't want to."

Courtney blinked at the challenge. "Sure," she said, her face still red. "Let's go."

The sun streamed down on us as we crossed the grass to the tables.

Darryl was already sitting in his usual spot. He's a sixth-grader, a year younger than I am, but he's already close to six feet tall. He looked up from his phone just long enough to smile.

"Hey, Kayla!" He nodded at Courtney. "'Sup?"

"Hey," I replied, sliding into a seat at the other end of the table. A moment later, Omarion and Jamar joined Darryl, and Shanita plopped down across from me, with Chemine right behind her.

Shanita is probably the girl I'm closest to these days. She's a scholarship kid, and she should be, because she's probably one of the smartest girls I've ever met. She understands everything the first time she hears it or reads it. She's gotten straight As since she started at Gatewood and gets extra work in a few classes, just so she isn't bored.

But as smart as she is, you can tell she lives over in Ludwig Heights. That's kind of a tough neighborhood, far from the pretty homes near the beach, where we live. When I told my mom where Shanita lives, she muttered, "That's the hood for real." There's lots of crime in Miami, even in the nicer parts, but Ludwig Heights seems to be where some of the worst of the headlines come from. I know Shanita has to be tough to survive where she's from, but every now and then, her edge seems out of place at Gatewood.

When she crumpled her dark brown forehead into a scowl, shook her shoulder- length braids, and growled, "What are you doing here?" at Courtney, she sounded pure Ludwig Heights.

"Sitting," Courtney replied testily. "You got a problem with that?"

*Uh-oh.*

If Courtney has ever been within five miles of Ludwig Heights, I'll eat dirt. But she's not the type to back down from anything. I've seen her argue with a teacher over half a point on a test and lawyer her mother (who actually is a lawyer) into agreeing to everything from a higher allowance to a later curfew. Some of the kids at school think she's rude because she likes to get her way and she's willing to go pretty far to get it.

In a way, I guess they're a lot alike, Shanita and Courtney.

The boys stopped playing with their phones and sat up a little straighter. You know how boys are: they love to see a fight. But Shanita didn't take Courtney's bait. Instead, she leaned across the table and rolled her bright brown eyes.

"Girl," she said to me, dropping her voice to a dramatic whisper, as if Courtney weren't there. "You have *got* to put these rumors going around about you to rest! You have got to set the record straight!"

"Rumors?" The sun was in my eyes. I started to reach into my bag for my sunglasses, but then I worried that slipping them on would look too Hollywood. Instead of sunglasses, I pulled my Look Book out from my backpack. When I told you I carry it with me everywhere, I wasn't kidding. Looking at beautiful clothes kills girl-drama, I've noticed. I wasn't sorry that Courtney had joined the table, but you didn't have to be psychic to know that a fight was brewing. I opened the book to some of the new stuff, things I'd added on the plane ride home from the Mickies: a sweet little floral two-piece swimsuit that I'd drawn a hat and caplet for, a hoodie with little clasps instead of a zipper, girly board shorts in neon colors. I marked the page, ready to launch a fashion show, and asked, "What rumors?"

Shanita shook her braids and rolled her eyes toward Courtney. "Some people are seriously confused. They think they're still your best friend."

"Who?" I tried to sound innocent, as if I had no idea whom

she was talking about, although it was pretty obvious she was talking about Courtney. Courtney's face was getting redder and redder with every fraction of a second. Seriously, if the girl got any redder, we would have to equip her with a siren and send her off to fight a fire. I know that sounds funny, but honestly, I didn't like it.

"Well, it's coming up in a couple of weeks. Thirteen is kind of a big deal for Jewish kids, so even though you're not Jewish, we were just wondering if you were going to do something," Courtney said quickly. "I was telling someone about how we had cake with your family last year, and I didn't know what you were going to do this year. That's all."

"No, that's not what you said!" Shanita spat angrily. "You were going on about 'only Kayla's real friends do this' and 'only Kayla's real friends do that'!" She crossed her arms over her chest, which, I have to say, considering that we were same age, was much fuller than mine. "You were trying to make it sound like we're not her 'real friends.'"

"Well, I've known her a lot longer than you have!" Courtney leaned over her hamburger as if she really wanted to reach across the table, grab Shanita's throat, and start twisting. "*I* was her friend from the beginning, when she and JJ first came from New Orleans and they didn't know anyone."

"Yeah, but she hasn't sat with you at lunch all year, has she?" Shanita fired back. "So maybe you *used* to be friends, but now—"

They were getting loud. Now it wasn't just the boys at the other end of the table who had stopped what they were doing to listen, it was the whole seventh grade.

"OK, stop it. Both of you," I said, not wanting to see

them pulling each other's hair and wrestling on the ground—especially, not over me. "You're both my friends. Courtney and I don't spend as much time together as we used to, but she's still my friend, Shanita. And you're my friend, too."

"So I'm coming to your house for cake on your birthday this year," Shanita concluded, shooting Courtney a superior look.

"Well, if you're there, I'll be there, too!"

"Not this time, you little—"

"Look," I interrupted. "I don't even know what I'm doing for my birthday, so—"

"That's easy," a familiar voice said.

I looked over my shoulder. That kid David from Mrs. Hinckley's class stood over my shoulder with his lunch tray. He didn't even ask, just nudged his into the empty space between Darryl and me and sat down, as if he was expected or something. It was annoying in one way . . . and kind of cool in another.

For a moment, Darryl and Omarion looked at each other, then at Jamar, who shrugged.

"This ain't your usual table, man," Jamar commented.

"Yeah, I just wanted to talk to Kayla for a minute . . . about English class." He shot me a look that made my ears suddenly get hot with embarrassment. He saw what I did with that paper; there was no doubt about it. I opened my mouth to say something, anything to keep him from telling that story to everyone, but he'd already changed the subject. "But then I heard all this talk about parties, and I just had to sit down. I *love* a good party." He paused to take a huge bite of his burger as if he hadn't eaten in a week. "Here's what you do: have a big party, and invite everyone," he muttered around the mouthful of beef.

"Hey, that's what I'm talking about," Darryl said. "It's been a while since there's been a party."

"Too long," Jamar agreed.

"Ooh," Chemine added in her faintly accented English. Her family is from Senegal, and she's only lived in this country since she was six. She speaks perfect French and does better with English than I do half the time—she's *that* smart. She's very dark-skinned and has her hair cut very, very short—like a boy's—but it looks good on her. Like me, she's tall and slim, with no figure to speak of. I've told her a hundred times she could be a supermodel, but she always laughs and says, "No, no. I want to study the stars, not be one."

But now she was grooving in her seat as if she could already hear the music at this party they had all decided someone should have. "With music so we can all dance."

"So it'll be a bat mitzvah, what Jewish kids have when we turn thirteen. It's supposed to symbolize that you're growing up. Becoming a teen and on the way to being a man—or a woman," David finished. "Mine is going to be in August."

Omarion nodded. "Yeah, didn't that kid Daniel have one of those last month? The whole school was invited. I didn't go—I really don't know him that well—but I heard it was some party."

"Oh, man, it was the bomb!" Darryl said, his eyes shining with enthusiasm. "He had that group, you know the one that had that song last year? They came and performed and sang 'Happy Birthday'! It was wild!"

"It was at that country club near the marina, right?" Shanita asked.

Courtney nodded. "They had it all done up like a haunted house, too. These actors would pop out of the scenery from time to time and scare you to death."

"But Kayla's not Jewish," Shanita said doubtfully.

"No problem," David said, grinning mischievously. "We'll just call it something different. A Kayla-ganza!"

Around the table, my friends started talking and giggling at once.

"I think the best party I ever went to was on the Fourth of July," Chemine said. "Cake, ice cream, music, *and* fireworks!" Her perfect white teeth appeared in the dark coal of her face. "The. Best. Ever."

"You ever see that show on MTV about the parties some kids have?" Jamar began, but Omarion interrupted him immediately.

"Dang! That stuff is just sick! They do all kinds of outrageous stuff like get brought in on litters and parachutes and helicopters."

"And everyone always gets—" Courtney began.

"A CAR!" they all shouted together and then burst into laughter.

I smiled. I'd never really thought of having a party before, a big party that I could invite the whole school to. A party with music and dancing and a fun theme. Just talking about a party had shut down the drama between Courtney and Shanita. Now they were so busy talking about parties that they'd forgotten all about whether I might have one.

Unfortunately, though, it didn't last.

"Isn't Jag U R coming to town this weekend?" Darryl asked.

Suddenly, the conversation stopped. When I looked up from my plate, everyone was staring at me.

Jag U R was a rap artist, and his tour had been selling out everywhere it went. He was also one of my dad's artists. Judging by the way everyone at the table was looking at me, there probably wasn't a single seat left for his Miami shows for any price.

"Are you going, Kayla?" Shanita asked at last.

I didn't want to answer. I *was* going, and Promise was flying down from Atlanta to go with me. I probably could have invited a friend, but saying that would start something I'd just done my best to kill. I was about to start talking about those neon board shorts in my Look Book when David's hand shot up like a rescue flare.

"Uh, this might sound like a stupid question," he said, stretching his eyes wide. "But who is Jag U R?"

The table exploded with laughter.

"Who is Jag U R?" Darryl guffawed. "Did he just say that?"

"You don't know that song?" Chemine started humming, snapping her fingers, and swinging her head from side to side.

Courtney belted out the hook, "She fine, we fine, it's all fine—"

The whole table joined in for the last line, "Pour some mo' Kool-Aid, it's party time!" and then burst into giggles when every head at all the other tables swiveled toward the serenade.

"Oh, so that's Jag U R," David said, nodding. "Yeah, I think I heard that before."

"Are you kidding, man?" Omarion joked. "Your mama hums that song in the shower." And they were all still laughing when the bell rang, signaling the end of lunch.

I don't know if he did it on purpose, but that stupid question got me off the hook, and I was so grateful I could have hugged him. I was eager for the school day to be over. I had an important question for my dad—if I could just work up the nerve to ask it.

# Chapter Four

## PROMISE

**W**hen I woke up, the sun was already shining brightly through the pale purple sheers at my bedroom window. At first, I thought it was Saturday, and I stretched slowly, pulling my zebra-print comforter up a little higher over my head in my queen bed. My bed is one of my favorite places: it's white and has a canopy of purple that drapes all around it like I'm Sleeping Beauty or something. I really like purple, but I also like animal print, so I guess my room has a split personality in a way. There are purple walls and lavender curtains, but I've got the slickest zebra-print comforter, and there are a couple of animal-print rugs on the floor. I even got this cool zebra fabric and draped it over the top of my white desk. I think it looks cool, but my mom says it gives her a headache.

As I said, at first I thought it was Saturday, and then, just as I was snuggling back under the covers, I remembered. I remembered what had happened the night before—and that it wasn't Saturday. I look at my clock in alarm. After nine A.M.!

Mr. Barker's class had already started. I wasn't just late, I was super late.

"Mom!" I yelled. "Deidre!"

*Deidre.*

That's when I remembered *everything* that had happened the night before. My stomach did a sudden sickening flip, and I ran out of my room and down the hall to the bedroom Deidre had lived in since Mom bought this house eight years ago.

"Deidre!" I banged on the door and then turned the handle, even though I know I'm supposed to wait until she says "Come in."

The room was empty. The bed was neatly and carefully made. It didn't look as if anyone had slept in it, either.

"Mom!" I yelled, leaving Deidre's room for my mom's. "Mom! Where's Deidre?"

But my mom's room was empty, too.

That's when I got scared. For a second, I had this crazy idea that the boys who'd robbed me last night had found their way to our house and that they had done something terrible to my mom and to Deidre. There was a part of me that wanted to run back to my room and lock the door.

But a second later, I realized that was stupid and that Deidre and Mom were probably just in the kitchen or something.

I hurried down the stairs instead, but both the kitchen and the family room were empty.

"Mom?"

The house felt empty. You know that silence that means you're all alone? That's how it felt, and I was just about to work myself up to a full-blown panic attack when the front door opened and Deidre walked in carrying a little white box.

I'd never been so happy to see anyone in my whole life!

"Deidre!" I cried, falling into her arms, laughing and crying at the same time. "You're still here!"

"Of course, of course, I am!" Deidre laughed, squeezing me hard. "I was a little nervous last night, too. I made a serious mistake when I left you in that car alone. Your parents would have been justified in letting me go."

"But they didn't."

"No." Deidre sighed in relief.

"Where's Mom?"

"She had an early meeting, and her flight to New York is at noon, so—"

Just then, the sliding glass door that led to the deck opened. A tall dark-skinned man stepped into the room and latched the door behind him. He was almost as wide as the door itself but moved with the ease of an athlete. He wore a black T-shirt tucked into black trousers and black shoes. Muscles bulged everywhere: arms, thighs, everywhere. Even his neck had muscles; he looked that strong. I'd never seen him before, but he acted as if he had every right to be there.

"Is Bella gone already?" he asked in a voice that rumbled like distant thunder. "Because I think we need to do a little work out there. There's a section of fence that's loose and I really think the whole thing should be replaced. And I'd cut a few trees. Eliminate cover for anyone watching the house." His eyes swept over me, and his broad face relaxed a bit. "Good morning! You must be Promise."

I glanced at Deidre, but suddenly, she was busily opening the white box in her hands and wouldn't look at me.

"Uh, who are you?"

"Name's Charles Williams, but most people call me Charley."

That didn't exactly answer my real question. I just stared at him, but it didn't look as if he was going to say anything until asked. It was annoying.

"OK . . ." I rolled my eyes impatiently. "Why are you here?"

The big man named Charley cut his eyes at Deidre, as if he expected her to say something, but Deidre refused even to look at him.

"Not my idea. Here." She thrust a small black square into my hand. "Your new phone. You have a new number"—she glared at Charley—"for security reasons. But most of your contacts and apps and music were backed up to the Cloud, so you just need to let everyone know the new number, and you should be all set." She shouldered her bag. "I've got a few more errands to run for your mom before she goes." She jerked her head at the big man, making today's earrings—copper triangles with little bits of turquoise in the center—swing like acrobats. "Charley will take you to school when you're ready."

"What?" I know it was babyish, but I grabbed Deidre's hand like a scared two-year-old. "You're leaving me with this guy? Who *is* he?"

"They didn't tell you?" Charley's smile faded. "I'm your new bodyguard. Your father hired me last night. From now on, wherever you go, I go. Period." Without the smile, he looked really mean. And he was roughly the size of a small house.

I took a step back. "No." Bodyguard? This big hulk of a

man going everywhere with me? No way. "Thank you, uh, Charley. But I really don't think I need you. I have my mom and Deidre—"

"Negative. That has proved insufficient." He sounded like a computer, which I didn't like, but I liked it even less that his words slammed Deirdre. I put my hand on my hip and was opening my mouth to tell him something about himself when he continued, "You should probably get ready for school. My instructions were to let you sleep as long as you needed but when you got up to take you to school."

"Your *instructions*?" This dude was beginning to make me mad. I mean, I'm a person, not an instruction! "Deidre—"

"I'm sorry, kiddo. I really am," she muttered, glaring at Charley. "I don't like it, either, but after last night . . ." She sighed, her shoulders hunched in defeat. "Well, what can I say?"

"But that was just bad luck. I really don't need a bodyguard!"

"Your father feels otherwise," Charley barked, as if anyone was talking to him. "Get dressed. If we can arrive by zero-nine-thirty, you can make the last few minutes of your first-period class."

I looked at him as if he'd just parachuted in from another planet. "Zero-nine-thirty? Are you serious? What is this, the Marines?"

Charley chuckled. "Negative. Trust me, Promise, I was a Marine, and you wouldn't last one day." He glanced at his watch. "You have fifteen minutes. Move! Move! MOVE!"

He clearly didn't know me very well. While he was shouting "Move! Move!" I was standing there wondering who the heck he thought he was talking to. I probably would *still* be standing there if Deidre hadn't nudged me.

"Go on," she said gently, patting me on the shoulder. "Maybe you can talk to your parents about him this afternoon."

School was a disaster. First, I was late. Second, Mr. Bodyguard embarrassed me in every possible way, following me around, checking every room, interrogating everyone I so much as looked at. And third, I had to miss the beginning of lunch—my only real free time—to go to Mr. Barker and apologize. That should have only taken a few minutes, but Mr. Barker wanted to "chat" with me about my recent behavior, as if he was the school psychologist or something. I was biting my tongue the whole time so that I wouldn't say "My only problem is that I can't stand you or this stupid class" and have to apologize all over again. By the time I reached the cafeteria, there was just time to plop down next to Tia and sigh—which would have been OK had I not spied Charley the Bodyguard talking to the cafeteria manager! What on earth was he still doing here?

"Where have you been?" Tia asked. "Why were you so late this morning? Why didn't you answer my texts last night?"

"Didn't you see?" I exploded. "You didn't see him? He's as big as a tree trunk! I don't see how anyone could have missed him. Anyone in the whole school!"

"See who?" Tia asked, her brow furrowing in concern. She glanced around the room as if looking for an actual tree. "What are you talking about?"

"Charley. My new bodyguard."

"Bodyguard?" Tia's dark brown eyes widened. "Why do you need a bodyguard?"

It wasn't until *after* I'd told her the whole story that I remembered I wasn't supposed to.

"So, I go and get ready for school, and when I came down in my uniform, you know what he did?" I was so worked up I didn't wait for Tia to reply. "He told me my uniform skirt was too short. I rolled it up at the waist the way we always do, and he had the nerve to tell me to roll it down! As if he's my father or something! And then he said that I shouldn't wear my backpack on my back but over my shoulder, because when it's on my back, it's easier for someone to grab me." I fumed. "It's a *back*pack! It's supposed to go on your back! And instead of dropping me off at the door the way Deidre would have done, he actually parked the car and walked me all the way to the classroom!"

"Oh, no, he didn't!"

"Oh, yes, he did! And even worse, he came *into* the classroom and went around and looked out of all the windows!"

"Get out!" Tia's eyes were wide in disbelief.

"As if I was the president's daughter or something. As if there were snipers sitting in the nearby trees just waiting to knock me off. And then I saw him walking the grounds with the headmistress, taking notes in some little notebook. As if the whole place is a security hazard. Can you believe that?" I shaded my face with my hands. "Oh, no. Here he comes!"

"Where?" Tia's voice was too loud, and her head immediately whipped around the room.

"Shh!" I whispered.

Charley lumbered past with the cafeteria manager, pointing to the doors and the windows. A moment later, they disappeared into the kitchen.

"OMG, Promise. That really is the biggest, scariest-looking dude I have ever seen," she whispered. "I guess that's what you want in a bodyguard, though," she added.

My phone buzzed, and a familiar number popped up on the screen.

"You're still at lunch, right?" My mom sounded tired.

"Yeah, for a few more minutes," I said.

"And Charley is still with you?"

"Yeah." I couldn't stop myself from rolling my eyes. "Speaking of that guy, Mom, does he really have to hang around school all day?"

"I don't think he'll do that every day, Promise. I think he's just checking things out. Getting to know your routines."

"But Mom, this is just stupid. I really don't need him."

"Don't start, Promise," my mother said wearily. "I'm not thrilled about it, either, but under the circumstances, I think we're both going to have to go along with your father on this one."

"Mom, you can't see what he's doing. He's going around the whole school checking on stuff like—like—"

"I know. The headmistress called me. Look, Promise, I've got nothing to do with this one. Your father thinks it's necessary, and as I said, given what happened, he might be right." Mom lowered her voice. "You didn't tell anyone about any of that, did you?"

*Uh-oh.* I had forgotten about that. I glanced at Tia. She wasn't "anyone," not really. I mean, Tia's twelve, like I am. She's not calling the tabloids to sell them gossip about me and my family. She's a kid! So I wasn't really lying when I said, "No, Mom."

"Good." Mom sounded relieved. "Well, I've been thinking. You've been through a lot these past few days, and unfortunately, I'm going to have to leave a little earlier than I thought today. I thought about dropping by the school to give you one last hug, but, well, we all agree that's probably too disruptive. It's probably best if I just get on up to New York and do what I've got to do, you know?" She sounded so sad that I felt my own tears wet my lashes. Even though my mom travels a lot, every time she goes, it's hard.

"When will you be back?"

She sighed. "Not for two weeks."

"Oh. Can I come up and watch you?"

"Not this time, baby. I'm going to be working really hard."

"I'll miss you, Mom," I said, and I meant it so much that I actually had to put my hand up over my eyes so Tia and the other kids wouldn't see me cry.

"Me, too, Promise."

Neither one of us said anything for what felt like a really long time.

"But you're going to see Kayla this weekend. And seeing Jag U R in concert will be fun. I'll call or text as often as I can. And I'll be back before you know it."

"Yeah," I said, but it wasn't true. Two weeks was a pretty long time. And with everything that had happened, and was happening, I just didn't like the idea of Mom being so far away.

"Hey, I know," Mom said brightly, forcing us both to focus on the positive. "Why don't you invite one of your friends to go with you? Maybe Tia would like to go. I'll call your godparents to make sure it's OK, but I don't think they'll mind. And you know Kayla. She gets along with everyone."

"Really?" I practically shrieked into the phone. "That would be great! Thanks, Mom! I'll ask her right now!"

"OK, then. I love you, Promise."

"I love you! Break a leg in New York. I know you'll be great."

"Thank you, sweetheart. 'Bye!"

I didn't even wait to put the phone away. "How would you like to go to the Jag U R concert in Miami with me this weekend?"

Tia screamed. All the kids stopped eating and talking to look at us. Charley shot out of the kitchen as if he'd been fired from a cannon and made a beeline toward me.

"Sorry, sorry!" Tia said nervously, her hands up as if she was surrendering to the police. "I was just excited, that's all."

Charley glared at her as if she'd stolen his money. "Are you OK, Promise?" he asked.

It was so ridiculous I couldn't stop myself from saying, "I don't think a little scream is gonna kill me, do you?"

Charley seemed to think about that for a moment. He opened his mouth as if he was going to reply but ended up just shrugging his massive shoulders, pivoting on his heel like a toy soldier, and retreating into the cafeteria.

Watching him marching back to the food line struck me as so funny that I had to cover my mouth with my hands to stuff the giggles back inside.

"I've made him mad," Tia whispered.

"That's OK. I made him madder," I said. "So, what about it? Can you go?"

"Yes!" Tia's eyes gleamed with excitement. "I mean, I'll have to ask, but my mom will say yes. What will I wear? I can't wait to go home and pack, only . . ." Her face crumpled with disappointment. "Oh, Promise, what am I saying? There's no way my mom can afford a ticket to Florida—or even the concert tickets. I'd love to go, but—"

"Don't worry about *that*." I dropped an arm around her shoulder. "You're with me. You won't need a penny. I roll all expenses paid!"

# Chapter Five

## KAYLA

"**D**ad . . ." My voice was shaking, but I knew I'd already waited too long to ask him if I could have a birthday party. But too many things had gotten in the way. He wasn't exactly happy with me. It was as if everything that could go wrong had been going wrong for me since the Mickies. Aurora quitting was pretty bad, but really, that was just the beginning.

My plan was to ask Dad about a birthday party right after school yesterday, since he picks me up every day when he's in town. My parents were never married, and they don't live together anymore, not since we moved from New Orleans after Katrina, but we're still a family in every other way. Dad meets me after school and takes me to dance class on Tuesdays and Thursdays, voice lessons on Mondays and Wednesdays, and straight home to meet Anne, my tutor, on Fridays. Then he heads over to the high school to pick up JJ after basketball practice. When we're all home, we have dinner together, just like one of those families in a TV commercial for Hamburger Helper or something. Then my dad goes to his studio and works, usually all night.

Since it was Wednesday and Aurora had quit, I was expecting to go home, but as soon as I got into the car, Dad said, "Well, I been thinking about what Aurora said. And she's right: you don't need no more voice lessons. We gonna try something different. I got someone I want you to meet. He's the dude who helped Madam Raka create her image: Lonnie Sonic. He's flying in from New York to talk to you, so we're going down to the airport."

My heart sank.

I'd been hoping that Dad would let the whole singing thing go for a while. I'd been hoping that he'd think about Aurora's words and decide to call the whole thing off. But Dad had done just what he'd promised to do: he'd found someone else.

"He might want you to sing a bit for him, so do your warm-up," Dad urged.

A rush of panic raced from my brain to the pit of my stomach. Immediately, my throat dried up. "Now?" I asked in a shaky voice.

Singing in front of my dad is one of the scariest things in the world to me. I mean, he's a music producer—he knows the difference between what sounds good and what sucks. I hate doing it even when I'm prepared and I have some kind of music accompanying me. But now, with just me and him in the car, without any background music to hide my mistakes and help keep me on key? If I could have stopped the car and taken off running, I would have.

"Sure," Dad said, patting me on the knee. "I know you're cold, so don't worry about it. Let's hear what you got."

He was staring at me, waiting for me to sing, with an encouraging smile on his face. I cleared my throat and tried to start out with one of the exercises Aurora had always begun our lessons with, singing the scale, but when I opened my mouth, all that came out was a squeak.

Dad laughed and reached into the Maybach's refrigeration compartment and handed me a bottle of water.

"Something warm would probably be better, but it's all I got. Drink up and try again."

I did as I was told. This time, I made it through the scale, but I knew it wasn't that great. I think I was pretty much on key, but the sound didn't have any power behind it. I sounded like one of those squeaky little recorders they give you in a preschool music class.

But Dad said, "That's better. You just need to work on your confidence. Again."

That's how we spent the next fifteen minutes: me singing the scale and doing a few other vocal warm-ups, over and over again. Dad kept saying "again" and trying to be encouraging, but I could tell he didn't like what he was hearing any more than I did.

"Don't worry about it, Queen," he said to me as the car rolled to a stop. "If confidence is the trouble, Lonnie can help. I know it."

We were at Opa-locka Executive Airport, a small private airfield that a lot of the charter jets used. As Tony pulled up to the curb, I moved close to Dad, expecting Lonnie to slide in beside me as Aurora had done, but Dad opened the car door instead and stretched out his hand for me.

"Come on. We're gonna talk on the jet."

It was a pretty nice plane, a little smaller than the ones my dad usually flies but still really comfortable. I wish I could tell you more about the plane—I know it had a TV and those big captain seats, and we sat together at a long conference table that looked as if it was made of glass—but once I saw Lonnie, I really didn't notice anything else.

I've never met anyone with a crazier look. He was a brown-skinned black man, probably a little older than my dad, forty-something, I guess. But there was something funny about the skin on his face that made me think he might be even older and just trying to look young. It was sort of shiny, as if he'd just covered it with Vaseline. When I looked closer, I realized he was wearing makeup; I could see the black eyeliner and some kind of plum-colored lip balm. He had long hair for a man, worn not in an Afro like a lot of the boys my age wear it but straightened and brushing his shoulders. Its natural color was probably black or dark brown, but he had dyed it an auburn red, which I probably would have really liked had it not been so confusing. He really looked like a lady, right down to the fringed scarf draped around his neck and his tight T-shirt, slim-cut jeans, and studded ankle boots. He had a computer open in front of him, a pair of headphones dangling from his neck, and a cup of hot tea steaming in the space near his hand.

"Lullabye!" His voice was low and masculine, considering how thin and delicate he looked. When he stood up and stretched out a hand to my dad, I saw how tall he was, at least six feet two inches, maybe more. "Thanks for flying me down," he said with a smile.

"Yeah, sure. Thanks for coming," Dad said. You couldn't

have imagined two more different black men than my dad in his sweats and ball cap and Lonnie Sonic in his retro punk-rock look. Dad took a seat on the other side of the conference table and started looking at his phone, as if he wasn't that interested in what was about to happen. I felt sort of mad at him right then; he was the one who wanted to do this, not me, but now that we were there, he was acting so laid-back you'd have thought the whole thing was my idea.

"And you must be Kayla," Lonnie said, turning his eyes to me. He looked me up and down, seeming to measure everything about me without taking out any kind of instrument. "OK, let's hear it. Sing."

Once again, everything inside me locked up. In my room sometimes, when I'm listening to my iPod and Rihanna or Beyoncé comes on the radio, I feel as if I might actually sound OK. I can sing my heart out—when I'm alone. But if you stand me up and tell me to sing? Forget it.

I stood there blinking at him as if I didn't speak English.

"Hmm," Lonnie said. He touched me gently on the shoulders and then turned me around so that I wasn't facing him and my dad anymore. I was staring at the rear of the plane.

"Try it now," he commanded.

"Do, re, mi . . ." I began in a shaky voice.

"Louder!"

"Fa, sol, la . . ."

"Louder!"

"Ti, do!" I practically shouted. The "ti" hadn't come out that well, but I tried to finish strong and in the right key.

"OK," he said firmly. "I'm going to touch you right here in the diaphragm." His slender fingers pressed my stomach.

"This time, I want you to sing a song, not a scale, OK? Sing from here." He pressed my stomach. "Not the throat."

Aurora had said the same thing, and I could never remember to do it.

I almost said that out loud, but I swallowed it down and asked instead, "What do you want me to sing?"

Lonnie shrugged and ran his hand through his red hair. "Anything you want, girl. What do you like? What's your favorite song right now?"

I don't know what was wrong with me. I like all kinds of songs. I listen to music all the time. But when he asked me, I couldn't think of anything. I couldn't remember a single lyric, not even to the songs Aurora and I had gone over and over in our months of lessons.

"I—I—I don't know," I stammered, feeling like the stupidest girl in the world. I glanced over my shoulder at my dad. He was still staring at his phone, but I could tell he was listening, probably wondering why he wasted his money to fly Lonnie down to Miami to talk to a girl too dumb to remember even one of the songs her own father had written.

"It's OK," Lonnie said reassuringly. "Sing the national anthem. Or 'We Wish You a Merry Christmas.' Or 'Happy Birthday.'"

"My birthday is in two weeks," I said, as if that was the question he had asked.

"Is it?" Lonnie smiled. "How old will you be?"

"Thirteen."

"Teenager." Lonnie sighed. "Big changes ahead, Miss Thing."

I don't know why, but that made me laugh, and Lonnie

laughed, too. I started to relax a little. I still didn't want to sing, but I wasn't as scared as I had been.

"Tell you what. Let's sing you 'Happy Birthday' together. It's a little early, but you can't get too many birthday wishes, right?"

I nodded.

"OK. On three. One, two, three . . ."

Lonnie started singing. To my surprise, he had this incredible rich tenor voice, like an opera singer. He sounded so good I just wanted to listen to him, until he nudged me, reminding me to join in.

I sang along. I didn't sound anywhere near as good as he did, but I didn't sound awful, either.

"Diaphragm!" Lonnie called out, and I tried to sing from my stomach the way Aurora had tried to teach me, but then I lost the tune a bit.

"OK." Lonnie stopped me. "That's enough. Have a seat, Miss Kayla."

Lonnie lowered himself back into his own chair and put his hands together as if he was praying, staring all the while at me. I was starting to get really, really nervous when he finally said, "So, Kayla. What kind of recording artist do you want to be?"

My dad looked up from his phone and swiveled toward me in his chair.

"What kind of artist?" I repeated.

"Yeah." Lonnie ran his thin hand through his hair again. He did that a lot. It must have been a habit, like the way some people lick their lips or bite their fingernails. For some reason, the way he did it reminded me of some of the girls I'd been on the cheerleading squad with last year. "When you imagine yourself up onstage, who are you like? How do you dress? Sound? What kinds of people come out to hear you?"

I shrugged. "I don't know."

"You don't know?" Dad repeated, chuckling. "You should see this girl striding around the house like every hallway is a runway, tossing her hair and being all *fierce* and stuff," he said. "If that's not a performance, I don't know what is!"

It's true. I do that all the time. But that was modeling, not performing, and I said so. "I never think about it that way. I never imagine myself onstage."

Lonnie cut his eyes at my dad. "OK, then let's start there."

"Yeah, maybe so," my dad agreed. "I'm not worried about the singing. We can fix that in the studio. But you can't fake confidence. Let's start there."

I stared at the two of them in confusion. "I don't get it."

"We're going to forget about your voice for a while. Instead, we're going to work on building your confidence as a performer. And for you?" Lonnie picked up his tea cup with a graceful hand—and for the first time, I noticed his black nail polish—and took a loud sip. "I think that starts with getting onstage."

I blinked at him. "You mean *imagining* myself getting onstage," I said slowly. "Right?"

He shook his head. "I have one assignment for you, Kayla. Just one. I want you to get up on a stage somewhere and sing for as many people as possible. I don't care if you sing 'Happy Birthday' or 'Twinkle, Twinkle, Little Star,' you just need to get up there and do it. Don't worry about how you sound; you can recite it if you want to. Don't worry about how you look, unless the look is a part of what makes you the performer you are. But until you know who you are as a performer?"

He settled back in his chair. "It's impossible to 'develop' an artist who doesn't have a clue about what kind of artist she is. Madam Raka is only a so-so singer. But she knows who she is as a performer, and that makes the difference. It gives her the confidence that makes up for what her talent lacks. Do you understand?"

I heard him. I even understood him. But all I could think of was standing up on a stage somewhere—in front of *people*.

"It can be at school or at church—or if you're feeling really ambitious, maybe your dad will let you open for one of his artists!" Lonnie chuckled; my dad didn't. We both knew that wouldn't happen until I was super ready . . . if I ever was. Lonnie didn't seem bothered by Dad's silence. He smoothed his hair again and said earnestly, "Will you do it, Kayla?"

*No.*

It was the only word in my mind. I didn't want to do this; there was no way I *could* do it. Just thinking about it was terrifying: I couldn't imagine myself ever doing it in a million, billion years.

"Kayla?" Dad leaned forward in his chair. "Answer the man."

But I couldn't. The only answer my dad wanted to hear was yes, but I just couldn't make myself say it. The only answer in my own head was no, and I couldn't say that, either. I stood there like a complete doofus and didn't say anything until, finally, my dad stood up.

"Thanks, Lonnie," he muttered. "We'll be in touch. C'mon, Kayla," he said without even looking at me.

He didn't say anything to me for the rest of the day, and I didn't dare ask him for anything as big as a party. I knew he was angry and disappointed; he'd gone to a lot of trouble to bring Lonnie down from New York, and I had embarrassed him. I wished I'd been able to say yes—I should have, I know it. I mean, I'm lucky. I have the kinds of opportunities other girls just dream about. The grateful thing to do would have been just to say yes. Just yes. Such a tiny little thing, considering all the wonderful things Dad does for me . . . and I couldn't do it.

I tried to tell him that when he picked me up from school, but he said he had to make an important phone call and that we'd talk later. But now, here we were at dinner, a whole day later, and he still hadn't said anything to me. Hadn't even looked in my direction. He hadn't said much to anyone, but he'd greeted Anne, my tutor, when she came in and asked her what was new.

"Don't ask, Lullabye." Anne rolled her eyes. She's young, twenty-six or twenty-seven, and really cute, with curly blond hair. She tells the best stories and gets so excited when she cares about what she's talking about that sometimes she's funny without meaning to be.

"That dumb man of yours still giving you trouble?" Dad joked, with a glint of mischief in his eyes.

"You know it."

"I say dump him." Dad grinned, flashing a mouthful of platinum.

"I know, I know." Anne sighed. "I have the worst luck with men!"

She is so much a part of our household that she has her own

key to Mom's house. She's been our tutor since we first came to Miami from New Orleans. She used to teach at Gatewood and she knows all the teachers and just about every student, too, which is sometimes a good thing . . . and sometimes not so good. Can you imagine having one of your teachers living in your house? That's kind of what it's like having Anne around.

Seeing her reminded me of Mrs. Hinckley's English quiz, which was still crumpled somewhere at the bottom of my backpack. I hoped Anne wouldn't find out about that. If she did, she'd tell my parents for sure. And then, for some reason, that started me thinking about that kid David and how he'd been like my knight in shining armor about my birthday and during that whole concert-ticket thing.

No one's ever done anything like that for me before. Was it on purpose? Or was he just a dork who happened to say the right thing at the right time?

"I'm serious, and move in with us," Dad was saying to Anne, still teasing her about her boyfriend.

"I probably should," Anne agreed.

"So you ready for the game?" Dad asked JJ, and then listened to him talk about what happened at practice and the team's prospects for victory against North Miami Academy.

"How's the car running?" he asked Mom, and then he told her to take it in for servicing because of the noise it makes when she puts it in reverse.

But to me? Nothing.

I cleared my throat. "My birthday is in a couple of weeks."

Mom looked up from her plate of chicken, mashed potatoes, and green beans. "I know. Did you want something special this year?" she asked.

I nodded. "I want a party."

Mom's eyebrows shot up, but she didn't say anything. She glanced at my dad, who finally turned his head to look at me. "What kind of party?" he asked.

I took a deep breath. "A big, fancy party that I can invite the whole school to. A 'welcome to being a teen' party, with music and dancing and food and all kinds of fun things to do. Maybe a Mardi Gras theme, you know? With floats and performers and beads and all that. I've never had a big party before; I just think all the kids would have such a great time."

Dad glanced at Mom. She shrugged her shoulders. JJ's head swung back and forth between the two of them as if he was at a tennis match. Mine probably did, too.

"A big party, huh?" Dad said slowly.

"To celebrate being a teen." I know, I'd said that already, but I guess I thought it would help convince them. After all, being a teenager was kind of a big deal. "A lot of kids do it." I told them about how Jewish kids celebrate, just in case they didn't know. "It's like saying you're growing up—that's what this kid David said, anyway."

"Oh, that's what David said," Dad repeated. He sounded a little annoyed, but I wasn't sure why. Just like I wasn't sure why my face felt warm or why every time I mentioned David's name, I kind of wanted to smile.

"And who is this David?" Mom asked. "I've never heard you mention him before. Is he one of the scholarship kids?"

"No, he's new. He just started going to Gatewood a couple of months ago. He's in my English class and on the basketball team. His parents are professors. They teach at the university. He said he turns thirteen in August and—"

I stopped. They were all looking at me. JJ looked as if he was about to burst out laughing, but Mom and Dad had very different expressions on their faces. Surprised, I guess, is the right word for how my mom looked. As if she had just realized that I really was going to turn thirteen in a couple of weeks and that I wasn't a baby anymore. Dad looked . . . worried. I guess he doesn't like the idea of me talking about boys at all. I don't know why they should have been surprised or worried, though. I'd talked about boys before. I know lots of boys. But I guess I'd never gone on and on about a boy like that before. I thought about explaining how David stopped Shanita and Courtney from getting into a big thing or about how he said "Who's Jag U R?" and made the whole table laugh the other day. Or about how today he and Shanita had decided to arm-wrestle for the brownie that I didn't eat and Shanita almost won so David split it with her. Or how, even though he's not a scholarship kid or black, he has this way of making everyone I really like feel comfortable—but I didn't. Talking *more* about him wouldn't help.

"Well, we've learned quite a bit about David today," Mom said at last. "Do you know him, Anne?"

Anne's curly hair bounced as she nodded. "Sure. He moved here from Montana about two months ago. His parents are both college professors at the university. I think his mother's going to be teaching a summer workshop at Gatewood in robotics or something," she added. "I don't think I've ever said more than hello to him, but he seems like a nice kid."

"He is." I don't know why I said it, but for some reason, I felt I needed to defend him. When everyone looked at me again, my face got so hot I wished I'd kept my mouth shut.

"Sounds like somebody's got a crush," JJ murmured slyly, and then quickly ducked his face back into his plate to avoid the daggerlike look I shot at him.

Dad didn't say a word. He started stirring the mashed potatoes on his plate as if he was trying to turn them into potato soup.

"So you want a party," he said slowly.

I nodded.

"OK. You can have a party . . . on one condition." He dropped his fork and fixed me with a serious stare while I waited, with a sick feeling of dread. "You're going to sing for your friends."

"What?" I shook my head. "But Dad—"

"We'll rent a club, get a DJ, the best food and treats, the whole nine. Invite the whole middle school, I don't care. You can even schedule one of those photo shoots you like to do so much and put the pictures on the invitations or hang 'em on the walls. I'll fly Promise down to take some shots with you, or we can do it Saturday when she's here for the Jag U R concert. Poor kid's been through a lot lately." He paused, probably thinking about the robbery and how Promise could have been killed. "Anyway," he said, "it won't be just 'a party.' It'll be THE party. We'll show them how we *do*. But before the night is out, you're gonna take that mike and sing one song. Like Lonnie said."

I felt as if my heart had stopped. Or someone had sucked all the air out of my body, as if I was a big balloon in the shape of a person.

A party . . . but only if I sang?

"That's not fair!" I didn't mean to say it out loud, but the words escaped from my brain and spilled out of my mouth.

"What's not fair about it, Kayla?" Dad's eyes flashed with anger. "You want a party, I said fine. Good. Great! All I ask is that you take a step toward what you want in the process."

"But Dad—" *That's what you want, not me! I want to be a model! I want to have a fashion line! I don't want to sing!*

I wanted to say all that . . . but I also really wanted a party.

"No 'buts,' Kayla. The party for a song. What's it gonna be?"

# Chapter Six

## PROMISE

**"I**'m all ready," Tia announced.

It was Friday afternoon, school was done, and Tia was standing in front of me with a bright pink duffel bag slung over her shoulder, as if she was going somewhere. Charley had finally found ways to occupy himself during the school day that didn't involve following me from class to class, but I was under strict orders not to leave the building until he came for me. I was waiting for him . . . but only because I didn't want hear his mouth.

"But Tia, I told you, we're not leaving for Miami until tomorrow morning. The concert's *tomorrow* night!"

"I know, but"—Tia shuffled her feet nervously—"I asked my mom, and she said I could sleep over at your house tonight. That's OK, isn't it?"

"Well . . ." I began. "I didn't ask my mom."

"I know, but I've been over your house a dozen times. She won't mind," Tia said, as if she'd already cleared the sleepover with my mom before she left for New York.

"Yeah, but I've also got rehearsal with the LOL Girls, tonight."

"Oh, cool! I'd love to watch that. I bet you guys are great!"

"Thanks. The choreographer is really strict, though. No one is allowed to watch the practices, not even our moms. He says other people are distractions when we're learning a new routine."

"Oh," Tia said sadly. "Well, I guess I'll just have to wait for you with Deidre, then, right? I mean, it's only, what, an hour?"

"An hour and a half," I corrected. I wasn't sure I even wanted to go to the rehearsal at all, but I didn't say it. I kept thinking about what happened last time and the whole robbery thing. Even though I knew the dance class wasn't anywhere near the storage place, I just felt antsy about it. Besides, we still had almost a month to practice, more than enough time. If I didn't show, the girls would be mad, but they were mad already, so what was the difference?

"Never mind," I told Tia. "I'll text Deidre and ask her to call them. I'm not going back there yet. I need just a little more time, you know? I'm the best dancer, anyway." My thumb flew over my keyboard with instructions for Deidre. "Done! Now we can hang out here tonight before we fly down to the concert tomorrow. I'll ask her if we can order in something from Applebee's."

"Yum! I love Applebee's."

"And we can watch a movie or something." The more I talked, the more I liked the idea.

"I'm just so excited, Promise. This is all going to be so much fun!" Tia was saying when a voice rumbled over my shoulder.

"Ready?" Charley stood over me, blocking the sun, taking

up more space than any one person should. "Stand up straight, Promise. You'll be a hunchback before you're thirty."

Immediately, I was irritated. My dad had security, but they always blended into the background of things, and you never noticed them unless something went wrong. Charley was the exact opposite. With his military expressions and his habit of correcting me as if I was a soldier in his boot camp, the guy was the ultimate in embarrassing. I looked around to see if any of the other kids were paying attention, but, except for Tia, no one else seemed to find him as annoying as I did. Most of them were busy chatting with one another or greeting their parents as their cars pulled up.

"Ready?" my drill instructor asked again.

"Sure."

"Good. Next stop, dance rehearsal. March!" He stepped off the curb to cross the street to the parking lot. "Walk behind me, like I told you."

"Is that really necessary?" I sighed. "I don't think anyone in this school—"

"You never know who's watching," Charley said cryptically. "And frankly, I'm appalled by the lack of security at this school." He lowered his voice and glanced around at the line of students waiting for their parents to pick them up in the carpool line. "Do you have any idea how easy it would be to snatch a student from this environment? There's hardly any adult supervision, and the cars just roll up. I could force you into a car and be gone before anyone even noticed. That's one of the first rules of self-defense, Promise. Don't ever let anyone force you into a car. Fight with everything you've got." He stopped and swiveled his block of a head toward Tia. "Young lady, are you following us?"

Tia's eyes widened as she glanced between us, drinking in his words like a person sipping a thick chocolate milkshake through a narrow straw.

"This is my friend Tia. She's coming home with me."

"Negative." Charley shook his head. "Next stop, dance rehearsal. No audience."

"I'm not going to dance rehearsal. I already texted Deidre. Tia's sleeping over, and we're going to take it easy and chillax before we go to Miami tomorrow."

"Negative."

"What do you mean, 'negative'?" I demanded. I'd put up with a week of his covert-affairs crap. I'd really just about had it.

"Negative. It means no." Charley said, as if he thought I was stupid or something. "Tia is a deviation from the schedule your parents set for you. I don't have the authority to allow any outsiders." He took out his phone and studied something on the screen. "See," he said, showing me a calendar entry. "She's on the list for Saturday but not for Friday."

"List? Outsider?" I took Tia by the hand and laughed. "She's not an outsider. She's my friend. And she's been to my house after school before plenty of times. She's on your stupid list for Saturday, so what difference does it make? My mom and dad wouldn't mind. So get out of the way and—"

Charley folded his arms over his chest and blocked us. I tried to step around him, but he moved again and again, blocking me every time I tried to get past. I heard some laughter behind me and realized that I finally had my audience—and not in a good way. It probably looked ridiculous: this massive bodyguard and me doing a two-step in the parking lot in front of my mom's Escalade, but I couldn't stop myself.

"Stop!" I shouted at him at last. "Just cut it out!"

"No one gets into the house without prior clearance, Promise!" he shouted back. "Period. She can come Saturday but not tonight."

"Clearance! What is this? The CIA? She's my friend, and you are completely humiliating me in front of her. Now, get out of the way!" I shoved him with all my might, but it was like pushing the Georgia Dome and expecting it to move. That made me even madder. "Move!" I screamed. "MOVE!"

"It's OK, Promise," Tia said. "I can just go home, and I'll see you tomorrow as planned."

"No!" I hollered, giving Charley's thick chest one more shove for good measure. "I'm calling my mom! She'll explain to you how stupid this is."

"Promise," Charley began. "Your mom—"

"Oh, shut up," I hissed, whipping out my phone like a diva calling her agent on a movie set. But unfortunately, my mom was on a *real* movie set. Her phone didn't even ring. I was dumped straight into her voice mail.

"Mom!" I began, ready to tell the whole story. Then I remembered that it might be hours before she heard it. Way too late for her to do anything about what was happening right now. "Never mind. This bodyguard guy is a complete jerk," I added before hanging up, and I didn't care how mad my mom got about me insulting an adult. He *was* a jerk.

Deidre answered when I called her, but she was no help. "It's OK with me, Promise, but it's not for me to decide," she said with a sigh. "New rules. Only your mom and dad can

OK these things now." She hesitated. "You can try your dad, I guess."

My heart sank. It wasn't that I thought my dad would say no, although he wouldn't be thrilled to hear that I wanted to skip rehearsal. He was always getting after me about my lack of discipline. "You can't just expect because you're my daughter, you're going to get to skip the hard work that goes with being an artist." If he'd said that once, he'd said it a thousand times. I'd get a lecture, and I might have to go rehearse, but he wouldn't have a problem with Tia coming over.

The problem was reaching him. He almost never answered his own phone, and going through assistants would probably take more time than I had.

"Maybe you can try a text," Deidre suggested before she hung up. "It's worth a shot."

I texted and waited.

No answer.

I tried his phone.

Voice mail.

Standing there in the parking lot—which was emptying car by car as all the kids got their rides and headed home to enjoy their weekends—I even tried my dad's assistant.

Voice mail again.

I sighed. This wasn't going to work. Time to try something else.

"Charley," I said sadly as I put my phone away. "She's my friend. She was coming over tomorrow, anyway. You're right, I should go to rehearsal, and Tia already agreed to wait. Please, please . . ."

"Negative." Charley sounded less like the commander

in chief and more as if he was genuinely sorry. "I have my instructions, Promise. Your parents weren't expecting Miss Tia until tomorrow. It might be fine, or they may have other plans for you. I don't know which. Until we get an answer from them . . ." He shook his head. "Negative."

I felt like crap, but I knew I was beat. I hugged Tia. "I'm really sorry."

Tia tried to smile, but she looked as if she was about to cry. "It's OK. I guess I should have asked first. The thing is"—she looked around the deserted parking lot—"I missed my ride."

I raised my eyebrows to Charley in one last desperate appeal. "Can't we at least drive her home?"

Charley shook his head. "That's not in my instructions."

I glared at him. "But how will she get home?"

"It's OK," Tia said bravely. "I'll manage. Sometimes Mrs. Rawls gives me a lift. If I run, I might be able to catch her before she goes home. See you tomorrow!" She hurried away, her pink bag bobbing sadly on her shoulders as she ran.

I felt terrible: angry and guilty and embarrassed all rolled into one. I stepped out in front of Charley toward the SUV.

"Behind me," he barked immediately, thrusting me behind him.

"Leave me alone!" I yelled. All the anger I felt came shooting out of me like hot lava. "I wish you'd just—just go away! I liked things better the way they were before you showed up. You're ruining everything! I just had to send my best friend away in tears because of you! You know she doesn't have a way home. She might end up having to walk—or, worse, take the city bus. We could have taken her. No big deal. But no! It's not in your instructions, so she has to walk! A girl! All alone!

Doesn't that bother you? Don't you care?"

"Of course, I care," Charley snapped. "But your safety is my primary responsibility. Later I might have more latitude. But right now, we're going by the book."

"Later?" I crossed my arms. "If I have anything to say about it, there's not going to be a later. I'm behind you, like you want. Let's just get into the car. I'm ready to go home."

"You mean rehearsal. Unless you're sick or something."

"Yeah, I'm sick," I muttered, sliding into the car.

"Negative. You're not."

"Am too." I said softly, after he closed the door and locked me inside. "Sick of you."

"I hate him," I told my mother hours later.

"He's just doing his job, Promise." Even over the phone, I heard the heaviness of her sigh. She sounded tired and a little down herself. "And I think it's good. You and Tia just assume that what you want to do is going to be OK with everyone else. The truth is, I might have had something for you to do this afternoon."

"But you didn't, and Deidre knew it. Why can't she just give permission like she used to?"

"Well, your dad's a little pissed with Deidre right now. He feels she shouldn't have left you alone in the car like that, given the time of night. He just doesn't trust her judgment right now."

"She just made one little mistake!"

"I know that, but it was a pretty serious one, Promise. You

could have been hurt—or worse. I'm sure in time, he'll come to trust her again, but for now, you're going to have to get used to Charley and a stricter level of security."

"I don't think this should be up to him," I said angrily. "I mean, Dad doesn't live with us. He's not here. He doesn't know. I already sent him a text, and when I get to talk to him, I'm going to tell him this is just not working. It's not working!"

Mom was quiet for a long time. "Promise, I know you don't like it, but I think Charley's here to stay. And maybe that's not a bad thing. The truth is, our lives have changed a lot. Your dad's career is on fire, my career is going well, and you're getting older. People are interested in you in a way they never were before. You have to understand that not everyone has your best interests at heart. We've gotten used to living as if we were nobody, but that's just not the case anymore. I'm sorry, honey, but you're not just *any* kid. You're the child of celebrities, and there are people out there who are so jealous and mean-spirited that they would think nothing of hurting you."

I thought about how scared I had been when those boys shot at the car, and I knew that what she was saying was right.

"But does it have to be *him*?" I complained. "Can't we find someone who's more . . ." I searched my vocabulary for the word, but I couldn't find it. "Can't we find someone who isn't such a jerk?"

For the first time in our conversation, my mother laughed. "He *is* a bit of a drill sergeant, isn't he? But that's his background. I heard he was in the Marines for, like, twenty years. He can't help it. But I'll tell you what, I'll call him in a bit and tell him it's OK for Tia to come over anytime, as long as it's

OK with him. You two can go over and get her first thing in the morning, OK?"

I grimaced. "Does he have to? Why can't Deidre and I do it?"

"You haven't been listening. Even if Deidre goes, Charley will be going, too, and there's no point in both of them going." She paused. "Tell me this: did you go to rehearsal?"

"Yeah," I muttered. I didn't tell her how badly it went or that the girls were still mad at me. I didn't tell her that I had been in such a bad mood that Derrick finally told me I was wasting his time. "Yeah, I went."

"Good." There was noise in the background on her end of the line and the sound of another voice, as if someone had just walked into the room. "Hold on, baby," she said. "WHAT?" I heard her yell. "What? Show me!"

"Mom?" I asked. She sounded really angry and a little scared. "Mom? What's the matter?"

She didn't answer me. I heard more muffled talking, and when she finally came back on the phone, she sounded completely different. There was an edge to her voice that hadn't been there before.

"Promise, I have a very important question for you, and I need for you to answer me honestly."

I was scared. She sounded super serious and even a little angry. "OK," I said cautiously.

"Did you tell anyone about the robbery the other night? Anyone? One of your teachers or one of your friends or one of the LOL Girls? Anyone?"

"No, Mom!" I said almost immediately. "I didn't tell anyone."

Of course, that wasn't completely true. I'd told Tia, but that was different. First of all, Tia was a kid like me. Second, she wouldn't tell something like that to anyone, let alone to media or anyone that mattered, I was sure of it. She wasn't that kind of girl. And besides, she probably didn't even read blogs or gossip columns. She probably didn't even know that people could get paid for selling stories about celebrities and that sometimes the money could be really good. If it hadn't been for how scary angry my mother sounded, I might have told my mom that, but I didn't.

"Are you sure, Promise?" Mom wasn't ready to let it go. "I know how close you and Tia are."

"I didn't tell her! I swear!" I insisted. "I wanted to, but you told me not to, so I didn't! Why?"

Mom blew an angry breath. "The whole thing is all over the blogs. One of my castmates just showed me that celebrity kids site, and the whole story is there. Some of the other ones are picking it up now, too. I don't understand it. The only ones who knew about it were you and me and your dad. And Deidre, of course." She groaned. "Someone told. Your father is going to *freak*. Oh, my God, what am I going to say to him? He's already annoyed with me for sending you out to the storage unit in the first place, and now this!"

I knew she wasn't looking forward to talking to my dad about the whole thing again.

And the last time I was in a blog story, it had been a complete nightmare. Some blogger reported that I was dead—killed in a car accident—and it went viral. People were reading about it all around the world. People were calling my parents to say how sorry they were about what happened. It was crazy! I had to go on TV and the radio to prove it wasn't true. I was only, like, seven or eight when that happened.

It wasn't something I was going to forget, not as long as I lived. I still don't understand why anyone would make up a lie like that. But as my mom has told me a thousand times, "Some people gotta hate."

That whole thing was horrible, but I'd never thought about how it must have been for my mom before. It must have been even worse for her than for me. Now that she was so far away and wouldn't be home for weeks, I realized how much she did for me. She was front and center at every show, every performance, and every school play. Well, she'd missed a few, but for the most part, she was there. And we talked about everything, almost like two sisters, and when it didn't interfere with school, she let me go with her when she traveled.

My mom is great, a terrific mom. And I'd just told her one of the biggest lies of my life as a reward.

"Other people knew, Mom." I just wanted to make her feel better; I mean, it wasn't her fault. She had just given me the whole lecture about how some people didn't have our best interests at heart, and now I felt she needed to hear it, too. "Lots of them. Dad's assistants knew, and his security team. And Charley. And maybe even the robbers figured it out. They had my phone."

"Yeah, you're right, Promise." She sounded relieved. "I hadn't thought of that. You're right. I don't think any of Dad's people would say anything—they're like Deidre. They've been with us for years. They've never sold him out before. Why would they do it now? But I forgot about your phone. That's very possible . . ." Her voice changed again. "All right. You should get to bed. You have a big day tomorrow with Kayla. Oh, did I tell you she's invited you to do some kind of photo shoot with her? That will be fun."

*Great, a photo shoot with Little Miss Perfect.* I rolled my eyes, but of course, my mom couldn't see that.

"I don't want you to worry about any of this, OK?"

"OK." Guilt did a funny little corkscrew inside me. "Mom?"

"Yes, baby?"

I missed her so much that I almost confessed that I'd told Tia, but I knew I couldn't.

"I love you."

"I love you, too. Now, go to bed," Mom murmured.

I did . . . but not before I had typed "celebrity kids blog" into my iPhone's browser and read the story and a few of the comments.

"Poor kid. She must have been terrified." Then: "Who carries around that kind of money? Dumb girl deserves what she got."

I shut the phone down and lay in the darkness, thinking about everything my mom had said.

# Chapter Seven

### KAYLA

**"W**here is she?" I asked my mom for probably the billionth time that afternoon.

Promise was supposed to have been at my house two hours ago, but she was late, as usual. She's always late—unless it's about her.

"Deidre says they had to take a later flight," Mom said, reading the text. "They're on the way to the studio now, but they hit some traffic." I could tell that she was getting a little annoyed, too. After all, the stylist, the lady who was doing the hair, and the makeup artist—plus the photographer himself—were all standing around looking at us. Sure, they were getting paid, but I could tell they didn't like waiting any more than I did.

"Why don't you just go ahead and take a few more shots of just yourself?"

"No, Mom." If she hadn't just suggested that exact same thing two minutes ago, it might not have annoyed me so much. "This is the outfit for the shots with Promise," I said impatiently. "I told you, I don't want to change clothes again."

"Well, you could do some close-ups. Just your face. Maybe we could use them for the invitations—"

"I don't want my face on the invitations!" I snapped. "It's a Mardi Gras party, Mom! Who puts their face on a Mardi Gras party invitation? It's stupid."

My mom's expression hardened. "Look, Kayla Jones, I know you're disappointed and upset that Promise is so late, but you need to watch your mouth. Right *now*," she said firmly, "or we can call this whole thing off. The photo shoot, the party, everything. Do you understand me?"

She was serious. I knew it . . . and she knew I knew it.

And there was a part of me that wanted to call the whole thing off. The party was still more than a week away, but I was already dreading singing. I had changed my mind about what to sing a hundred times. The only thing I knew for sure was that it had to be short. Very, very short.

I had told my friends about the party the very next day, and of course, everyone was thrilled. Courtney sat at the "black table" with us again. Shanita rolled her eyes, but she didn't say anything, so I thought it would be OK.

I was wrong.

"So you never told us," Courtney began. We had been talking about the previous night's basketball—Gatewood had beaten Starrow. "Why weren't you at the game last night?"

The memory of Lonnie Sonic and my new assignment flashed in my mind, triggering a tickle of nervousness in the pit of my stomach, but I tried to play it cool. "I had some other stuff I had to do. But I heard that David was the star."

"That David kid, he's good!" Jamar said respectfully. He didn't add "for a white boy," but I knew he was probably thinking it. When I first started sitting with the scholarship kids, Jamar told me that the school he'd gone to before Gatewood had been all black and Hispanic. He didn't really know any white kids at all until last year, but I never would have known it if he hadn't told me. With his big curly 'fro (he wears all that hair in cornrows close to his head during the basketball season) and easy dimpled smile, he's the kind of kid who gets along with everyone. I knew for a fact that half the cheering squad—all white girls, except for me—had a crush on him last year, because he's handsome and has muscles that pop when he lifts his arm to take a shot.

I admit he's got a nice body compared with a lot of the boys at Gatewood, but I never thought of him that way. He reminds me of JJ, my brother, too much.

"Aww, man, that last shot was amazing!" Omarion agreed.

"I know!" Courtney said. "We won the game because of him. The score was tied and—"

"Sank it from the top of the key." Jamar lifted his arm, replaying the shot with an imaginary basketball. "Swish. Nothing but net." He looked around the pavilion. "Where is he?"

"With the Bloody Red Queen," I said. "Getting some extra help, I think."

"Well, he better be in science," Shanita said. "He's my lab partner. I don't want to have to make that fruit battery without him." Shanita fixed her eyes on me. "You should have seen him. Too bad you missed the game."

"Yeah, almost everyone was there. Starrow is one of our biggest rivals!" Courtney added. "Remember last year, when you were on the squad and they beat us by ten points? Boy, we were all depressed for a week." She shook her head. "I wish you were still a cheerleader, Kayla. It's too bad you had to quit." She paused for a split second, then changed subjects on a dime. "What do you want for your birthday?"

The question surprised me. To be honest, I wasn't expecting presents at all. I know a lot of kids look forward to getting birthday presents, but I don't really need any presents; my parents pretty much get me everything I want. The gift I wanted was to see my friends get together and have fun—and I said so.

Courtney wouldn't leave it alone. "Oh, you *have* to have presents," she insisted. "Presents are the way the guests acknowledge that they've had a good time. My mother told me it's rude to show up at a birthday party without a present. Only the most low-class person would do something like that."

That's when I got it. I glanced at the rest of the table, but no one would look at me. Of course, they wouldn't: except for Courtney and me, all the other kids at the table were scholarship kids. I didn't know if they could afford presents, and I didn't care.

"I don't want presents, Courtney," I repeated firmly. "I want *friends*—"

"I'll talk to you later, Kayla," Shanita mumbled, picking up her trash and leaving the table. She kept her head down, but it sounded as if she was about to cry. As she walked away, it seemed to me that her stride didn't have its usual confidence.

"I'd better go see if she's OK," Chemine said softly, leaving the table, too.

The boys sort of pulled away from us, settling into a quiet conversation that had nothing to do with parties or presents or anything we girls had been talking about.

"What did you do that for?" I hissed, turning to Courtney angrily.

"What?" Courtney stretched her eyes wide, her voice rising as she faked innocence. "What did I do? I just said—"

"Yeah, I heard what you said. You were trying to make everyone feel bad. You were trying to rub it in that you have money and they don't," I muttered in a low voice. "As if that matters!"

"I didn't say they had to have money. I said that it's right to bring a present to a birthday party."

"And I said I don't want any presents!" I repeated angrily, and stood up. "Honestly, Courtney, that was just mean. If you're going to be that mean, maybe you should go back to sitting with your other friends."

Courtney blinked her big eyes at me. "Gee, I'm sorry, Kayla. I didn't mean to be mean," she said, but I didn't really believe it. I think she meant to cause exactly what she caused . . . and was only sorry because I was mad about it. "Where are you going?"

"To find Shanita and Chemine," I answered.

She stood up, smoothing the skirt of her khaki uniform. "I'll come, too."

I threw my palm up like a stop sign. "No. You've caused enough problems."

Shanita's not the type to let on that her feelings are hurt, so when I found her crying in the bathroom while Chemine patted her arm and handed her tissues, I was even angrier with Courtney than I had been before.

"If I could get you something, I would," she said, while big, fat tears rolled out of her black eyes and down her cheeks. "Maybe I should just not come."

"Stop it," I said, hugging her. "I want you there. I couldn't care less about presents. In fact, if anyone brings me a present, I'm going to give it right back and send them home."

Shanita laughed. "No, I wouldn't want you to do that."

"But I will," I declared. "In fact, I'm going to ask my mom to have the invitations printed to say 'No gifts.' I'm that serious." I hugged her again, taking in the smell of her coconut hair crème. "Are we good?"

She sniffled one last time but nodded.

Chemine dropped an arm around Shanita's shoulder. "I told you Kayla wasn't like that," she said.

"Like what?" I asked.

"A rich snob," Chemine explained. With her accent, it sounded like "reech snub." "A rich snob. Like a lot of kids in this school."

*A rich snob?* Shanita had said that about me?

I tried to laugh it off, but it bugged me, even though I knew I wasn't one . . . or at least, I didn't think I was.

"I can't believe you were friends with that girl," Shanita said, her lips twisting with disgust. "I really hope you aren't taking her to the Jag U R concert. I mean, I don't even know if you're going—you never said—but if you are, I hope you don't take her. She's not a real friend. She's just trying to see what she can get."

"She's not so bad," I answered, because it was true. Courtney had never acted like this before . . . but then, until last year, all the kids at Gatewood had been rich. And as for Jag U R, I was going, but given the dynamics with my friends right now, I'd decided it was probably better that I go with Promise and not invite any friends from school this time.

"Not so bad!" Shanita gave me a look as if she'd changed her mind and chalked me up as a rich snob after all, then shook her head. "Poor Kayla. You've been living in this little bubble for so long, you don't even know any better."

*What does that mean?* The question was on the tip of my tongue, but just then the bell rang, signaling the end of lunch.

"Come on, girls," Chemine said. "We must hurry, or we will be late to social studies."

I didn't get to ask.

It was still on my mind the next day when I got ready for the photo shoot.

We'd quickly found a location for the party and decided to cover the walls with shots of me, and there wasn't a minute to waste to get all that together. I was already uptight about school and the party, and I knew the pictures needed to be perfect. Promise being late was the last straw.

Normally, when I'm nervous, thinking about what I want to wear helps to calm me down. But even that wasn't working, because I was screaming at my mother like Naomi Campbell having a diva moment.

"OK, I'm sorry. I'm sorry. But I had a whole concept planned out." I pulled out the Look Book and pointed to the page where I'd drawn a picture of Promise and me, back to back, sort of leaning against each other. "I wanted the two of us posing together. Like—"

"Mary-Kate and Ashley," my mother finished. "I know. I've only heard it a thousand times. I get it. Your dad says he wishes you'd put just a tenth of the energy you put into this photo shoot into thinking about your performance."

"I *am* thinking about it!" It wasn't a lie. I was thinking

about it all the time—I just hadn't come up with anything. Right now, I just wanted Promise to hurry up and get here so that this whole thing could be over with.

I've been in lots of photography studios for one reason or the other, and this one was definitely nice. There were several dressing rooms with lots of light, so you could change clothes and do makeup and hair. The photographer went by one name— Willis—and I knew he'd done a lot of high-fashion shoots for glossy magazines such as *Miami Style*, and now he was doing some cover shots for national magazines such as *Gossip* and *Real Stars*. He was really hot right now, and people were standing in line to hire him, but my dad had fixed it, and here I was.

Still, there were some things that bugged me, such as the dark blue backdrop he'd picked for several of my shots. It reminded me of school pictures; there wasn't anything exciting about it at all.

"You're the star. Not the backdrop," Willis said when I asked if he had another color. He was a white guy, a little heavier than I had expected, wearing a black T-shirt and black jeans and bright yellow eyeglasses.

"But I don't think that color blue will do anything for me," I insisted. "My skin has a yellow undertone, and the skirt is—"

"It'll be fine." Willis sounded as if he would have patted me on the head if I were standing close enough. That was part of the reason I was mad.

I fingered the short- tiered skirt and denim jacket the stylist had picked out for me and wished for the dark jeans and frayed vest I'd planned to wear. Sometimes I can visualize something, even without drawing it in my Look Book, and I knew this look wasn't right.

"I had different clothes planned," I muttered so the stylist wouldn't hear. I really hated the outfit. I'd gone along with it because she's a professional, but the truth was, no girl my age would ever wear anything this cutesy. I looked like a ten-year-old in that flouncy skirt with that huge white flower headband sticking out of my head.

"Your father asked for this look, and you look adorable," Willis said.

*Adorable?* I sighed. It wasn't at all the description I wanted—not for my thirteenth birthday—but I knew if Dad had asked for it, there wouldn't be any use in arguing. I'd just have to find a way to make it work.

"Let's take a few," he continued, and started snapping my picture before I'd even had time to strike a pose or figure out my best angle. And when the next outfit was as bad as the first, and Willis still wouldn't change that drab blue backdrop, and Promise still hadn't showed, I was just about done.

By the time I heard voices in the hallway, I was in a really, really bad mood. The studio door swung wide, and a beefy dark-skinned man in a black T-shirt stepped into the room. He took a quick look around before speaking to my mom.

"You must be Mara," he said. "I'm Charley Williams. Promise, Tia, and Deidre are in the changing room, getting ready—"

I didn't listen to the rest of it. I stormed out of the studio toward the makeup room, ready to give Promise a piece of my mind.

For a second, I thought I was looking at Bella, Promise's mother. Promise still had on her sunglasses, and she was sitting in the hairstylist's chair with the same "look at me" grace that seems to come so easily to her mom. She was laughing and talking with someone behind her, and I expected to see Deidre standing there, but instead, another girl stood beside her chair. An older girl, I thought at first, because of the very tight short skirt and high-heeled shoes she wore. Her long reddish hair brushed her shoulders, and she had on as much makeup as I did—but then, I was made up for photos. This girl apparently walked the streets that way. When I walked in, she looked my fluffy skirt up and down and cut her eyes at Promise, with a look that I knew meant they'd laugh about me later.

"Well, don't you look cute?" Deidre said from behind me. She carried a big garment bag that must have held the clothes Promise had brought for the photo shoot. *She* would get to wear what she picked out for herself. I knew that without asking. But me? The weight of my father's control settled like a rock on my heart. I wanted to cry, but I swallowed it down and focused on how mad I was instead.

"Hi, Kayla!" Promise said in a loud dramatic voice. She jumped out of the chair and opened her arms wide, kissing the air beside my cheek the way they do in Hollywood. "You look great!"

"You're late."

"I know. I overslept, and we missed the first flight, and then we had some security trouble at the airport," she said, and the made-up girl started giggling, remembering some story I didn't know. "But I'm here now," she finished quickly. She reached out and grabbed her friend's hand. "This is Tia. She's my BFF from school."

"Hey," the girl said. We stared at each other the way girls do, checking each other out. Now that I was looking right at her, I could tell that she was probably my age, maybe even a bit younger, and it was the makeup that made her look so old. It made me wonder about my own face. Maybe the makeup artist had gone at it a little too heavy. I scratched at my cheek a bit with a fingertip and felt something waxy beneath my nail.

"I've heard a lot about you," the girl said at last.

I raised an eyebrow at her. "Really? I haven't heard anything about you. Not even that you were coming."

Promise's mouth dropped open in surprise. "But my mom said she talked to your mom. She thought since I've been having such a rough week and she had to go away that it might be more fun if a friend came with me."

More fun? I remembered when Promise and I used to have fun *together*, without having to bring along other friends, but whatever. I had other friends, too. Plenty of them. Only one of them was acting like a mean girl, and the other thought I was a snob.

"She must have forgotten to tell me," I said nastily. I didn't even bother to say hello to Promise's friend. I would have pretended she wasn't even there if she hadn't gotten in my face.

"Promise tells me you're going to be having a birthday party soon," Tia said, smiling as if we were on the road to becoming best friends. "That sounds soooo fun."

I just looked at her as if she was a CGI alien from some movie and then turned my head.

"Hurry up, Promise," I said. "We've had the photographer waiting for more than an hour." I reached for the suitcase that Deidre had dropped on the carpeted floor between us. "The stylist picked out these outfits for us. I think she's going for an updated naughty schoolgirl or something, but the shoes she brought are even worse than the skirts. I refused to wear them." I flipped the lock on her bag. "Did you bring anything black?" There was a shoe box right on top. "Oh, what are these?"

"Kayla! Don't!" Promise cried, but it was too late. I'd already opened the box and found . . .

A pair of fuchsia Louboutin ballerina flats.

I pulled them slowly out of the suitcase and studied them. They looked just like the shoes that had disappeared from the Mickies last weekend. They were even my size.

Promise's feet are smaller than mine.

"Oh, crap!" Promise muttered. "What did you have to do that for? Now you've spoiled everything."

"*I've* spoiled everything?" I screamed. All the feelings I'd been trying to keep in came exploding out of me, and I threw first one shoe and then the other at her. "You stole my shoes, when you knew how important that night was to me and my family! And *I'm* the one who spoiled everything?" I grabbed a handful of her clothes, then another and another, and threw them at her, too. I was about to pick up the whole empty suitcase and throw at it her when my mom came bursting into the room, with the bodyguard at her heels.

"Kayla! Put that down!" She looked first at me and then at Promise, then at the clothes and shoes littering the space between us.

"What on earth is going on here?"

"Ask *her*," Promise spat in an ugly tone. "I felt bad about her losing her shoes at the Mickies, so I bought her another pair for her birthday and—"

"You *took* my shoes at the Mickies, Promise!" I countered.

"You took them, and now you feel bad, and you're trying to play it off as if they're a present!"

"They *are* a present!" Promise screamed.

"Liar," I hissed.

Promise's face tightened with rage. "What—did—you—say?" She said every word as if she wished it was a punch. "What did you call me?"

"I called you a liar, because that's what you are."

"If I'm a liar, you know what you are, Kayla Jones? You're *nothing*, that's what you are!" Promise screamed in my face. "If you didn't have a dad who could buy you a career, buy you some talent, buy you some friends, everyone would see you for the pathetic loser you really are."

"Well, at least I'm not so desperate for attention that I'll do or say any stupid thing."

"No, you don't do or say *anything*—unless your daddy tells you to!"

"That's enough, both of you!" Mom sounded angry, but when I glanced at her, her dark eyes seemed more shocked than anything. "What's gotten into you two? This is no way for sisters to behave! Kayla, apologize to Promise, right now!"

"Me? Apologize? Did you hear what she said to me, Mom? She stole my shoes and then had the nerve to say all that crap about me."

"I didn't steal her shoes!" Promise wailed. "I bought her a new pair to replace the ones she lost."

"I didn't lose them! You stole them!"

"Kayla Jones, that's enough!" The surprise was gone. Now Mom was just mad. "One more word, and you're going home."

"WORD," I said angrily. It wasn't like me to be this disrespectful, and I knew I would be in serious trouble, but I didn't care. "Now, let's go home. I don't want to take a picture with her, anyway." I pushed my way out of the room and into the hallway. As I stomped toward the other dressing room, I heard my mother apologizing for me.

"She's been on edge all week. I think this whole party thing is getting to her."

In a minute, she'd come find me, tell me how disappointed in me she was and how she'd have to tell my father. And she'd make me apologize, and I would. I'd even smile and take the shoes—my "present." But I wouldn't mean it. And I certainly wasn't going to spend the weekend with Promise and her friend laughing and talking together, while I sat quietly and watched. *She* needed a friend? *She'd* had a tough week? Promise needed just a *single* day in my world. Then she'd know what real pressure—pressure to be perfect, to be talented, to be a star—was about.

I found my bag and grabbed my phone. Mom would tell me I should have asked first, but since I was already in trouble, that didn't matter much. A wild feeling I couldn't describe or explain seemed to have taken me over. I was going to invite a friend to go to the concert and sleep over without talking to her first. All I had to do was decide: Courtney or Shanita?

If I picked one, the other would be mad. I was doomed either way . . . unless I invited both of them, and I couldn't see how that would work.

"She's a little full of herself," Courtney told me after meeting Promise at my house last year. "I mean, she's nice and all that. But she acts as if she's the famous one, not her parents. You know?"

At the time, I had actually been stupid enough to defend Promise. Today, though, those words were going to earn Courtney concert tickets. Shanita would be really, really mad, but I told myself I would make it up to her somehow.

"What on earth is going on?" Courtney whispered when she climbed into the car and saw Promise and Tia in the rear seat. Promise had a small scratch on the side of her cheek, but other than that, you couldn't tell to look at her that we'd been fighting. I hated to admit it, but she looked cute in a pair of white shorts and a long blue tunic over a white T-shirt, with her favorite new Jordans on her feet. Tia, on the other hand, had on a skimpy little sundress that was just barely long enough to cover her behind.

"Long story," I muttered. "Tell you about it later."

"Well, thanks for inviting me," Courtney said. She was wearing black leggings, a bright pink top with sequins along the edges, and a pair of gladiator-style flat sandals. "Though I'm a little surprised. I thought you'd probably invite Shanita or one of the other kids this time."

I didn't say anything. I didn't want to think about what Shanita would say when she found out, especially after all that "snob" and "bubble" talk.

From the rear seat of my Mom's Land Rover, I heard Promise whisper something, and her friend started giggling. They were talking about us, I was sure of it. That might have started another round, but Mom shot me a dark look, and I kept my mouth shut. I was on such thin ice, I didn't dare say anything else until I was away from her. If she'd had her way, I'd be sitting at home in my room, doing homework or flipping through fashion magazines. But when she told my dad, to my surprise, he took my side.

"She and Promise always fight like that," he said, chuckling. "It's how they show love. It don't mean a thing." As for inviting Courtney, he just shrugged and went back to the phone call he was on.

Courtney didn't say anything else, and even Promise and Tia finally stopped their whispering. The car was quiet until we arrived in the parking lot of the Miami Intercontinental Hotel, a very nice but low-key place about twenty minutes from the AmericanAirlines Arena. Mom ignored the front entrance and drove around to the back, where three large motorcoach buses were waiting with their engines running and their doors closed.

"We're here," she said into her phone, and a moment later, I saw my dad get out of the middle bus and wave.

"OK, girls," Mom said. "Have fun. See you later."

One by one, we slid out of the car.

"Hello, Parran," Promise said to Dad, using the French name for "godfather" that she'd called my dad her whole life. "This is my friend Tia."

Tia's eyes widened. "H-hello . . . sir," she said nervously, pulling at the top and the bottom of her dress. It was sky-blue, too tight, and too short and made it really obvious she was trying hard to look older. "It's amazing to meet you."

I've seen so many people look at my dad that way, as if they're talking to Jesus or something, and usually it makes me feel both proud and annoyed at the same time. I mean, it's nice to see my dad getting such adoration and respect, because he totally deserves it. He works all the time, and he always tries to do the very best he can in everything he does. But he's not God. Seeing that look and watching how people sometimes fall all over themselves over him make me want to scream, "Hey, he's a person, just like you!"

Dad just nodded at her. "All right, y'all. The concert starts in forty-five minutes. Time to roll."

Jag U R wasn't on our bus. My brother, JJ, was, but he didn't even take his ear buds out of his ears or slide over to make room for us. Deidre was on the bus, along with members of Jag U R's traveling entourage, but no one else I knew, since Dad had hopped on the bus with the performers to encourage them and vibe on the preconcert energy. I was glad to be away from that; it would just remind us both about his expectations for me, and I didn't feel I could pretend to be interested in that right now.

We followed a special route to the stadium and arrived at the rear of the venue only about thirty minutes before the show was supposed to start.

"Do you think we'll get to meet Jag U R before the show?" Tia asked Promise.

"No," Promise replied. She sounded bored. "Afterward . . . if at all." Promise had toured with her dad, so she knew what would happen. When the bus stopped, one of Dad's or Jag U R's security guards would hustle us inside to get our backstage passes. Then we'd probably be escorted to the green room—a place set up for the performers and the people who work with them to relax and hang out before and after the show—until it was time to go to the special seating area they would have set up for us. Of course, since we were with my dad, we definitely would at least get to say hi to Jag U R and hang out a bit backstage but not until later. Deidre would stay close to us and walk with us if we needed to go to the bathroom or anything like that—or at least, that's what I thought until I saw Charley, Promise's bodyguard, standing by the bus door waiting for her.

"Oh, great," Promise muttered. "I was hoping I wouldn't see him again until we were back in Atlanta."

Tia giggled. "Here we go again," she whispered.

My dad jogged over from the lead bus. "Guess what, Queen?" He smiled, showing us a glint of platinum. "There was a change in the schedule. Nu Gee's opening. You remember him, right?"

Did I remember Eugene? That was like asking if I knew my own name. Eugene was one of my father's artists, a kid only a year older than JJ. Dad signed him last year when he was just fifteen, and he spent the summer with us while he and Dad worked on his album. He was nice, very talented . . . and cute, and all summer long, every time Promise visited me, she'd say, "Eugene likes you, Kayla. He *likes* you likes you!" until I started to believe it.

Of course, other than Promise's teasing, there wasn't any more to the story. I'm not boy-crazy—I swear I'm not—so Eugene's like another brother to me. We just hung out when he wasn't working, watching TV on the couch or playing Wii or whatever. I'd been sorry when the album was done and he started touring to promote it, because I'd gotten so used to having him around.

The last thing I'd heard about him, though, was that he wasn't doing as well as my dad had hoped on the road, but I wasn't sure why.

"Thought you might like to go see him after his set. You and JJ," my dad continued. "You'll miss a bit of Jag U R, but—"

"Yes," I said a little too quickly. Promise giggled, and I heard her stupid whispering behind me. I wanted to turn around and tell her to shut up, but with my dad standing there, I didn't dare. I took a deep breath and told myself it didn't matter; seeing him would be the best thing to happen to me in a long time. Maybe I'd get to talk to him a bit about performing. He might even have some tips for me. But I didn't want to sound overeager or anything, so I shrugged and added, "I mean, if JJ wants to."

"JJ's gonna hang backstage with me, but . . ." He touched Deidre on the shoulder. "Will you walk her back there at the end of his set and keep an eye on them for me?"

"Sure, Lullabye. Glad to," Deidre said with a smile. "Now, come on, girls, let's get inside and get our backstage passes. Nu Gee will be a gray old grandfather before we even get into the arena at this rate!"

A booth was set up for us in the auditorium to the right of the stage at an angle that gave us an unobstructed view of the stage and yet separated us from the fans. It was draped with a silky-looking fabric and had a bank of seats facing the stage, along with a few tables and a little mini-fridge stocked with water and soda. We slipped in through a special door cut into the hallway behind the stage.

Charley took a position inside the booth near the entrance and stuck a pair of ear plugs in his ears. A moment later, he planted his feet wide apart, settling in for a long night of standing and crossing his arms, his eyes fixed on the crowd, not the stage.

"Why can't he stand outside with the rest of the security?" Promise muttered, but that was all she had time to say—or at least, all I heard. With a sudden blare of sound and light, Nu Gee sauntered onto the stage. The crowd seemed willing to give him a chance, because, like me, they were all on their feet, screaming and cheering.

My enthusiasm died quickly. Nu Gee's set was just OK. He bobbled some of the lyrics; he didn't seem to know where he was supposed to stand and kept messing up the dance routines. It was obvious that either he hadn't practiced or something else was wrong with him.

I could hardly believe how different he looked or how much he had changed as an artist. Gone was that quiet kid with the amazing voice I remembered listening to in my father's studio. This guy reminded me of a much older performer, one who didn't care about his fans anymore. The only time he seemed to find his groove was on his one hit song. For three minutes, the whole audience practically pulsated along with him, until he left all of us roaring with appreciation for his talents and jazzed for the coming appearance of Jag U R. But when Nu Gee tried to close his part of the show with another song off his latest album, the crowd seemed to get bored.

"I'll be back," I yelled over the crowd to the other girls.

Promise stood up, too. "I want to go. He's my friend, too."

"Negative," Charley interjected, putting out a hand to stop Promise. "That movement is not authorized."

"But she gets to go!" Promise whined.

"Mr. Jones authorized it, and Nu Gee is expecting her. Deidre and Miss Jones's father's security will escort her, and you will stay here."

Promise gave him a look that might have wilted a lesser person, but Charley seemed able to stand it just fine. If I hadn't been so excited to see Eugene, I might have laughed at the two of them bickering like an old married couple. But it was time to go.

"Do you want me to go in with you, or . . . would you like a minute?" Deidre asked when we reached a door with Nu Gee's name on it.

That surprised me, and it must have showed on my face. I mean, I never go anywhere by myself. Never. My mom or my dad or some adult or some kind of security is always with me. I was about to say that, when Deidre said, "Go ahead. I'll give you twenty minutes on your own with your friend, and then I'll come in and assume my official role as chaperone."

"But—"

"Well, I remember what it was like to be young. Sometimes I feel really bad for you kids. It's hard to grow up when there's always security or some other adult around. If you don't get to spread your wings sometimes, all by yourself, while you're a kid, I don't know how you'll ever learn to trust them when you're grown." She patted me on the behind. "Go on."

I turned the handle and stepped inside a little sitting room with chairs similar to those in the green room, but there was no one sitting in any of them. There was a small table piled with food and another television, now alive with the image of Jag U R as he paced the stage with his microphone, shouting his lyrics into the screaming crowd. A few feet ahead of me was another door, which I figured must lead to Eugene's changing area.

I didn't know what to do. I figured Eugene was expecting me, but I wasn't sure I should just barge into his private area, especially without JJ. After performing, he might have been showering or changing clothes or something. Walking in on that would be bad, and embarrassing for both of us, so I sat down on one of the chairs and tried to wait.

That was hard. First, I kept thinking of Eugene and how much I was looking forward to seeing him. I wanted to ask so many questions—about singing, about performing in front of people, about how his life had changed since I'd last seen him.

On the closed-circuit television, Jag U R segued into his next song and then another.

I started to worry. My dad was pretty busy. What if he hadn't had a chance to talk to him? Or what if Eugene had forgotten about me? Maybe he didn't even know I was out there waiting.

I stood up and knocked, softly at first and then more loudly.

"Come on!" a familiar voice cried.

Eugene was still dressed in the jacket, low-slung jeans, and heavy chains he'd worn onstage. He even still wore his sunglasses and his Balenciaga sneakers. He sat on a long, low sofa that almost filled the small room, making the tiny space seem even tighter. But what really made the room seem small was all the girls crammed on the little sofa with him. Two girls were snuggled up under his armpits, and two more were sitting on the low coffee table that his sneakered feet rested on. One of the girls kissed him on the cheek, and the other nuzzled his neck. Another one rubbed his leg, and the fourth was telling him how great his set was. Although they were all different shades and sizes, they were all dressed in skimpy little dresses and high-heeled shoes. Stripper wear. I mean, there's no design in it; it's just about showing as much body as you can.

"What's up, little girl?"

He and his girls all turned toward me as I stepped into the room in my jeans, little purple top, and flat sandals. My hair was pulled back into a ponytail. I'd loved the look when I left the house, but standing there looking at those glamorous older girls in their tiny dresses spilling boobs and behinds out of every inch of fabric, I probably looked like a dorky little twelve-year-old. I suddenly felt stupid for thinking that I could just sit down and talk with Eugene the way we used to do at my dad's studio. I was angry at Eugene and disappointed that he liked these kinds of girls. I knew all about groupies — all of my dad's artists had them. I just never thought of Eugene as the type.

But as mad as I was at him, I was even madder at myself for thinking for a single second that maybe Eugene might have kind of liked me.

And even more than that, I wished more than anything that I'd never come.

"Kayla!" Eugene cried, jumping up. "I—I—forgot."

"It's OK," I said. "I'll talk to you later." And I turned around to leave.

He stopped me before I reached the outer door.

"Don't go, Kayla," he said.

He swept off his sunglasses so I could see his face. His eyes were the same sweet brown that I remembered, but other than that, he seemed so much older now. Older and different.

"It's OK, really."

"No, don't go. Your dad told me you were coming by. I just got kinda . . ." He paused, searching for the right word that would explain the groupies in the next room. "Sidetracked," he finished lamely.

"Whatever," I said. To be honest, I felt like sinking into a hole in the ground and disappearing forever, but there was no way Eugene—or Nu Gee or whoever he really was these days—was going to know that. "I just wanted to say hello before you go back onstage. Hello. Now, good-bye."

"Wait!" Eugene put his hand on the door and stopped me from leaving. He paused a moment, then smiled a smile I could tell he thought was sexy. It probably worked on lots of girls, but it wasn't working on me. Not at all. In fact, I really wanted to slap it off his face—and I might have, except that I was pretty sure my dad would find out. "Um . . . you're not mad at me, are you, Kayla?"

"Why would I be mad?"

"Well, you know . . ." He turned up the smile another notch, so it was like those big bright lights at a football game. "Long time ago, you and me, we used to hang out a little."

"Like you said, that was a long time ago," I reminded him.

"Now, if you don't mind, I'm missing the concert. I want to get back to my friends."

"Sure," Eugene said, but he didn't move. "It's just, well . . ."

"What?"

"You won't mention this to your father, will you?" he blurted out at last, and that was when I noticed that he looked really scared. Really, really scared. "'Cause I know how tight you two are. I'm still new to this game, and I owe him a lot. I just don't want him to get pissed off with me because I dissed his little girl."

"Is that all you have to say? That you're worried about what I might say to my dad?"

Eugene looked unsure of himself. "Well . . . yeah. I mean, I don't want him mad at me. If he gets mad enough, he could switch my producers or take me off this tour or even drop me from the label."

"Is that the only reason you were ever nice to me, Eugene? Because you were trying to get in good with my dad? Because you didn't have to bother. My dad believes in your talent. If you're using it and the audience is into it, it's not going to matter whether I like you or not. But if you're just goofing off . . ." I shrugged. "I used to think you were so cool," I muttered angrily. "But after what you just said, I don't care if I ever see you again."

"Well, you might have to. Just before the show, your dad invited me to perform at your birthday party. He said I was gonna introduce your singing debut. He's gonna have some cameras there and stuff, release it on YouTube if it goes OK. He said he thought it might kick-start my career a bit—"

"*What?*"

Cameras? YouTube? What was my father thinking? There was no way I was ready for all of that! I had a million questions for Eugene, but he was too focused on his own problems to answer me.

"You won't say anything, will you, Kayla?" he begged. "I'm already in trouble. Please, Kayla? Please?"

Just then, Deidre's broad face appeared in the doorway behind us.

"Oh! I'm sorry—"

"It's OK, Deidre," I said. "Your timing is perfect. I'm ready to go back."

Eugene's eyes begged for an answer, but I didn't say a word. My head was reeling at the thought of the preparations my dad was making for what had started out as just a song, and I couldn't have cared less about Eugene's career right then. But I wasn't going to tell him that. Instead, I followed Deidre back into the corridor and left him standing there, wondering just what I'd say to Dad about him—and when.

# Chapter Eight

## PROMISE

"So . . . how's Eugene?" I asked Kayla after the concert.

We were sitting in her living room in our pajamas, eating the ice cream sundaes Aunt Titi—my nickname for Kayla's mom—had made us. Tia was talking so much I finally just stopped listening to her, and she gave up on me and wiggled her way into the conversation that Courtney and Kayla were having.

I was alone.

I was still really pissed with Kayla after all those awful things she accused me of at the photo shoot, the kind of low, rumbling anger that makes the pit of your stomach warm, and every single look or word she spoke made me wonder if I were going to blow up like some kind of human volcano. I faked it pretty well through the concert, and Jag U R was great and everything, but every time I looked at Kayla, I felt like screaming or crying. She actually thought I'd *steal* something from her? We used to be so close. What happened?

OK, so I knew. Lately, we'd been moving in opposite directions. She likes fashion; I like music. She lives in Miami, and I live in Atlanta. She has her own friends, and I have mine.

But I never expected things to get this bad between us. She's the only other person I know who really knows what it feels like to have a super-famous parent. She's the only other person I know who gets to wonder if people really like you for you, or if they like you because of the cool things they get to do with you. She was the only other kid I knew who had to worry that everything she did might make her parents look bad. Only Kayla somehow always managed to keep from goofing up, while I —

Whatever.

I felt angry and betrayed and sad and disappointed and hurt all at the same time, but like it or not, Kayla and I were two apps on the same phone: we had different features and did different things, but we used the same operating system. We were linked. And Eugene was my friend, too. I could ask about him if I wanted to.

Kayla stopped talking to her friend Courtney long enough to roll her eyes. "His name is Nu Gee now."

Courtney and Tia looked at each other in confusion, but I busted out laughing. "Oh, so he's gotten famous now, huh?"

Kayla nodded. "The room was filled with groupies."

Tia's eyes swung between us in curiosity. "What do you mean?"

"It means that he's not the guy we knew anymore. He's an *artist* now. That changes people," I explained.

"He used to be really sweet. Really talented. But it was almost as if he didn't know it. Just another kid, you know?" Kayla added. "But now he's a celebrity. A star."

"But you're a celebrity, too!" Now that Tia had washed her

face and put on a T-shirt for bed, she looked like the rest of us: twelve years old. I remembered something my mom said about her being too grown for her own good. "Why would he act that way around you?" she asked Kayla.

"Well, I guess he didn't, exactly." Kayla looked sad and sleepy at the same time. "When I walked in, he was hugging on the groupies and putting his hands all over them and acting like some nasty old man. He's only sixteen!" She shook her head. "I just . . . I wasn't expecting that."

"Oh," Tia said. "I've had the biggest crush on him ever since that song 'Girl, Say No.' 'Don't go with him, girl. Say no, no, no!'" she sang in a slightly off-key voice. "I love that song. I was really hoping I'd get to meet him." She sighed. "Oh, well. At least I got to see him in concert. And he's still really, really hot!"

"Not to me," Kayla grumbled. "Not anymore. I really don't care if I ever see him again. But my dad asked him to perform at my birthday party."

"Oooh!" Tia said. "That's going to be amazing! Can I come, Kayla? Please?"

Kayla cut her eyes at me. For just a second—for the first time in a long time—it was like the old days. I knew exactly what she was thinking, and she knew what I was thinking. I tried to smile at her to let her know I was right there with her—and I hoped that maybe, if I could get her to smile, we could stop being so mad at each other—but instead of smiling, she rolled her eyes at me.

"You brought her," she muttered, jerking her head toward Tia, and then she got up. "I'm going to bed. Courtney, you're in my room." She glanced at Tia but didn't look at me at all. "You two are in the guest room."

She left the room without saying another word. Courtney waved and then followed her.

"I don't think Kayla likes me very much," Tia said.

"Well, you just invited yourself to her birthday party," I snapped.

"What's wrong with that? We're friends now, right? She's inviting her entire middle school. I thought we were having a good time. It's not like one more person would make any difference."

I just looked at her. It crossed my mind to try to explain it, but I had the feeling that Tia would never understand—and that made me feel sad and lonely all over again.

Silence settled over us for a long time. You know how sometimes you start thinking about something that makes you feel bad or sad, and then suddenly everyone and everything around you sucks?

That was me.

"What's with her and Nu Gee?" Tia asked at last, sliding down a little lower on the sofa and flipping channels until she found a rerun of *The Game*.

I shrugged. "I think she really liked him."

"*Liked* him liked him?"

I nodded. "I thought he liked her, too. He always used to ask if she was coming to the studio and stuff. But . . . well, you never know about things like that."

"Why?"

I sighed. I mean, I like Tia and everything, but sometimes she seems really dumb to me. You have to explain everything, or she just doesn't get it.

"Her dad's kinda like his boss, Tia," I said, trying to translate the situation into regular-people language. "He might have been pretending all along so that Parran would like him better and help him more with his career."

"Oooohhhh!"

I could almost see the light bulb flash on in Tia's brain. I couldn't stop myself from muttering, "OMG, you are so slow sometimes, Tia."

"I am not!" she said defensively. "You and Kayla just need to make up and stop fighting with each other. If two people in the world had no reason to fight, it's you two." She looked around the vaulted ceilings of Kayla's huge family room. "I mean, you have everything. Everything!"

"Sure. Everything," I repeated sarcastically. "Including a bodyguard who thinks he's still in the Marines, people writing nasty things about me in the blogs, friends who want to hang out with me for the concert tickets, and parents who are never home. It's great!"

Tia stood up. I could tell by the look on her face that I'd hurt her feelings, but I felt too sorry for myself to care.

"I don't just like you for the concert tickets, Promise," she said, sounding as if she was about to cry. "But if that's what you think . . . I don't know what else to say. I'll just go to bed."

She left me alone.

That's when I started crying. I sat there on the sofa alone, with tears rolling down my face, wishing more than anything that I could take back everything I'd ever said or done that made me feel this alone.

"Are you girls just about ready?" Titi asked us the next morning after breakfast.

I didn't feel much better. I'd fallen asleep on the couch with the television going and had ended up spending the night there. When I went to the bedroom to shower and get dressed, Tia refused even to look at me. At the breakfast table with Kayla, Courtney, and Tia, I wondered if I had a single friend in the whole room.

The last thing I wanted to do was walk around the Aventura Mall with three girls who weren't talking to me. If you've ever done that, you know it's pretty much a disaster situation. They walk ahead of you, and you end up bringing up the rear, where you can't even hear them talking about you. And if you want to go into a different store from the one they want to go into, you're just screwed, because no one's going to come with you. You're going to end up doing what they want to do and being ignored at the same time. Without a friend on my side, I could have suggested we all hop on helicopter to Disney World, my treat, and I'd probably still lose.

"I just need to get my purse," I replied with a sigh.

"Good," Titi said. "Charley's going to meet us there to help me keep an eye on you girls."

"Charley!" We hadn't seen him since we piled into the limo to come home with Kayla's dad. "But Titi! I've been to the mall here with you and Kayla a hundred times, and we never needed a bodyguard. Why does he have to come?"

Titi shook her head. "I'm sorry, Promise. Those are the new rules. When you go out in public, Charley goes. But don't worry. I'm sure you won't even know he's there."

"Won't know he's there!" I shouted. "Have you *seen* him, Titi? Do you know how he acts?"

"Oh, come on, now, Promise," Titi said reassuringly. "It can't be as bad as all that. Run and get your purse. It's time to go."

I obeyed her, but I didn't run. Far from it. I dragged my feet toward the chair where I'd thrown my bag, because I knew exactly how Charley would carry on at the mall, and it would make what had already started out to be a bad day that much worse. I caught my reflection in the mirror over the chest of drawers, and for a second, I thought my mom had come into the room to surprise me. But that was impossible: Mom was in New York, and I hadn't heard from her since I left Atlanta.

Staring into the mirror, looking at my reflection, I missed my mother so much. She would have defended me. She would have taken my side. She knew I wasn't a shoe stealer or a bad friend. She knew I said crazy things, but I didn't meant them. Not deep in my heart.

Thinking of my mother might have been where I first got the crazy idea that ended up changing everything.

The mall was crowded with Saturday shoppers and plenty of people who weren't really interested in shopping but just wanted a place to hang out for a few hours. The minute we walked in, I felt as if the whole place turned to stare at Charley, who stood behind me with his arms crossed over his thick chest as if he was expecting bullets to rain down from Nordstrom on the second floor. Kayla stood by her mother; Courtney and Tia stood near them. Tia glanced at Charley from time to time as if she was a little afraid of him, which, considering how he had left her standing in the school parking lot with her duffel bag, was kind of understandable.

"What is our destination?" Charley asked Titi.

"Destination?" Titi's smooth brown forehead crumpled with confusion. "Well, I don't really think we have one of those. I usually just let them walk around a bit. Go in and out of the stores. Look around."

When Charley stared blankly at her, I couldn't stop myself. "You know, browse?" I snapped. "Shop? Haven't you ever just walked the mall just to look?"

Charley shrugged. I looked him over. I'd never seen him in anything but a black T-shirt and black jeans, even though in March, it's already getting warm in Atlanta and even warmer in Miami. And with his skin tone, black wasn't all that becoming.

"Browse," he repeated. "Affirmative." He glanced at me. "I'll follow you, Promise."

"Great." I sighed and took my place as the tail of the unhappy little group. Just as I'd thought, I couldn't hear what the other girls were talking about, and even though I kept telling myself that I couldn't care less, I did. I hate being left out. To me, it's the worst feeling in the world.

"I love it," Kayla said, admiring the Regalia Trinity suede rucksack in Juicy Couture. The tag said the color was camel, but to me, it looked more like a dusty pink. The bag was sharp—and only two hundred dollars. "I think I might get this."

I picked up the blue one. "I'll get the blue one. Then we'll kind of match," I said, trying to break the ice with Kayla and get out of the doghouse. But she shut me down pretty quickly by putting the bag down in a huff.

"You're such a copycat, Promise," she muttered, and walked away.

That volcano in the pit of my stomach fluttered to life as if Kayla's words had dropped a match on it. I threw the bag down . . . but then I realized that if I didn't buy it, it really would look as if I only wanted it because Kayla had it, and that was so not true.

Tia picked up the black one. "Hey, if I get this one, we'll be like twins!" She smiled at me for the first time since I'd said what I said on the couch. "What do you think, Promise? What about it?"

"Sure," I said, relieved that someone was talking to me, at least. "That's cool."

I headed to the register with Tia at my heels.

"These two?" the clerk asked, scanning my blue bag and reaching out for Tia's black one.

"Wait a minute," I said, stopping the clerk. "I thought you were getting that one."

"I am. I mean, I thought . . ." Tia looked confused. "I thought you were buying them. One for me and one for you."

"But . . ." I shook my head. "Really, Tia. Don't you have any money of your own?"

"No," Tia said defensively. "Not everyone is like you, Promise. My dad can't just hand me a stack because he's in a good mood. And besides, you told me when you invited me that I didn't need any money. You said that it was all expenses paid." She snatched the bag off the counter. "But that's OK. I don't need it."

I was completely screwed. If I didn't buy her the stupid bag, by the time we got back to school on Monday, Tia would have told everyone that Promise Walker was cheap with her friends. She would have made it sound as if I was some kind of miser, and knowing how the kids in my school love to gossip, it would take days—or even weeks—for the story to die down.

"No," I said heavily. "You don't have to put it back, Tia. But I can't buy you anything else, OK?"

Tia threw her arms around me, but the hug didn't feel right now. "Thanks, Promise," she squealed. "I'll carry it forever!" As soon as the clerk removed the tags, she took the new handbag. "I'm going to get rid of this old thing right now," she said of the purse she was carrying, and hurried off to find a trash can. I spotted her a few minutes later, showing Kayla and Courtney the new purse as if she'd bought it for herself.

I was so ready to leave—all of it, the girls, the store, Miami. I glanced around the store. Charley was standing with his feet wide and his arms crossed over his massive chest in front of a display of bright pink tees with the words "Juicy Loves Miami" emblazoned on the front in silver sequins, watching me. If he'd seen the whole thing with Tia, he probably thought even less of me than ever.

Finally, they were ready to get out of Juicy. As we left, a group of girls around our age tumbled inside, giggling. I turned back to double-check, but they didn't have any adults hanging over their shoulders—and certainly no bodyguards.

*I wish I was with them. It must be nice to go the mall with your friends without having any adults around. I bet they'd be fun and talk to me and be interested in me and—*

I stopped, my head pivoting back toward the girls. An idea tickled at my brain.

"Something wrong, Promise?" Charley asked. "You—"

"Hi, Kayla!" A good-looking white boy with a shock of brown hair had stopped in front of us.

Kayla got a really funny look on her face. I think if she could have blushed, she would have. "Oh! Hi, David. What are you doing here?"

The boy gestured to a tall woman with bushy graying hair talking to Kayla's mother. "Mom says I need new jeans."

"Oh," Kayla said. "Where are you going to get them? Seven?"

David laughed. "No, I don't need all that! Just some jeans. The Gap, probably. Can't wear them to school, anyway, right?"

"Yeah, the hated uniform," Kayla joked.

"Hey, have you started that paper on *Romeo and Juliet*?" he asked.

"No," Kayla said, laughing. "Have you?"

"No. Well, maybe we could talk later. Kick around some ideas." He lowered his voice. "Just as long as you promise you won't crumple them up and throw them away."

Now Kayla really did turn a funny shade of maroon. She cut her eyes guiltily toward her mother.

I wondered what Little Miss Perfect was up to.

"S-sure," she stammered. "Only . . . my number isn't . . ." Kayla began.

"Yeah, it's not in the school handbook," the kid finished for her. "I know. I checked." He blushed a little. "I can understand why not. I guess some people would take advantage of that because of your dad and all. Mine isn't, either, though. Too new." He pulled his phone out of his pocket. "So if you want to talk . . ."

Kayla was fumbling in her bag faster than a rocket. I'd never seen her act like that.

Something was definitely up.

I watched them exchange numbers while their mothers talked about Kayla's party and Courtney and Tia stared into the window of Hollister as if they were memorizing the placement of every item in the display.

"Come on, David," the woman who must have been his mother said at last. "Nice to see you, Mara. 'Bye, Kayla!"

"We'll talk later, OK?" the kid said to Kayla.

It might have been my imagination, but it seemed to me Kayla looked sorry that the conversation was over.

That's when I realized it. Charley wasn't standing behind me anymore. The whole wide free space of the mall beckoned behind me. In the far distance, I saw those other girls, walking and talking without chaperones. There was nothing, no one, between me and the same kind of freedom.

I took off running.

"Promise!" I heard him roaring my name, but I didn't look back. I kept my eyes on avoiding the people meandering here and there in front of me, praying that I wouldn't run into someone and fall down. Skipped the escalator for the stairs and ran down to the lower level, skipping the center concourse for one of the more deserted arms and finally racing into the biggest store at that end: JCPenney.

I took the escalator two steps at a time and ended up in the juniors department.

I might have enjoyed being there if I hadn't been so out of breath. But Charley was nowhere in sight. I suspected that, like a lot of big, muscled people, he wasn't that fast. A kid like me, who had dance rehearsals almost every week and who was wearing Jordans, would lose in a fistfight but could beat him in a race any day.

I collapsed at the feet of a mannequin wearing a polka-dot bikini and sat there, sweating and thinking about my next move.

I was free.

Free! At least for a while.

I knew they would be looking for me, but if I had anything to say about it, they wouldn't find me until I was ready. After all, it was a huge mall—but one that I knew so well I didn't feel scared of being alone or anything. And I still had a few hundred dollars left from the stack my dad had given me the last time I'd seen him. If I was lucky, I could shop a bit and then maybe find a way upstairs to the food court for a little lunch or even duck into my favorite restaurant, Applebee's, for a bacon double cheeseburger and fries before they found me.

Just thinking about it made me feel better. Sure, I'd be in trouble when they caught up to me, but I was already in trouble. I mean, I'm not like Kayla; everything I do is always wrong anyway. When you're always in trouble, after a while, you stop trying to do what people think you ought to do and only try to see what you can get away with.

"Are you OK?"

I looked up. A girl about my age was staring down at me.

She was brown-skinned, with a bad weave in a shade lighter than her natural hair brushing her shoulders. She wore a pair of bright red shorts and a top that didn't quite cover her belly.

"Yeah," I said. I probably looked ridiculous sitting there beneath the mannequin as if it was a chair or something, so I stood up and brushed the back of my own shorts with my hands. "Just taking a rest."

The girl nodded as if that made sense to her. "Uh . . . I wanted to ask you something." She glanced over her shoulder, and I saw several other girls standing a few feet away. "See, I said you looked like Promise Walker, IDK's daughter. But all my friends say you're not her. They say she wouldn't be in no mall in Miami 'cause she lives in the ATL. But I told 'em you could be here because you come here to Miami sometimes. IDK got a house here — I read it in a magazine. So what I want to know is . . . are you Promise Walker, or do you just look a lot like her?"

I started laughing. I don't know why. I guess I was just thrilled to be recognized or something. That hasn't happened to me that much, although it's something I dream of, especially since it happens to my parents all the time. I felt like a real celebrity when I said, "Yes, I'm Promise Walker."

"I told y'all!" the girl in the red shorts shrieked. She threw her fist up in the air. "I *told* y'all it was her, and it's her!" She turned back to me. "Can I get a picture with you?"

The other girls joined her before I could answer, all talking at once. Their cell phones flashed and clicked as they took my picture.

"OMG! You look just like Bella! I watched her show."

"Me, too. It's on channel fifteen."

"Her dad's like the greatest rapper alive!"

"True dat! I have all his songs in my phone."

"Can I get a picture?"

"Me, too!"

"And me!"

"Sure," I said, striking the pose I'd practiced for the red carpet: right foot forward, hand on hip, chin up, and smile. The red-shorts girl stood beside me, grinning, then her friends, one after another.

"I want one!" a voice said, and a heavy-set man stepped out of the circle of people who had gathered around me. He handed his phone to his friend and put his arm around me, smiling as if he'd won a Mickie.

"Me, too!" said another guy. He put his hands on me, too.

I didn't like that so much. I didn't know these dudes! But I couldn't figure out how to stop it.

"And me!" An older woman stepped up.

"OK, that's enough," I said. "Thanks, everyone, but I've — I've got to find my friends."

I tried to step backward, away from the flashing cameras and phones in front of me, but there were people standing behind me now, too. In fact, there were people everywhere. When I looked up, I saw people standing on the displays to get a better angle, taking my picture from a distance.

"Excuse me," I said loudly, trying to move through the crowd. "Excuse me!"

But it wasn't working. People surged forward to touch me, to shake my hand and take pictures. It was starting to feel as if the whole mall had decided to come hang in the juniors section of JCPenney — and all I wanted was to be somewhere, anywhere else.

"Excuse me, but I really have to go!" I yelled, pushing against the people closest to me, but the crowd seemed to surge in closer, with people calling my name, asking for pictures.

"Take this to your father!" someone yelled, throwing a CD toward me. I ducked but not in time. It hit me on the side of the head, and I felt the sting of freshly cut skin.

"Ouch!" I cried, grasping at my forehead. When I looked at my hand, there was a tiny drop of blood there. "Let me out of here!" I screamed. "Let me go!"

But no one moved, and now the circle seemed to draw in even tighter. People were brushing against me, touching me all over, and pulling me in one direction and the next, until I felt like the rope in a tug of war.

*I'm going to get trampled,* I realized in a panic. *I'm going to get trampled by these people. That's why Dad travels with security. That's why Mom always has Deidre or someone. So they can get away . . .*

"BREAK IT UP!" a voice roared.

The walls of people moved aside, parting like those Bible stories about Moses and the Red Sea, until Charley's massive shadow appeared in front of me. "That's enough, everyone. Thank you!"

Then he scooped me up like a wayward four-year-old and carried me out of the store.

# Chapter Nine

## KAYLA

"Take Tia to your room, Kayla, and stay in there until I come to get you," Mom said as soon as we walked into the house. Promise was still crying, and Charley hovered over her like a worried father.

"Yes, ma'am," I said. I could tell from the tone of her voice and the look on her face that this wasn't the moment to put up an argument. Courtney was the lucky one: she'd been dropped off on our way home. My dad was already at the house when we got there, which never happened. Usually, he was asleep at this hour, and JJ and Mom and I would see him in the late afternoon. He looked a little as if someone had awakened him from a really good dream, and it was pretty clear that he wasn't very happy about it.

We were in for a bumpy afternoon.

As angry as I was at her, I felt kind of bad for Promise. I was even a little sorry that I'd been so mean to her, especially now, when you could just look at her face and see that this time, she was scared to death. But Promise had made her own bed . . . and besides, I had problems of my own.

Tia followed me to my room.

"I've got some homework I need to do," I told her, picking up my backpack and dumping everything inside it onto my bed. I kept forgetting about English! It was as if I had a mental block or something. I hadn't even asked the Bloody Red Queen if I could make up that quiz, and if it hadn't been for David, I would have forgotten all about the English paper we'd been assigned for the weekend, too. All the stuff about singing and performing had pushed school to the back of my mind, but not my parents' expectations for good grades. After the disaster with the quiz, I needed a decent grade on that paper. If I ended up with anything lower than a B in English, Mom would start the lecture that began with "We pay all this money for a tutor" and ended with her taking my iPhone and computer until my grades improved.

I just couldn't deal with that now, on top of everything else. Not this close to the party . . . and not since I'd just given David my phone number.

"What's this?" Tia asked, grabbing my Look Book as it slid out with all the school junk.

I reached for it, but she stepped away, flipping the pages. "Nothing. Just a book I made of clothes I like."

"Oohh." Tia pointed to a hoodie idea I had been thinking about: the bottom is a regular zip-up, but the top is almost like a cowl neck that you can pull up over your head. I was thinking the neckline could be two-tone, so it could be a different color from the body when you pull it up and wear it as a hood. I'd drawn it because I'd never seen a piece anything like it anywhere. "I *love* this! Where can I get it? Is it in Forever 21, or is it only in one of those fancy boutiques that girls like me can't even go in without being followed by security?"

"No, it's not in Forever 21," I said, taking the book from her.

"Oh," she said sadly.

"I mean, it's not anywhere," I explained. "It's just something I drew."

Tia's light eyes widened. "You mean you came up with that yourself?"

I nodded.

"That is gorgeous, Kayla! You know you could totally sell that, don't you?"

I studied the drawing. "You think so?"

"Absolutely." Tia nodded. "I know I'd buy it. You know, in some fun colors?"

I liked her a little better for saying that. So when she asked, "Can I see your computer?" I pointed to the laptop on my desk, and Tia sat down.

The English paper.

Anne always made me write something—anything—before she'd help me, which always seemed unfair to me. I mean, what's the point of having a tutor if she won't even help you get started? But Anne wouldn't even be there until much later, and if I was doing my homework, I wouldn't have to talk to Promise's friend. There was something about that girl that I really didn't like. She was the sort of friend Promise always fell for, the ones who just liked to hang on and see what they could get. I'd rather do homework than deal with that kind of girl. I lay on my stomach on the bed with *Romeo and Juliet* open in my hand and my notebook open in front of me, trying to think of something to write.

I didn't have the first clue.

I flipped through the pages of the play, skimming the dialogue. I covered the blank pages of my notebook . . . with drawings of girls in cute little outfits. I drew the hoodie again and again, imagining colors, then pairing it with jeans, leggings, and shorts. It really *was* cute. It was exactly the kind of thing I'd love to wear if Gatewood didn't have a strict uniform policy.

As for *Romeo and Juliet*? I gave up.

"This is the stupidest play ever," I muttered, but Tia must have been too focused on whatever she was doing on the computer to notice.

It wasn't until I remembered what David had said about tackling the paper this afternoon that I felt anything other than annoyed by the whole project. I found his name on my iPhone and hit call before I even thought about the fact that I still had company.

"Hey, Kayla!" He sounded genuinely glad to hear from me. "What's up?"

"Nothing much," I said. "Except I'm starting that stupid paper."

"You're better than me," he said with a laugh.

"But you at least understand it."

"That's just because I've watched more movies," he said. "Seriously, Kayla. I know we weren't supposed to, but it helped."

"I don't think I'm going to get to do that until after I finish reading the whole play. Besides, it's been a busy weekend."

I glanced at Tia. She was staring at the computer screen so intently she was barely moving. But that didn't mean she wasn't listening. In fact, she was probably listening as if her life depended on it. "Hold on a second," I muttered into the phone.

I slid off the bed and headed into the bathroom, closing the door behind me. But that wasn't enough, I decided, so just to make sure I could talk in private, I turned on the shower. I sat down on the floor, my back propped up against the wall. "OK," I said. "I can talk now."

"What's that noise?" David asked.

"Dishwasher," I lied. "I'm in the kitchen." I couldn't exactly tell him I was sitting across the room from the toilet, could I?

"Oh," he said. "So did you have fun at the mall with Courtney and those other girls?"

I sighed and then dove into the whole story—and when I say the "whole story," I mean I went all the way back to the shoes. No, I went back even farther than that: I told him all about Promise and me and how close we'd once been—and how off track everything was now. Except for the occasional question, David didn't interrupt me once.

"Well," he said when I finally wound down. "I guess it's pretty hard for her."

"For her?" I couldn't believe it! After listening to everything I'd told him, he was actually going to take Promise's side?

I was about to explode when he said, "Yeah. I mean, you're a tough act to follow, Kayla. You're smart, and you're pretty. You get along with everyone. You're . . . I don't know. You're just really cool. Probably the coolest girl at Gatewood. And that's not because of who your dad is. I thought you were cool long before anyone told me about him."

I wasn't expecting that. The room suddenly felt warmer, as if someone had cut off the air conditioner on one of Miami's one-hundred-degree days. Or maybe it was the shower. I reached into the tub and turned the water off.

"You really think so?" I wasn't sure he was right, but it was something to think about.

"Yeah. Must be hard for the other girls. They probably all want to hate on you and be just like you at the same time." He laughed. "Listen to me. I sound like Dr. Phil or something!"

I giggled. "You have too much hair to be Dr. Phil!"

For a while, we were both laughing too hard to say anything much. It was weird, but I felt better than I had since we'd gotten back from the Mickies.

"How many different places have you lived, David?"

"I don't know. Fifteen or twenty. I lost count."

"Do you like traveling?"

"Sometimes. I like seeing places. But it's hard to always be the new kid. It's hard to make good friends when you might be gone in six months."

"What was your favorite place?"

"Fiji," he said immediately. "Best beaches in the world. Sorry, Miami!" He laughed. "How about you? You've probably been everywhere with your dad."

"Not really. New York and Los Angeles, mostly," I said. "I've been to Puerto Rico and few other islands. That's about it. Dad's been everywhere, but I stick close to home with school and all."

"Do you go back to New Orleans much?" he asked.

"Not that much," I answered. "Our relatives there usually come to see us."

"I guess it's kinda hard," David said. "After Katrina and all that. Were you there then?"

"Yeah. You know, we just barely got out ahead of the storm. My dad was in Miami, and we were trying to go there, but the state troopers and the National Guard wouldn't let us go that way. We ended up in Houston, and the trip . . ." I hated remembering that time. "It was awful. I mean, money isn't any good when there's no place to buy *anything*. We had to stand in long lines just for food and water and gas."

I stopped talking. Even though I was little when that happened, I remembered it as if it was yesterday.

"It's a sad thing, but I guess it's important to remember. Because what really matters to me isn't the stuff. It's the people I love. And I guess that's part of the reason . . ." I hesitated, knowing that if I shared the whole thing about performing with him, he'd be the first friend I'd told. But a moment later, I lost my hesitation. David had listened better than any of my girlfriends had. Why not tell him? So I just said, "I guess that's why I try so hard to be a performer like my dad wants me to be. Because I love him."

"Yeah. I guess I can understand that."

For a long moment, neither of us said anything.

"OK, I got something serious to ask you," David said.

"OK."

He hesitated. "Kayla, what do you want for your birthday?"

"Oh, you don't have to get me anything. In fact, please don't." I quickly filled him in on the drama between Courtney and Shanita. "That's why it's written on the invitations," I concluded. "I really don't want or need anything. And I don't want anyone to feel they have to get me something."

"See what I mean?" David said. "You're a cool girl. I know lots of kids who are all about the presents, no matter what. But you're not like that."

I didn't know what to say to that, so I didn't say anything. I sat there feeling all happy and good inside, and I wouldn't have rushed that feeling for any present in the whole world.

"I want to get you *something*, Kayla," David insisted. "But it's tough, because, well, you know. You really *are* a girl who has everything."

He was right. I honestly can't remember a time when I didn't have just about everything I wanted. And the truth is, most of the time, I don't even want that much.

"So what can I get you?" he asked again.

I thought about some of the things I like: cute stuffed animals, clothes, and jewelry. But I didn't want David to get me any of those things. They were all way too . . . *personal*.

And that's when I thought of it. "I need a good luck charm," I said.

"A good luck charm?"

"Yeah. See, I'm trying to be a performer, but . . ." I sighed. "I'm just not that good at it. It's gonna take some major luck for this all to work out. But David? It has to be small. And you can't let anyone else know. I don't want the other kids to feel bad because they didn't bring me anything."

He got quiet. I could almost hear him thinking.

It was funny how easy he was to talk to. It was weird, but he was just about the only person in my life who brought absolutely no drama whatsoever. All my other friends, my parents, Promise—it felt like all drama, all the time. And then suddenly, something clicked in my brain. Romeo and Juliet were just a couple of kids around the same age as David and me who were able to escape from the drama of their lives with each other. Their parents and relatives, who had picked out other people for them, were willing to fight one another to keep them apart and to maintain their family honor. I kind of understood how Juliet must have felt: she liked a boy, but everyone around her had other ideas about what she should do and who she should be, and they were watching her every move. I always felt a little like that, too.

"Does this good luck charm have to be happy?" David asked suddenly.

I wasn't sure what he was asking. "Happy?"

"You know, rabbits' feet and four-leaf clovers and that stuff. Does it have to be happy, or can it be . . ." He hesitated. "I don't know. Just special."

It was a good question, and to be honest, I didn't know the answer. "I'll love anything you pick," I said.

"OK. See you tomorrow?"

"Sure thing."

He stopped talking. I wasn't sure if he was one of those people who just doesn't say good-bye, so I waited a couple of seconds. When he still didn't say anything, I was about to hang up.

That's when he said, "Kayla?"

"Yeah?"

"Thanks for calling. I like talking to you."

I'm not boy-crazy—I swear, I'm really not—but my insides

did this funny little flutter as if there was someone inside my chest, tickling me from my heart to my stomach.

"Me, too," I heard myself saying. "'Bye."

I stood up and left the bathroom, feeling a little as if the carpet beneath my feet was made of clouds. I had to take a couple of deep breaths before I could scribble down the sentences that had come into my mind while David and I were talking. I knew the ideas didn't belong in the same paragraph and that my thoughts were nothing but a jumbled mess—it wasn't perfect—but I tried not to let that bother me for once. I just kept writing and writing. For a good twenty minutes, I kept at it, and I didn't draw a single dress or top. I wrote and wrote.

I might have really gotten going on it had it not been for Tia. All of a sudden, she scraped the chair away from the desk and turned to me.

"Not sure what Promise's mom is going to say about *this*."

"What?"

She pointed at the screen. "Promise is trending on Twitter."

"What?" I hurried over to the laptop and leaned over Tia's shoulder. She had logged into her Twitter account, and sure enough, there was "#spotted" followed by Promise's name.

"Yeah," Tia said absently. "That was fast. I wonder . . ." Her fingers flew over the keyboard. "Hey, there's already a story up on RapCelebKids. It's short, but there's a picture. Ugh, Promise isn't going to like that one. She's making a weird face. See?"

I hesitated. I definitely wanted to see, but my parents had strictly forbidden me to read the celebrity blogs. The first time I'd ever looked at them was after the Mickies, and then it was after my mom had printed out the stories and pictures that she thought were appropriate.

"Those blogs are usually just a place for mean-spirited people to spew their hate, and you don't need that. We don't need to read ugly gossip about the people we know, and we certainly don't need to read about what people who don't even know us have to say about us." That's what she said, and to make sure I knew she was serious, she added, "If I find out you've been reading those blogs, I will take your computer and your iPhone, and you'll be twenty-five before you get either one of them back, do you understand?"

Trust me, she's not exaggerating. My mom doesn't play. She'll take my phone in a heartbeat. I glanced over my shoulder, straining my ears for the sounds of voices from the other parts of the house. If Mom came in here and found me reading celebrity blogs, Promise wouldn't be the only one in trouble.

"Look," I warned Tia. "If anyone comes through that door, you've got to close that down quick. If my mom sees that, I'll be in so much trouble . . ."

"Really?" Tia's eyes shone with excitement. "I've got you, Kayla. Don't worry about a thing. But . . ." She blinked innocently and gave me a smile. "I'd *really* like to come to your birthday party with Promise next week."

See what I mean? Promise always has friends like this. I mean, what kind of girl blackmails you for a party invitation? At first, I couldn't imagine any of my friends *ever* doing anything like that . . . but then, when I thought about it, I wasn't sure. Lately, every day seemed to be a battle over who was the "better" friend. Maybe Promise knew exactly what she was dealing with. Maybe it was easier to have one friend who wanted to do everything with you than trying to be friends with everyone. If she'd been there right then, I might have asked her about it. After all, Promise is the only other person I know who has to deal with stuff like "does she like me for me, or does she just want to hang out with famous people?"

And at least I knew for sure which camp Tia was in. She didn't even *know* me enough to like me. She wanted to come to my party because she thought there would be famous people there — and that was all.

"Oh, all right," I agreed. "I suppose it will be OK."

I'll be honest. I felt a little weird about it, but considering that the whole middle school of Gatewood was invited, she wouldn't be the only kid there whom I didn't know very well. I knew my mom and the party planner were ordering extras of everything, from the beads and coins I would toss from my special float to gift bags for the guests.

Tia clapped her hands. "It's going to be so fun! Now, come here. See what I'm talking about?" Tia giggled. "I bet that's the worst picture she's taken in years."

She was right. Promise's eyes were stretched wide, and her lips were crunched together as if she was trying not to cry. There was a little line of blood on her temple, and her hand hovered in midair as if she were trying to push someone away. Her hair wasn't neat and sleek the way it had been when she'd started running; it was messy, and a long, lank piece stuck to her cheek as if she had been sweating.

She looked terrible . . . and really scared. And this time, I didn't feel angry at her at all anymore. I felt really bad. Promise does a lot of crazy stuff, but she *is* my sister — or the closest thing I have to one. I didn't like the thought of anyone hurting her or scaring her, even if a lot of the time, she's being completely obnoxious.

"There're already a few comments, too," Tia continued, her eyebrows crinkling as she read. "Well, *that* one was kinda mean. Think we should post a nice comment to counter it?"

I couldn't see it from where I was standing, and I suppose it didn't help that my eyes were on the door. "What does it say?"

Tia cleared her throat. "'Promise Walker is one ugly girl. She got none of her mama's pretty and all of her dad's jacked up looks.'"

"It *says* that?" I couldn't stop myself. I forgot about door watching and leaned closer to the computer. "Look at her eyes. She's scared to death," I said angrily. "Can't they see that?"

"Apparently not," Tia muttered. "I'm going to write a comment and tell that heifer to leave her alone."

Tia started typing, while I grabbed the chair from the corner near my mirror and slid it close to the desk.

"There," Tia said as she read over her work. "Take that, haters."

She pressed send, and a moment later, her words appeared on the screen under the handle "Promisefriend." I liked her a little better for that.

"Do you do that a lot? Post comments?"

"Sometimes. To be honest, Promise isn't in the blogs that much, but every now and then, when she is, I post. Especially if it's something that I feel people need to be set straight about. If I'd known you last week, I would have posted something then, too."

I stared at her. "What are you talking about?"

"You don't know? There was a whole bunch of stuff about

you in the blogs after the Mickies, people talking about your hair and the outfit and all that. And when people got word about the party—well, let's just say that hater-aid is a popular drink on these sites."

"But how do they know about the party?"

Tia rolled her eyes and shook her head as if I was missing something completely obvious. "Um . . . you're only having one of the biggest parties anyone's ever heard of, Kayla. Your family has rented a club on South Beach for the evening, and there's going to be a whole Mardi Gras parade, beads, king cakes, and coins with your face stamped on them for the guests." She laughed. "And that's the stuff I read about *last* week. I bet there's a bunch of *new* stuff on here now. Wait, I'll just do a quick search—"

"No, I mean, how do they find out this stuff?" I asked. "I know I didn't tell them, and I'm guessing my parents didn't, either. How do they know all that?"

Tia shrugged. "I don't know. I guess people talk. The people at the club where the party's going to be. The people making the floats and the cake and the kids you've invited and their parents and—" She sucked a sharp breath between her teeth, making a sudden whistling sound. "Oh, wow." She pointed at the screen. "Look at this."

"HEARTBREAK for KAYLA!" blared a headline in neon red letters above two pictures. The first was of me—an old photo from when I went with my dad to a concert a few months back. The second was of Eugene, taken while he was onstage performing somewhere. The editors had made the pictures look as if they had once been one photograph and someone had ripped it into two pieces.

"Oh, no!" I said. "What does it say?"

Tia read quickly. "It says Nu Gee dumped you for his groupies yesterday at the concert, and now he's scrambling to make sure your father doesn't dump him from the label."

"I don't believe this." I jumped out of my chair, my fingers curling into angry balls. If Eugene had been in the room, I don't think I could have stopped myself from scratching his eyes out. "That creep! Why would he let them write something like that?"

"Maybe he didn't, Kayla. It could have been anyone. Even your girl Courtney."

"Courtney? No way. She wasn't even there. No one else was there! Just him and me. Well, Deidre, but she was in the hallway. And I guess those trampy girls might have been listening . . ." I shook my head. "It's not even true—not really. We were never boyfriend and girlfriend. We were just—I just—" I couldn't figure out what I wanted to say. "It doesn't matter. Where did they get this from? How did they know this? How do I make them take it back?"

"Well, at least you're not blaming me."

"What are you talking about? Why would I blame you?"

"Promise's parents thought I might have said something to someone about her getting robbed when that showed up in the news." She shrugged. "I didn't do it, but I guess you never know. Some kids do stuff like that when they have famous friends. And I heard sometimes the tabloids pay good money for stories, so—"

"But Courtney doesn't need any money," I snapped. I didn't really think about how it sounded until Tia blinked at me as if I'd slapped her for not having rich parents. It was the same look that had been on Shanita's face when Courtney made that comment about presents.

*Rich snob.* The words echoed in my brain as though Chemine were in the room with us right now. Tia didn't call me one, but her eyes spoke loud and clear.

"Well, I may not have the kind of money she does, but that doesn't mean I'd sell out my friends," Tia flashed back. "If that's what you're thinking. Maybe you could ask your dad about who might have."

I shook my head. "I can't ask him. I'm not even supposed to be looking at this."

"Well, if you're this upset with the story, then you definitely don't want to read the comments. I thought some of the comments about your party were harsh, but this is a whole other level."

"Why?" I asked before I could stop myself. I knew I should just close down the computer and find something—anything— else to do. But you know what they say about curiosity, and now I had to know. "What do they say?"

Tia stood up and gestured toward the computer. "You read them. I'm not getting blamed for anything else today. But if you want a summary, most of them think you're nowhere near pretty enough to get a guy like Nu Gee." She tossed her head and stomped toward the bathroom, slamming the door behind her. I heard the shower go on. I guessed she had a phone call of her own to make.

I scooted into her seat and scrolled down. She was right: the comments were mostly mean. Hardly anyone who had posted seemed to take my side or have my back. I didn't know these people, and they didn't know me, but somehow their words seemed to dig into me and make me not ever want to do anything that might attract any attention ever again.

Someone knocked on the door.

Faster than lightning, I shut the laptop and scurried away from the desk as if it had scorched me, just as Anne's face appeared in the doorway. She didn't smile the way she usually does. In fact, she looked more serious than I remembered seeing her in a long time.

She looked around the room. "Where's the other girl? Tia, is that her name?"

I nodded. "In the bathroom. Is it time for tutoring already?"

Anne stepped into the room and closed the door behind her. "No. It's time for explanations." She thrust her hand out and opened her fist. There on her palm was a crumpled test paper. "I found it in your backpack."

"When?" I cried. I looked over the mess of papers on my bed and realized I hadn't even noticed the paper wasn't there. "What were you doing in my backpack?" I exploded, grabbing it out of her hand. "Can't I have any privacy in this house?"

"When I was at Gatewood on Friday, Mrs. Hinckley told me she was missing your test."

"Then she must have lost it. I turned it in."

"That's what I said . . . at first. But then I started thinking about the way you've been acting lately, and I decided to have a look." She sighed. "What's going on, Kayla?"

I told her everything: about going to the Mickies and Khrissy and modeling and how my dad just said no without even listening to her or to me. And then how hard it was to read the play after Aurora told Dad he was wasting his time and his money, because I couldn't sing and I never would be able to, only Lonnie didn't think that had anything to do with it, as long as I knew what kind of artist I wanted to be. And I was going to make it up. I had started my English paper already, because talking to David had given me some ideas about the themes and—

"You won't tell them, will you, Anne?" I grabbed her hand and squeezed it hard. "Please? I won't do it again. I don't know why I did it in the first place. It just sometimes seems I can't do everything they want me to do, and since I can't, why keep trying?"

It's sometimes hard for Anne to look really serious, because her hair is so curly and bouncy and she's so young. But right then, she looked so sad and serious I thought she might burst into tears. She sighed. "You're putting me in a tough position, Kayla. They count on me to help you with your schoolwork, but it's more than that. They trust me to be honest with them and do what's best for you. Lying to them—"

"It's not lying!" I insisted. "It was just one stupid quiz, and I would have made a zero on it, anyway."

"Let me finish," Anne said gently. "I agree. I don't think one quiz is that big of a deal, Kayla. But these feelings you're having *are*. I really think you need to talk to your parents— your dad, in particular—before things get any worse."

"I've tried!" I said. "He won't listen, Anne. He really believes that because I'm his daughter, I must have his talent. But I don't! I hate singing! I don't want to be a performer— at least, not like that. I don't know how to make him understand!"

"I've worked with a lot of kids your age," Anne said with a smile. "Heck, I *was* a kid your age not that long ago. I remember all those feelings: that I wasn't good enough, that I couldn't please the people I cared about. And that no one really cared about me and who I really was inside."

I try not to cry in front of people—I guess I'm like my dad, because I want to seem as if nothing really bugs me that much—but as she was talking, it felt as if my heart was kind of squeezing together. It got hard to breathe, and then, before I could stop myself, I was crying those big, hard, hiccupping tears that make your nose run and your chest hurt.

Anne pulled me into a hug, rocking me gently as she patted my back. "It's OK, Kayla," she murmured into the top of my head. "It's going to be OK. Your dad loves you. He doesn't want you to do anything that will make you this unhappy—I know he doesn't. You have to try to talk to him again, Kayla. Otherwise, all these feelings—"

"W-w-will you talk to him for me?" I asked, pulling away from her and wiping my face. "Please? He likes you. He'll listen to you."

"Now, you know I can't do that." Anne said. She stuck her hand in the pocket of her jeans and pulled out a crushed bit of tissue. "Wipe your face and blow your nose. That's better. Now, I'll make you a deal. I won't say anything about the quiz—"

I threw my arms around her neck. "Thank you, Anne! Thank you, thank you!"

She disentangled herself, giving me a stern look. "I won't say anything about the quiz, because *you're* going to. And you're going to tell him how you really feel about singing at this party and all of the other stuff."

"But if I don't sing, I can't have the party at all!"

Anne stared at me solemnly. "Kayla Jones, is a party really *that* important to you? More important than being honest? More important than telling the truth about who you are and what you want?"

I had to think about that for a moment. The truth was, I was starting to get excited about the party, and as much as I dreaded performing for my friends, I didn't want to lose the party completely. But I also didn't want to spend the rest of my life doing something I hated, just because it was what my dad wanted for me.

"I'll talk to him," I said softly.

"You promise?"

I nodded. "I promise. Tomorrow, on the drive home after school."

Anne shook her head. She stood up and stretched out her hand. "Never put off till tomorrow what you can do today."

I stared at her in horror. "Now? But he's already upset because of Promise and what happened at the mall!"

"Yes, but that's for Promise's family to deal with. Right after they sent her to the guest room, your dad told your mom how glad he was that he could be sure you'd never do anything like that. He said he was proud of how honest and level-headed you are."

"He said that?"

I was a little surprised. Lately, the only thing I ever heard from Dad was criticism and pressure to do better. He hadn't told me he was proud of me since forever.

"Of course, he said that!" Now Anne seemed surprised. "He's always talking about you, about how you carry yourself like a young lady, how well you do in school, how you get along with people from all different backgrounds no matter what color or religion they are or how much money they have in their pockets." She raised an eyebrow at me. "I can't believe you don't know all that, Kayla! You and JJ are everything to him. He might be disappointed at first, but if you just tell him the truth, I know he'll not only listen to you, but he'll be your biggest fan. You'll see." She nodded toward the bed. "Bring the Look Book, Kayla. Show it to him. Talk to him about it. Now, come on." She stretched out her hand to me again. "This is something you need to do for yourself, but I'll walk with you to the living room."

I stood up as if I had been sentenced to death by lethal injection or the electric chair or whatever they do to people who commit really serious crimes and headed for the living room.

"I think she's just desperate for attention," Mom was saying in a low voice when I walked into the room. For a second, I thought they were talking about me, and I was about to protest, but of course, they weren't. They were still talking about Promise.

"Mom . . . Dad . . . can I talk to you?"

They were sitting in the living room. My mom was sitting on a corner of the couch, and my dad was in the deep armchair nearby. When they turned toward Anne and me, they both had weary, worried expressions on their faces.

"I'm going to go see how JJ is coming with his algebra," Anne said. She winked at me and squeezed my hand one last time, then let me go. I watched her disappear up the stairs.

Dad sat up and spread out his arms, gesturing for me to come to him. To my surprise, he settled me on his lap and squeezed me tight.

"Sure, Queen," he said, kissing my cheek. "But first, I need to ask you to do something for me."

I nodded. "What?"

"Look out for Promise," he said solemnly.

"Look out for Promise?" I repeated. At first, I thought he was warning me that Promise was up to something and I needed to watch my back. "Why?"

"Try to talk her out of these crazy ideas she gets."

"You're so level-headed and calm compared with her," Mom chimed in. "I don't know what's going on with that poor child, but—"

*Poor child?*

I forgot all about how bad I'd been feeling for Promise. *Please!* Yeah, I knew Promise was in trouble *again*, but that's Promise. She's always stirring up something and then looking for help and sympathy when it blows up in her face. Meanwhile, there I am, always trying to walk the straight and narrow, worried to death about what they're going to do me over a single quiz grade while I tie myself into knots trying to be what they want me to be—and my reward is to "look out for Promise"?

It made me so angry I wanted to jump off my dad's lap and screech, "Forget Promise! I've got problems of my own!"

"That Promise loves an audience. Onstage, that's a good thing, but it can cause all kinds of problems in real life." Dad peered into my face. "You understand what I'm saying?"

"I know, Dad, but Promise is—"

"What's this, Queen?" Dad said, taking my Look Book from hands and flipping the pages.

"It's . . . just something I like to do, clothes and stuff."

Mom rolled her eyes. "That's the 'Look Book,' Lullabye. I've told you about that before. Any spare moment she has, your daughter is cutting up fashion magazines and drawing pictures. I swear she spends more time with that book than she does doing her homework, and I know she spends more time on it than she does singing."

"I do not!" I began, even though I knew she was right.

"Mmmph." Dad grunted. He flipped a few more pages and then handed it back to me. "What was it you wanted to tell us?"

"Well . . . about this whole performance thing. At the party," I began, and then stopped.

"I was wondering when you'd give us some clues about what you want to do," Dad said, giving me a squeeze. "We need a song, and we gotta get you some accompaniment. You want a live band or a pianist, or are you just going to work from a CD?"

I cleared my throat and started again. "I'm not sure I—"

"Well, it's time to get sure. This thing is less than a week away," my dad said sternly. "You're dragging your feet, Kayla. That's not the way to get stuff done, I've told you that a thousand times. You got to stay on top of things. Keep grinding. You're my daughter, and the bar is higher for you. Higher than it is for anyone. I expect you to be great, you hear me?"

"But Dad . . ." My mind was scrambling, trying to figure out a way to make him understand. "I mean, do I have to do this at the party? Lonnie just said to sing in front of people. Do I have to do it in front of my friends? I mean, what if I mess up?"

"Stop thinking like that. Think about success. And it's good to do this in front of your friends. They'll be a friendly audience, right? And it's what, seventy-five people? Eighty? Nice small audience."

*Seventy-five is small?* I swallowed hard. Performing in front of seven would have terrified me. Seventy-five?

"I—I just don't know if I can."

"I said that I don't want to hear any more of that," Dad barked. All of the gentleness had drained from his face, and he looked at me like the serious music industry genius he is. "What are you going to sing?" he demanded. "And don't tell me you don't know. It's time to decide, Kayla. Right now!"

"I—I—I'm gonna sing Kasha's song 'Maybe, Maybe,'" I heard myself saying.

"Good choice," Dad said, showing me a mouthful of platinum. "It's nice and upbeat. Maybe you can work on a little dancing to go with it. You're good at that."

"I don't know," I said slowly trying to figure out just who or what had taken over my mouth. "It's hard for me to sing and dance at the same time."

"Think of it like cheerleading," Mom offered. "You were really good at moving while you were doing those cheers." She stood up. Her raspberry linen dress, so crisp and summery this morning when we'd all headed to the mall together, was now a wrinkled mess. "I'm going to go get a shower and change. I might even try for a nap once Promise and Tia are gone. It's been one heck of an afternoon," she said. "And you need to go on back to your schoolwork. Anne is waiting, and we can't go to dinner until your work is done."

At the mention of Anne's name, I felt a little guilty, but I couldn't bring myself to come clean now.

"That's right. Go get your work done." Dad slid me off his lap and stood up, too. "I'm counting on you to do well, Queen. In everything you do. Excellence. That's how we Joneses roll. Now, I gotta go to work—and so do you."

I was halfway up the stairs back to my room when he called, "And Kayla? Less time drawing dresses and more time singing. You got it?"

I nodded and climbed the rest of the stairs. The Look Book felt like a heavy stone in my hands. Anne was waiting outside in the hallway near my bedroom door.

"Did you talk to them?" She looked so sure and confident in me that I couldn't tell her how badly I'd failed.

"Yeah," I lied.

"And what did they say?"

I wiggled a bit, desperate to escape into my room and avoid her piercing gaze. "They said . . . they want me to do well and that . . . they were disappointed that I didn't at least *try* to do the quiz."

Anne waved my explanation away. "And about having to sing this weekend?"

I don't know where it came from—I guess it was what I wished would happen—and the words sprang to my lips and spilled out as if they were true. "Dad still wants me to do it," I said, managing to smile. "But he said he'd look at my drawings as soon as the party is over with. He says if Khrissy can put out a fashion line, so can we."

Anne grabbed me and squeezed me hard, practically jumping up and down in her excitement. "That's even better than I hoped, Kayla! I'm so proud of you—and so happy for you!" She pulled away and peered into my face. "Aren't you excited?"

"Oh, yeah," I said, but just then, I heard the sound of Mom's flip-flops on the stairs.

"Promise!" she called. "Tia! Deidre and Charley are here to take you back!"

I pulled Anne into my room.

"Don't you want to say good-bye?" she asked me, her blue eyes wide with surprise.

I shook my head. "I want to finish this paper," I told her, hoping that I could keep her away from my mother long enough to figure a way out of my lies. "Besides, if I were Promise, I wouldn't want to see anyone right now. Would you?"

# Chapter Ten

## PROMISE

**a**fter Parran got done lecturing me—and Mom and Dad weighed in by speaker phone—they put Tia and me and Deidre and Charley on the very next plane back to Atlanta.

It was the quietest ride ever. I had just about cried myself sick, so I just sat there, feeling numb and empty. The worst part was, I really couldn't explain why I'd done what I'd done, and that was what everyone wanted to know. I felt they all thought I was just an awful, rotten, spoiled brat. And maybe I was, but there was more to it. I just didn't know how to explain it.

Deidre tried to smile her encouragement now and then, but I wasn't really feeling it. Charley hadn't said a word to me since he scooped me up and carried me out of JCPenney. Nothing. He answered Parran, he talked to my mom and dad, but to me? Nothing.

Tia talked, though. She talked and talked and talked. About blogs and pictures and Twitter feeds and Kayla's birthday and the rumors about Kayla and Nu Gee.

"She acted almost as if she thought I did it," Tia said huffily. "Can you believe it? Everyone's got it in for me. It's as if they think I've got 'rat' stamped on my forehead." She shook her head. "I didn't have anything to do with it, Promise, I swear. I mean, seriously, that girl Courtney probably knew more about the whole thing than I did, and I said as much. Then she made some snippy comment about me needing the money, and that was that. I don't think I said another word to her until her mother came and said for me to pack up because it was time for us to go home . . ."

I stopped listening. I couldn't listen. I like Tia a lot, but I've never been so glad to see her go inside her apartment building as I was when we finally dropped her off. The new handbag I'd bought her swung from her shoulders as she waved good-bye and disappeared inside. There wasn't a doubt in my mind that she'd be on the phone as soon as we pulled away, telling everyone at school every detail about what happened at the mall—from her insider's point of view.

Charley drove us home but didn't come inside. I heard his Land Rover's engine fire up and then grow fainter as he pulled away.

"Where's he going?"

"Home, I guess," Deidre answered. "Tomorrow's going to be a big day for him, too."

"Why?"

Deidre shook her head so hard her earrings danced. She rolled her eyes in Promise's direction. "Why do you think? It can't be good for him that you went to such extremes to get away from him, Promise. He's probably gonna get fired tomorrow. And good riddance, I say. I get that we need a little extra help, but that guy . . ." She made her earrings swing. "What a piece of work."

Her phone rang. She glanced at the number and started walking away from me toward the privacy of her bedroom.

"I've got to take this. Go unpack, Promise. I'll get us some dinner in a minute."

Normally, the sight of my lavender walls and zebra-striped comforter made me feel happier. I'd remember the day my mom and I designed it and feel surrounded by good memories. But right now, all I could think of was what Deidre said about Charley getting fired. Yesterday that news would have had me Dougie-ing around the room. But it didn't feel right now. Don't get me wrong; I still hated his guts. But if Charley hadn't shown up when he did back at the mall . . .

I shuddered at the thought of what might have happened.

Deidre appeared in the doorway. "Your mom's on her way home from New York, and your dad will be here tomorrow morning."

*Uh-oh.* This was bad, very bad. "But I already talked to both of them with Parran. Why are they coming?"

"They want to talk to you."

"But tomorrow's Monday. I have school. Will they be here before it's time for me to go?"

Deidre crossed the room and sat down on the bed beside me. "School is the least of your problems right now, don't you think?" She sighed. "Are you hungry?"

I shook my head. There was no way I could eat with the thick ball of shame and sadness stuck in my throat. The thought of facing my parents made what had to have been the very last few tears left in my body seep out and roll down my face. I could already see the hurt and disappointment on their faces.

"I . . . didn't mean to . . . I just wanted . . ."

Deidre dropped her arm around my shoulder and squeezed me tightly. "I know. But it's done now, and now you're going to have to face the consequences, whatever they are. Remember, your parents love you. They just want to see you be the best you can be, right?"

I couldn't talk. I thought I'd cried myself empty at Parran's house, but I guess I was wrong. There were a lot more tears left than I realized, and they were determined to come out. Deidre handed me a wad of tissues, patted my shoulder, and stood up.

"I'll make you a little snack," she said gently. "Then you should think about getting some sleep. Tomorrow's going to be a long day."

"Wake up, Promise," Deidre was standing over my bed when I opened my eyes. The sky was just barely light, and Deidre still had on the old T-shirt and shorts she usually slept in. "They're here. Both of them."

I sat up and rubbed my eyes, surprised that I'd actually fallen asleep. It felt as if I'd stared at the ceiling for hours. "OK. I'll get dressed—" I started to say, but Deidre shook her head.

"No. Just go as you are. Your dad can't stay. He's got to perform in Houston tonight. He needs to get back. Good luck," she added, giving me a kiss on the forehead.

I could hear their voices as soon as I got to the bottom of the stairs. Mom was sitting on the edge of the white suede couch, leaning toward Dad and talking in the fast, urgent way she always did when she was really upset. Before we'd left for Miami — when it was just Deidre and me — the room had been pretty neat, but now there were a bunch of papers on the glass coffee table, as if Mom had been working on her script or going through her mail before Dad had arrived, and two big coffee cups. Her big Gucci bag was sitting on the floor with all kinds of things spilling out of it: a thick scarf and a pair of gloves, more papers, some thick envelopes. All that stuff reminded me of how busy she was, and I knew I was in deep, deep trouble.

Dad slumped in the matching white suede armchair, listening. He looked the way he usually did when he wasn't performing: jeans, unlaced Jordans, T-shirt under a warm-up jacket. His long dreadlocks were gathered into a ponytail at the base of his neck. He must have been tired, because he was wearing his glasses. He didn't look like a superstar right now; he just looked like a guy. He could have been any of my friends' fathers coming home from a late-night shift where the dress code was casual and employees could have a lot of tattoos. Unlike my mom, he didn't have any stuff. Just himself.

"I'm telling you, Terry, I really think these new friends have a lot to do with it," I heard Mom saying. "That one girl especially."

"Maybe," Dad murmured. "But there's got to be more to

it than that. We're both so busy now, and she's growing up, Bella—"

He noticed me standing at the edge of the room and stood up.

"There she is."

I didn't know exactly what to do. Normally, when I see my dad after having been away from him for a long time, I run into his arms and give him a big hug. But under the circumstances, I wasn't sure that was a great idea.

"What? No hugs?" he said, opening his arms wide.

The moment his arms went around me, the tears came back *again*. I mean, he's my *dad*. I love and admire him more than I know how to explain, and I just felt so bad about everything— everything. My parents divorced when I was four, and even while they were married, he wasn't around that much, because he was always working and touring and building his career. I love him, but sometimes I feel he doesn't really know me and I don't really know him. With Mom, it's different. Until the last few years, when her career started taking off and she got so much busier, we were together all the time. She knows me inside and out. We love each other, but we also annoy each other.

I don't see my dad often enough for all that. And when he hugged me, all I wanted was for him to feel proud of me, instead of feeling that I'd dragged him from his work because I screwed up. Knowing that he loved me even though I had disappointed him hurt worse than any punishment he could give me.

"Hey, hey," Dad said. He sat down and pulled me into his lap. "Why don't you tell me what's going on?"

"I—I just—I wanted to get rid of Charley, but now I don't— because of all those people, and Kayla was mad at me—but the shoes were a present, really, and no one would talk to me— and I just wanted to make some new friends—but there were too many until Charley came and—you're not going to fire him, are you? Because it's not his fault that it's all over the blogs and TMZ and—" I pleaded with him, trying to read his brown eyes. "I'm sorry, Dad. I didn't mean to embarrass you or Mom. I really don't know why I did it. But I promise I won't ever, ever do that again. I've learned my lesson. Just don't fire Charley, OK?"

My parents looked at each other.

"Charley quit," my mother said at last. "Yesterday, after he brought you home. He said if you were willing to put yourself in jeopardy just to be free of him, he couldn't stay."

The words washed over me but wouldn't take hold. It never occurred to me that Charley might quit. I always imagined myself making the decision about when and how he'd go. Now I felt a little as if I'd been dumped for being difficult. It was weird and wrong, and I didn't like it.

My father was watching me, waiting for me to say something or do something, but I felt as frozen as a "Love It" cup from Cold Stone.

"It's too bad," my dad said after a while. "He's one of the best in the business. But he told me at the beginning that he'd never worked with a teenage girl before, and he wasn't sure it would work. Guess he was right."

"So . . ." I said slowly. "Does this mean things go back to the way they were before? Just me and Deidre?"

"I don't think we can go back now. Those days are gone for

good," my mom said with a sigh. "Your dad has hired another company. I know you didn't mean for it to happen, but with all this publicity you've been getting lately . . ." She shook her head. "If anything, you need *more* security now. Not less. And . . ." She paused just long enough to take a deep breath and glance at my dad, as if she hoped he would take over the conversation. "We've made some other decisions, too."

I swallowed hard. There was a whole movie in that big breath and that look. They'd decided something really big. Something really big that I probably wasn't going to like at all.

Dad sighed. "Your mom and I have decided to pull you out of the LOL Girls."

I jumped off his lap. "What? Why?"

"Lots of reasons. Some of it has to do with stuff I'm creating for my own career. I see you being a part of that someday, and I don't want you to be committed to another group when the time comes. But the other reasons have to do with you and how things have been going for you right now."

I stared at him as if he'd sprouted horns. Nothing he was saying made any sense. I knew I hadn't been giving the LOL Girls the best of my attention lately, but that didn't mean I didn't want to do it. I did, and now that they were taking it away from me, I realized just how important the group was to me. The truth was, I had this whole plan in my mind: I'd be like Beyoncé. She'd started with Destiny's Child and then gone solo. That's what I was going to do, too . . . only it wouldn't work if I had no group.

"Your dad and I think that you need a bit more growing-up time before you start your career," Mom chimed in. "Being a performer is a lot of work, and if you're lucky enough to get some success, you have to be ready to deal with it. Everything you've been doing right now makes us think that you're not ready. You need a few more years to grow up a little bit. To have fun and be free and make mistakes. To be a kid, not a professional. Do you understand what I'm saying?"

I shook my head. More tears — now hot, angry ones — rolled down my cheeks. I'd expected them to be angry, to yell and scream and take away my television, computer, and iPhone. But the LOL Girls? A few weeks before our big performance at the Georgia Stars of Stage and Screen concert?

"This is cruel and unusual punishment!" I insisted. "I can work harder. I'll take it more seriously. And I won't do anything like what I did with Charley anymore."

"It's not just that, Promise!" Dad's voice was sharp and firm, and I knew that no matter how much I pleaded or cried, he'd made up his mind. I shut my mouth and sank onto the couch beside my mother, completely defeated. "You're not ready. For now, it's better if you concentrate on yourself. There will be time for singing, and I want you to keep working on it, but your time isn't now. You understand?"

I nodded. There wasn't any point in saying anything else, but I couldn't stop the tears. I sat quietly and wiped at them with a thick wad of tissue. Inside I felt that everything I'd ever worked for was being taken away, and it was my own fault.

"There's something else." My dad's voice was soft again, but he still sounded very determined. I braced myself for more bad news.

"It's about Tia," my mom began.

"Mom!" I interrupted. "Tia didn't have anything to do with the stuff on the blogs. It was my fault. I'm the one who —"

Mom held up her hand. "I know she didn't have anything to with that, Promise. It's the other stuff."

"What other stuff?"

"A lot of our family's very personal information has been finding its way into gossip columns in the past few months," Dad said. "Fights you've had with your mother. Texts you've sent me. Details about the way our houses run. It's a problem, and it's dangerous. I don't know who the leak is, but your mom seems to think . . ."

"It all started around the time you and Tia got tight," my mother finished.

"But Mom, I've told you! It's not Tia. I don't tell her things like that!"

I could tell by the look on her face that she didn't believe me. "Look, Promise, I was twelve once," she said. "I know how girls talk to one another, especially best friends. There aren't any secrets, not when you're as tight as you and Tia seem to be." She raised an eyebrow at me. "Am I right?"

I wanted to defend my friend to the end, but I couldn't. I knew in my heart that I had told Tia all those things. I just couldn't believe that Tia had done more than gossip a little at school. She didn't seem, well, *smart* enough to do more. But saying that wouldn't do me one bit of good. My parents had made up their minds.

"OK," I said heavily. "I'll tell her we can't be friends anymore."

"I'm sorry, Promise, but I don't think that will work, either, and I don't know what else to do." She took a deep breath. "I'm going to pull you out of Riverside. You'll start at Atlanta Girls Prep as soon as the paperwork can be finalized."

*Atlanta Girls Prep!*

"But that's a boarding school!"

"I know."

"And it's on the other side of the city!"

"I know."

"And isn't it one of those kinds of schools where the girls ride horses and have nicknames like Buffy and Bitsy? And Mom, it's a *girls'* school! All girls! Do you know what that means? It means there are no *boys* there. None at all!" I shook my head so hard my hair fell into my face. "No. No. I'm not going there. And if you send me, I'll figure out a way to run away. I don't want to go to Atlanta Prep! Please don't do this to me. I promise I won't say anything to anyone. I'll live like a hermit with no friends at all. But please, please, don't make me change schools! Please!"

I knew I was out of control, but I couldn't stop myself. I started sobbing, covering my face with my hands. I felt my mom's arms go around me, but I shrugged her away. Why were they doing this to me? No LOL Girls. No Tia. And now this? This was love? This was protection? Why couldn't they just ground me or take away my privileges the way other parents did?

"Promise . . ." My mom sounded as if she wanted to cry herself. "Please, honey, don't cry. It'll be fine. Really, it will. You'll make new friends . . ."

That made me cry even harder. I didn't want new friends. I wanted my *old* friends.

"Well." Dad's soft voice rose above the noise of my tears. "There may be another solution. At least in the short term."

"What?"

"Well . . ." He hesitated. "This can't be forever. Just until the end of the school year and through the summer at the longest. But if Promise would rather, she could join the tour and travel with me."

I jumped up and threw my arms around my father's neck. "Yes! Yes! That would be great!"

"But what about school?" Mom asked. She didn't sound nearly as thrilled as I was.

"We could hire a tutor to keep her on track," my father suggested. "She won't be allowed to do anything fun until her schoolwork is done. And you know how touring is, Bella; things can be kinda dull between shows. There'll be plenty of time for her to do her work. I'll see to it."

Mom didn't say anything, but I could tell by her face that she wasn't convinced.

"She'll be away from this friend you're concerned about for a while. In fact, she'll be surrounded by our people. People who have been with us for a long time. If you pull the trigger on that other thing, Deidre can come, too."

*Pull the trigger on that other thing?* Other than being pretty sure that they weren't talking about killing someone, I didn't have a clue what they were talking about—and I didn't want to get sidetracked by it, no matter what it was. A girls' school was still on the table, people! A school for just girls, without any boys at all!

"I don't know, Terry," Mom said with a sigh. She stood up and paced the room, her brow furrowed. I wanted to say something—I was about to—but Dad gave me a stern look and put his finger over my lips.

It felt like forever while Mom walked back and forth,

tapping her fingernail with her teeth the way she sometimes does when she's thinking really hard. It was driving me just about out of mind, knowing that my fate depended on what she might be thinking and not being allowed to say anything about it. I mean, if she didn't let me go on tour, my next stop was Atlanta Prep! Did I mention that it's an all-*girls* school?

"Deidre!" Mom called out at last.

Deidre hurried down the stairs, now dressed for her day. "What's up, Bella?" she asked cheerfully.

"Can you call Promise's school and see if they can help us find a tutor? She's going to try touring with her dad and being taught from the road for a while."

A broad smile covered Deidre's face. "Sure." She winked at me before pulling out her phone. "There should be someone at the school by now," she added, and disappeared down the hall toward the office.

"Thank you, Mom!" I began, jumping up to hug her. "You won't be sorry."

Mom disentangled my arms from her neck and stepped back, fixing a stern face on me. "This is temporary, Promise. Just temporary, you understand?"

"Yes, Mom."

"Don't bug your father too much. He's working."

"I know."

"And Promise?" My dad's voice was soft but serious. Very serious. I don't think he'd ever spoken to me in quite that tone before. A sudden chill crept down my back, and I almost shivered. "This is it. This is absolutely your last chance. Just one more stunt, one more lie, one more anything, and it's over. I won't hear any excuses, and I won't listen to any explanations.

One more thing, and it's Atlanta Prep." He stared hard into my face. "You understand me?"

I nodded.

"Go get ready, then. I've got to get back. I've got a show in Houston tonight."

I turned to go but had only taken two steps before I stopped. I knew I was on thin ice, but there was one more thing I had to do.

"Mom, Dad . . ." I began, and then paused to gather the strength I needed for what I had to say. "I don't want another security guard."

"Promise," Dad said firmly. "We've already been through this—"

"I know," I said quickly. "I know I have to have security, Dad. That's not what I meant. I meant I don't want a *new* guard. I want Charley back."

Mom looked at me as if she thought it was time to take me to the psych ward. "But I thought you hated him."

"I do. I mean, I did. I mean . . ." I sighed. "I don't like him. I think he's too strict. But I don't feel right about him quitting because of something stupid I did. It was my fault, not his. And I want him to know that I respect what he does and that I'm glad he was there. I owe him"—I took a deep breath, hoping I wouldn't have to repeat the words I was about to say ever again—"an apology."

My parents looked at each other as if I was an alien in a Promise suit.

"I think someone grew up a bit today." Dad sounded proud, and I know I stood a little straighter after he said that. "I don't know if Charley will come back, but I'll call him."

"And I guess I should talk to Deidre while you do that . . . about the other thing," Mom said with a sigh.

Dad nodded. "It's time, Bella. Past time, really."

"I know. It's just hard, that's all."

I wanted to ask them what they were talking about so much I could already hear the words in my head, but I didn't dare speak another word. I hurried out of the room to pack and wondered just what Mom was going to say to Deidre. Something else was going on here, and I couldn't help but wonder if I'd saved Charley and brought the ax down on Deidre in the process.

# Chapter Eleven

## KAYLA

"So I heard you took Courtney to the Jag U R concert Saturday night."

Shanita poked her lips out angrily and crossed her arms over her chest. There was an ugly crease in her forehead.

"Yeah, well, Shanita," I said impatiently. "Courtney's my friend, too, so—"

"You knew I really wanted to go to that concert, Kayla!" Shanita interrupted me. "She went to a lot of things with you last year, and this year, you two don't even hang out that much. How come you invited her? I thought we were tight."

"We are! Look, Shanita, I really like you. You're smart and funny and lots of fun to be around. The only reason I didn't invite you was—"

I was going to tell her the truth about Promise and the photo shoot. I was going to admit that I'd been really mad, and I just wanted to be around someone who already knew how full of it Promise could be. But I didn't get the chance.

"It really doesn't matter," Shanita interrupted in a voice as ugly as a slap. "I don't know, Kayla. Sometimes I really think you've spent too much time in places like *this*." She gestured to Gatewood's bright, clean hallways. "Around white kids like these. Courtneys and Davids and people like that. Maybe you should just go on back and sit with the cheerleader girls like you did last year. You've forgotten where you came from. You've forgotten who's like you and who's not."

Then she turned and marched away from me as if she'd accomplished something, her hips swinging indignantly under the khaki brown of her uniform skirt.

I told myself I didn't care. I mean, I had bigger problems. It was just a matter of time before Anne figured out that I hadn't told my parents the truth. Compared with that, some girl being mad about a concert wasn't anything to get excited about. *She'll get over it*, I told myself. But the truth was, it bugged me. It bugged me almost as much as the certainty that the clock was ticking on my lies.

Usually, I could shake myself out of a funk by imagining that the hallways were runways. I'd suck in my stomach and stand up straight and concentrate on walking, one foot directly in front of the other, every step smooth and fierce. I couldn't stomp it out the way I would have on a real runway, but it made me happy to think I was working toward my future, right there on the way to science or gym. But today the runway seemed so far away it might as well have been on Jupiter. Or the sun. Or—

As soon as I walked into Mrs. Hinckley's class, she pulled me aside. "I guess you know I've talked to your tutor," she said.

"Yes, Bloody—I mean, Mrs. Hinckley," I muttered, feeling

my cheeks get hot with embarrassment. I'd almost called her by her not-very-nice nickname, and I could tell by the way her face flushed pink that she knew it.

"Well, I've thought about it, and I've decided that I can't let you make up that quiz. It's really not a makeup circumstance, Kayla. You understand that, right?"

I nodded.

"So you'll be getting a zero," she told me, somehow managing to look even younger than normal, even though her thin lips were pulled in a sharp line. Up close, I wondered if this was her very first job out of school and if, in a way, she was trying as hard to prove she was a grown-up as I was. "I'm very disappointed in you, Kayla. You're usually a model student. If you needed extra help, I would have been glad to help you. And of course, you have Anne Epstein."

"I'm sorry, Mrs. Hinckley. It won't happen again."

"I hope not," she said firmly. "Do you have your paper?"

I nodded. I slipped it out of my homework folder—a plain folder that I'd covered with pictures from my favorite fashion magazines and then laminated so they looked slick and glossy—and handed it to her. She read the first few lines. "This is much better. More like what I've come to expect from you." I got the feeling she wanted to smile or give me a pat on the back or something, but she wasn't sure if she should. It was the first time I'd seen her that way, as someone who was as uncertain about what was the right thing as I felt a lot of the time.

She didn't hug me. "Take your seat," she said at last, and that was that.

Most of the class was already in their seats by then, and I expected to find David in his.

He wasn't there.

I didn't realize how much I'd been looking forward to seeing him until he wasn't there, which was sort of weird. The girls had been teasing me about him all weekend—at least, until Promise had ruined it all—and I'd denied that I liked him that way. But after talking with him on the phone yesterday, I wanted to see him. He was the only one who listened to me.

He missed science and socials studies, too. He didn't come to the table to have lunch with me, and when I looked around the pavilion, he wasn't sitting with the other guys on the basketball team, either.

Courtney was standing near the table I used to sit at last year, when I was a cheerleader—where most of the cheering squad ate—but when she saw me, she grabbed her tray and headed in my direction.

"Do you know what's up with David today?" I asked.

Courtney opened her mouth but didn't get the chance to answer.

"What are you doing here?" Shanita glared at Courtney.

"I'm talking to Kayla," Courtney snapped. "You got a problem with that?"

"No problem, just surprised. I mean, you got what you wanted, why do you need to talk to her now?"

"What are you talking about?"

Shanita leaned toward her. "You know what I'm talking about, Courtney. You think I don't know what you're about? You come sidling over here last week, just in time for Jag U R's concert? You've been sitting over there with all the other little white girls all semester, but when there's a show in town, here you come. Kayla might fall for your act, but I see right through you."

I didn't believe that—I mean, Courtney and I had been friends for years before Shanita even came to Gatewood—and if it hadn't been for Promise bringing Tia, I probably wouldn't have invited anyone. I was about to try to explain it all one more time, but Courtney jumped in and made it worse.

"It just kills you, doesn't it, Shanita, that Kayla invited me and not you?" Courtney's voice was syrupy sweet and bitterly cruel all at the same time. "And by the way, *you're* the one who keeps talking about concert tickets, not me." She crossed her arms over her chest like a lawyer on TV presenting the ultimate piece of evidence before the jury. "So I guess we know who likes Kayla for herself and who likes her to see what they can get."

Shanita jumped out of her chair. Her face was as hard as her fists. "You take that back," she hissed.

Courtney swung her ponytail and stood up slowly. "No," she said in the same sickeningly sweet voice. "I'm not taking anything back. It's the truth, and you know it, so if you want to step to me, go ahead!"

*Step to me?* Coming out of Courtney, that was funny. I mean, she's the ultimate nice Jewish girl. Hearing her try to talk black was like hearing someone as old as my mom call someone "ratchet." If I hadn't been so afraid that they were about to pound each other into meatloaf, I might have laughed. Instead, I stepped between them.

"Cut it out!" I muttered. "Sit down, both of you." I pushed Courtney into her seat and glared at Shanita until she sat back down. "If this is the way you're gonna act, I'm not asking any-

one at this school to do anything ever again. I invited Courtney this time because Promise was here—"

"Promise? Promise Walker, IDK's daughter!" Shanita's
eyes glittered with excitement. I was right. Shanita would
have been totally starstruck by Promise. "I missed the chance
to meet Promise, too? Oh, man."

"You didn't miss anything. She brought this other girl, and
she had to leave early—"

"I was just reading about her," Shanita continued as if I
hadn't said anything. "Were you with her when all that stuff
happened at the mall?"

"No." I sighed. That whole thing was on the long list of
things I really didn't want to talk about. "Anyway, she wasn't
here long, and she brought this friend," I repeated. "I knew
you wouldn't get to spend any time with her, so I figured I'd
invite you the next time she's in town, and you can really get
to meet her. And anyway, you'll have the chance to say hello at
my birthday party. She'll be there."

I could see that Shanita was thinking, weighing every word
I'd said against what she knew about me and what she'd read.
"Well, I guess," she said at last, but her eyes told me she was
only half-convinced.

"Besides, IDK is coming in July. I thought you'd rather go
to that concert, and of course, Promise will be there then. In
fact, she's touring with her dad right now, anyway."

"Wow!" Shanita exhaled. "I can't imagine what that must
be like, touring with IDK! Do you ever do that? Tour with
your dad?"

I shook my head. "Not lately. I haven't done that since I
was little. Back when we lived in New Orleans."

"I want to go to the IDK concert," Courtney interrupted, her lips turned down into a pout.

*Really, Courtney?* I'd just tied myself into knots trying to keep her from getting her butt kicked, and that's all she had to say? I could have slapped her. No, even better, I could have let Shanita do it.

"No way. You went to see Jag U R," Shanita said angrily.

"So? Kayla can invite me to both if she wants to."

"She just said that *I* was going to the IDK concert with her, not you!"

"Kayla's dad runs the whole thing. If she wanted to invite this whole school, she could. Right, Kayla?"

They both looked at me, each waiting for me to take her side against the other. In fact, the whole table was staring at me—Chemine, Omarion, Jamar—all waiting for the answer, hoping for the next invitation. Suddenly, every face seemed hungry, ready to eat me alive for concert tickets. Had those looks always been there and I was just noticing them for the first time? Or was it my imagination?

Suddenly, I just didn't want to be there anymore. I didn't want to look at any of them or listen to two girls who both said they were my friends fight anymore.

"I've gotta go," I lied. "I've got to go take a quiz for Mrs. H."

I dumped my tray full of uneaten shrimp fried rice—even the eggrolls, which were normally my favorite—and headed for the bathroom.

It was cold and white, very clean and very empty. I caught a glimpse of my own face in the little square mirror over one of the sinks and didn't like what I saw. It wasn't that I looked any different. I still had long dark hair, pulled off my face today with a white headband. My skin was still light brown, my eyes a darker brown. I hadn't magically grown any boobs overnight. But everything about my face seemed wrong: nose too big, eyes too small, hair too lank.

"And you wanted to be a model," I said to that ugly girl, and then I started to cry. I thought about Khrissy and that moment when she'd asked me to model her line, that terrific picture we'd taken together, and my Look Book and how everyone seemed to like my stuff except for my dad, who thought it was all a waste of time. Even if I'd found the nerve to tell him that I didn't want to be a performer—that I'd much rather model or have a fashion line—it probably wouldn't have mattered. He wouldn't have listened. I was just screwed. This weekend, I would try to sing and dance. By Monday, I'd either officially be an "artist in development," or I'd be disowned.

I scurried into one of the stalls and closed the door behind me, locking it. I covered my mouth with my hands, hoping no one would hear me as the tears started to fall. The last thing I wanted was for someone to come in and ask me what was wrong. I couldn't tell anyone. No one would understand. Besides, the way things were going, if I let anyone comfort me—if I let anyone know anything about how I was really feeling inside—she'd probably declare herself my best friend and ask for concert tickets.

I don't know how long I was in there before I calmed down enough to think of David. Where was he? When we'd talked yesterday, he hadn't said anything about missing school today. I missed him. I wondered if any of that mess with Shanita and Courtney would have happened if he'd been there. He'd been the only one at the table last time who hadn't wanted tickets—because he didn't even know who Jag U R was!

I giggled a little in the bathroom, just remembering it.

And that made me want to talk to him even more. I pulled my phone out of my backpack and texted: "Where r u?"

I was expecting a text in answer, but to my surprise, a few seconds later, my phone rang.

"Hey!" I said. "Are you cutting school today? Didn't finish your paper?"

When he answered, his voice sounded slow and heavy. As if I'd woken him up before his alarm clock.

"No . . . I . . ."

"Are you OK?"

"I broke . . . I broke . . ." He spoke in a low, slurred voice. "I broke my arm . . . had some surgery today . . . to fix it."

"Oh, no, David! What happened? When? Are you OK?"

"OK . . ." he said after a pause. "I'm a little . . . sleepy . . . you know?"

"It's OK. Go to sleep," I said, even though I had a million questions. I wanted to know what happened, what kind of surgery, when he would be back at school. But it was pretty clear David couldn't answer me right then. He probably shouldn't have been on the phone at all.

"Go to sleep, David," I said gently. "I'll call you later to check on you, OK?"

Another long pause. "OK, Kayla . . ." he murmured sleepily at last. "And Kayla?"

"Yeah?"

"You're the prettiest girl at school, you know that, right?"

A warm feeling spread over me, erasing the feeling of

hopelessness that had driven me into the bathroom in the first place.

"Go to sleep, David," I said, laughing. "I'll talk to you later."

I hung up, feeling ten thousand times better. I sailed through the rest of the school day. Drama swirled around me, but I didn't care anymore. I forgot all about Courtney and Shanita, about Anne and my grades. I didn't think about singing or the party or anything. Nothing could touch me. I was Juliet expecting Romeo, and since I still hadn't read the whole play, I figured I'd just pretend I didn't know how badly things worked out for them in the end.

# Chapter Twelve

## PROMISE

**M**y dad had chartered a private jet to take us to Houston. I had hoped that when we got to the airport, I would find Charley standing there in his tight black T-shirt, waiting for me with his arms crossed over his chest.

But he wasn't there.

Maybe he'd had enough. Maybe he'd decided I was too much trouble. Maybe he just didn't want to deal with me anymore, no matter what my dad was willing to pay him.

I could understand that, but I hoped it wasn't true. Maybe he'd meet us in Houston later today or tomorrow. Maybe he'd give me one more chance and he'd find out that I really wasn't such a rotten kid after all. I mean, he must have done some crazy stuff when he was my age, too.

I love flying in private planes, and this one was super nice, probably the nicest one I'd ever been in. There were two long cream-colored leather sofas right in the middle of the plane and two seats on the right and two more on the left, both in front of the sofas and behind them. I could smell something good cooking in the galley, even though I couldn't see it. There was a closed door at the rear of the plane and another one up front where the captain sat. I wanted more than anything to snap a picture of myself reclining on one of those sofas and post it to Instagram, but I quickly changed my mind.

Might be better to lie low, at least for a couple of days.

"I'm going to stretch out, Promise," Dad said. He sounded tired, and I felt bad. Yesterday was supposed to have been a rest day for him, but it wasn't, because of me. And he had to perform tonight; he had to go out onstage and give the audience that 110 percent he was always lecturing me about.

"You want one of the couches?" I asked. I had planned to plop down on one of them, but I didn't have to. I could sit in one of the chairs and let my dad rest.

But Dad shook his head and nodded to the closed door behind me. "There's a bedroom back there. Besides, I figure you have plenty to think about."

He patted me on the shoulder and disappeared behind the door. I wondered if they'd make him put on a seatbelt at take-off or if they'd leave him alone because he was IDK.

"Would you like anything?" a thin young white woman in a very slim black skirt and crisp white blouse asked me. Her blond hair was swept up into a bun. "Breakfast?"

"Please," I said, taking the card she handed me. "I'll have the bacon and egg sandwich."

"Orange juice?"

"Yes, thank you." I stretched my legs out on the couch and closed my eyes. *Yes, sir,* I thought, *I could definitely get used to this.*

The only problem was, there wasn't anyone to share it

with. I know some people don't mind being by themselves, but that's just not me. I love to have company, someone to talk to and share experiences with. Alone, nothing is the same. Alone is boring. Lonely.

I thought of Tia and my other friends at Riverside. Was I just going to leave them, without even a word of explanation or good-bye?

It didn't seem right, and no one had told me that I couldn't at least text them and tell them where I was. I pulled out my phone and tapped Tia's name in my contacts list.

"Touring with my dad, I typed. Getting a tutor. Will send pix when I can. See ya when I see ya!"

I hit send just as the flight attendant brought my orange juice. I was lonely, but as far as punishments went, this one wasn't half bad.

The first couple of days were like summer vacation. The tutor hadn't arrived yet, and I was on my own. I hung out with my dad's girlfriend and with his assistant. We went to the mall in Houston before one show, but the only thing I bought was an XXL white T-shirt that said "TRUKFIT." It reminded me of Charley. He hadn't shown up yet, but my dad said that was because he was still thinking about it. I got Serena—that's Dad's new girlfriend—to help me mail the shirt to him, along with a note I'd written trying to apologize. We sent it express, so it should have reached him the very next day, but I didn't hear anything back from him one way or the other.

We went to a movie the next day, and the day after that, we

all loaded up in the tour bus and hit the road for three shows in Dallas.

"Your tutor will meet us there," Dad said. "Time for you to get back to work. And you might have a little company soon, too."

"Charley?" His silence had me completely freaked out. I'm not used to people staying mad at me, and it really had me tripping.

Dad smiled. "You'll see." And then he sat down next to me for the whole four-hour ride. It was the most I'd seen him in three whole days, since before we'd left Atlanta.

When we got to the hotel, my new roommate was already unpacking.

"Deidre!" I cried, hugging her. I was glad to see her, but I'll admit, I was a little disappointed. Sometimes when I get something in my head, whether it's an idea or a person or whatever, I can't let it go. Deidre was great, and I was glad to see her, but my brain was fixed on Charley. "When did you get here?"

"About half an hour ago." Deidre stuffed a pile of multicolored T-shirts into a drawer. "I don't know why I'm unpacking — we're only here for, what, three days?" She sighed. "This is some punishment, Promise."

"I know!" I grinned. "Isn't it great?"

Deidre frowned. "Maybe for you. Not for me. Do me a favor, will you? Next time you think you want to run away from someone, just tell me. I'll help you do it so that you won't get into the kind of trouble you did last time. This . . ." She shook her head. "You might think it's a vacation, but from where I'm sitting . . ." She sighed. "Touring is hard. Right when you start to get settled, it's back on the bus. I can't believe I'm here instead of in New York, and I didn't even get to fly in the private jet," she muttered, then flashed me a quick smile. "But if you're happy, I'm happy for you. You'll get to spend a bit more time with your dad."

"Yeah, sort of," I replied. "But other than when he's onstage, I've barely seen him. He's either sleeping or working."

Deidre sat down on the bed beside me. "Well, that's what it takes for him to stay on top. It's much harder to be a successful musician than most people realize. Something to think about if that's the path you're going to choose." She paused. "You also have to be willing to drop people," she muttered. "Just cut them off like—"

I would have asked her right then what she was talking about, but her cell phone exploded in a ringtone I recognized. It was an old song of my dad's, an angry song with some dirty words in the title. Deidre quickly silenced it before I could hear the worst part.

"Yes, Bella?" Deidre said into the phone.

Mom! I reached for the phone, already wanting the chance to say hello, but Deidre elbowed me aside and stood up.

"What?" she cried in alarm. "No, of course not! No, I don't know who would—they've always treated everything with the strictest confidence!" Deidre cut her eyes at me. She looked so worried and upset that I stood up, too.

"What happened?" I asked urgently. "Is Mom OK? What's wrong?"

Deidre showed me a single finger. "Wait." Then she said into the phone, "I don't know. I haven't really checked anything. I just got here. No, she's right here. Wait, I'll ask her."

I knew from the expression on her face that something really bad had happened. "Promise, did you say anything to anyone at school about going on tour with your dad?"

My stomach tightened. "Why? Is something wrong?"

"There's been another story about you in some of the gossip columns," Deidre said in a low voice. "It's not very nice. Your mom wants to know if you talked to anyone. That friend from school, Tia, for example. Did she know you were leaving school?"

I'd sworn off lying, so I had no choice. I told her the truth. "Yeah," I said with a sigh.

"Yes, Bella. Promise said she talked to her."

Even though Deidre was holding the phone close to her ear, I could hear every word Mom said. She must have been screaming into the phone. "Restraining order to stay away from my daughter!" I heard her saying. "I'm gonna put that little girl or her mother or whoever is behind this on notice that this is libel! I'll be calling my lawyers today to put a stop to it!"

"I understand," Deidre said soothingly. "I think that's an excellent idea. Do you want me to make the call to the attorney's office for you?"

"No . . . yes. Yes, thank you, Deidre. Tell them to call me around four P.M. New York time. I should be able to talk by then. Now, put Promise on."

"You bet, Bella. Try to calm yourself down, you hear me?" Deidre said gently. "You know you don't do well when you cart a bunch of anxiety onto the set. Take a few deep breaths. Do you have your meditation tape?"

I heard my mother's tone shift. She exhaled. "Yes, thanks, Deidre. You're right. We'll get the lawyers on this now. This is the last straw."

"OK, now, here's Promise."

"Mom?" I asked hesitantly. "What happened?"

"There's a new rumor going around that you were kicked out of school and that's why you're traveling with your dad," Bella said. "And I think your so-called friend Tia might be behind it."

I wanted to say something, but I couldn't. There wasn't anything left to say. Even I didn't see the point in protecting Tia anymore. Almost everything I'd ever said to her had ended up in a tabloid or on a gossip blog. At some point, even I know when I'm being played.

As soon as I was alone and had the opportunity, Tia was going to hear from me.

"Hey, Promise!" Tia sounded cheerful and excited. "What's up?"

I guess a hotel room is as good a place as any to "break up" with your best friend. It would have been worse if I'd been in my own room, where I'd have to keep looking around and remembering how awful it felt. This place, with its plain cream walls and boring wildlife pictures, meant nothing to me, and after three days, I'd never see it again. Still, when I heard Tia's voice, my heart pounded as if I was running the fifty-yard dash for Olympic gold.

"That's what I wanted to ask you," I said angrily. "What is up with you, Tia? How could you do this to me, huh? Why? Was the money that good?"

"What are you talking about, Promise?"

"Come off it, Tia. I know. I saw it myself. The story on the RapCelebKids website? The one with my picture and the big screaming headline, 'Kicked Out!' The story about how I'm touring with my dad because no school in Atlanta will take me because I'm such a diva and a drama queen and a troublemaker and I don't know what else!" I yelled. My hands shook so badly the phone almost slipped out of my hand. "Why, Tia? I defended you! I thought you were my friend!"

"I am! I didn't do it."

"Right," I scoffed. "You expect me to believe that the headmistress leaked it? Not likely."

"Maybe not, but it wasn't me!" Tia sounded as if she was about to cry, and for just a moment, I wondered if I had made a big mistake. "I swear, Promise, it wasn't me! I don't know why you don't believe me. Is something happening there? Are you in trouble again? Isn't the tour fun?"

"As if I'd tell *you*," I spat. "I don't want to read about it on the Internet tomorrow, so consider this conversation over. Don't call me anymore."

I hit the red end button on my phone. I should have felt better, but instead, I felt worse, even sadder and lonelier than before. I was surrounded by people on the tour, but they were all adults. Just thinking of Tia and the kids at my school had made me feel connected to them, connected to middle school and the gossip and that whole world that I'd loved being a part of. But now, in a single minute, it was all gone, gone for real.

I scrolled through the story on the blog once more, trying to find my anger again, anything to make the sad feelings go away. The story was sickening, by far the most embarrassing thing I'd ever read about myself. Reading that story, you'd think I was the worst, most spoiled and ill-behaved kid on the planet.

And maybe I really was, because some of the things in the article were things I'd actually said or done. Such as daring Mr. B to call my dad on tour or being jealous when Mom came to school and stole all the attention. Who else knew those things about me but Tia? Tia, whom I'd told everything since we'd first gotten tight. Tia, whom I'd trusted like a sister.

*Sister.*

In a sudden desperate need for comfort, I called Kayla.

"Please answer, please answer," I prayed. "Please answer, Kayla. I need you."

But a moment later, the perky recording of Kayla's voice invited me to leave a message. Like Charley, she was still mad at me, too.

I put my head down and curled up on the bed. I was alone in a hotel room, miles and miles from my mother. My dad couldn't talk to me now; he was about to go onstage in front of tens of thousands of people. Deidre was helping my mother try to get me out of yet another mess, because my best friend at school had sold every word I had ever told her. Sure, I had money, I had famous parents, and I was living a life that other kids only dreamed of. But at that very moment, I would have given everything for one single friend I could count on.

# Chapter Thirteen

## KAYLA

When David finally came back to school on Thursday, he didn't look so good. The doctors said he'd broken his arm in a couple of places and that it would take a while for everything to heal. You could see that he'd had a rough time of it: he looked a little thinner, and there were dark shadows under his eyes, as if he wasn't sleeping well. But when he saw me, he smiled like himself, and the weight of the world rolled off my shoulders.

"Hey, superstar," he teased. "What's up?"

I sighed. Every day after school, I was spending hours practicing "Maybe, Maybe." My dad had my dance teacher helping me work out some moves, and instead of waiting for me in the car as he usually did, he'd started taking a seat in the studio to watch the whole lesson.

"What's the matter with you, Kayla?" Susan, my dance instructor, asked after I'd missed the fourth step in a row. "You act as if you've never been here before! It's walk, walk, walk, turn." She showed me again. "Try again."

I glanced at my father and then hung my head.

Why wouldn't he leave? He was making me nervous. I'm not a bad dancer, but somehow having him there was making me seem like one. Every time I tried to sing *and* dance, I messed up. And every time, Dad leaned forward in his chair, as if he wanted to shake me.

"Walk, walk, walk, turn. Head up, Kayla! Attitude! Think runway, girl!"

That helped. Immediately, I stood up straighter, dropped my shoulders, and let my legs swing from my hips, not my knees.

"Walk, walk, walk, turn!" Susan hollered. "Better! Sing! I can't hear you!"

I opened my mouth . . . but nothing came out. I couldn't even remember the words. Susan stopped the music and sighed. "OK, we'll try it again."

But I didn't get better. Every time I tried to sing, I got scared. If I could have just danced, I might have been OK . . . maybe.

"I'm gonna buy all your time after school for the rest of the week," Dad told Susan in a low voice when we were done. "She needs more practice."

"She'll get it," Susan said. She always wears the same thing: black bicycle shorts with a black leotard on top and little black jazz shoes. She has a ballerina's figure, very thin, with narrow hips and shoulders. The only thing that isn't ballerina-ish is her hair, which is jet-black and cut in a short pixie. With her pale skin, she's very graceful and pretty. "But maybe if she worked on it without an audience—"

"I'm no audience," Dad snapped. "I'm her father."

Susan didn't say anything else. That's the thing about Dad:

most people back down when he gets angry. I guess it's partly because of his look — the tattoos and all that — but it's also that he has lots of money. People don't like to make him unhappy, even when making him happy makes me miserable.

"I just want to get through it," I told David later that night, after Anne left and my homework was done. Maybe it was the painkillers he was on, but he listened to me rant on and on about dancing and singing as if he was interested. "If I can just get through it —"

"Your dad will schedule another one. And another one. He'll start writing songs for you, and the next thing you know, you'll be on a world tour," David said.

"I don't think it will go that far."

"I know it will, Kayla," David insisted. "Anne was right. You have to talk to him."

"But what if I suck?" I said. "Don't you think that will discourage him? And that's not even an if, David. I promise you, I'm going to suck. I can't sing! Today I tried just to rap the words — I gave up on singing them — and I couldn't do that, either. I don't have any sense of rhyme or flow or anything." I sighed. "If I'm bad, don't you think he'll give up?"

"No," David said. "What happened after that lady — Aurora — told him he was torturing you? What happened?"

"He hired someone else," I said sadly.

"Bingo. You're going to have to talk to him, like Anne said. That's the only way out of this, Kayla."

"I can't, David."

"Then hello, world tour," he said. "Can I get some concert tickets?" he added, mimicking Shanita's accent almost perfectly.

I burst out laughing.

He was a good friend—who happened to be a boy. And who sometimes happened to make my heart flutter and my stomach spin. So when he walked up to me at school that morning, I was so happy to see him I had to talk to myself to keep from throwing my arms around his neck and kissing his cheek. I mean, first of all, that might have hurt him—you could see the thick white cast on his left arm, resting in a dark blue sling that looped over his shoulder. And second, if anyone saw us hugging in the hallways, within an hour, the whole school would know. And if the whole school knew, Anne would know . . . and then my parents would know, and that was the *last* thing I needed.

So instead of hugging him, I just said, "Welcome back!" with the hugest smile in the world on my face.

"Had to make it back in time for your party! I wouldn't miss that." He leaned close, so close I could smell him. He smelled like soap and exercise and . . . I don't know. Boy smell. It was kind of nice, and I got a little sidetracked from what he was saying, thinking about how nice he smelled and how his breath tickled my ear. "I gotta make that party 'cause I broke my arm getting your gift!"

*Huh?*

"What? But how? What on earth did you get me?"

He laughed. "I'm not saying. At least, not yet. If I tell you now, it will ruin the surprise. I promise I'll tell you, at your party when you open your present."

OK, he had me. I was dying to know what this present was and how it could have caused him to hurt himself so badly. I know I said I didn't need any presents, and I didn't. But David had promised to get me a good luck charm, and that was different. And now he'd added a mystery to it, making it the very best kind of present: the kind that drives you crazy trying to guess what it could be. I stared at him for a long time, trying to think of what to say next.

I'd always thought he was nice-looking, for a white boy, but I'd never thought I'd find him as cute as I did right now. What is it about really getting to know people that makes them better-looking? He was as cute as Eugene to me, and I hardly noticed that he was white at all anymore.

"So are you ready for Saturday, or are you going to talk to your dad?" he asked.

Saturday? What was he talking about? I was so busy noticing how his eyes were the exact same shade of brown as my dad's that my brain had gone blank.

"What happens Saturday?"

"Duh. Your party?"

"Oh, yeah!" My cheeks felt as if they were on fire. Being stupid is always bad. Being stupid around a boy you like is The. Worst. Ever. "I'm, like, so tired and busy I don't know what I'm doing anymore," I said, trying my best to save the situation.

David shifted his backpack off his good shoulder. The motion must have caused him to bump his injured arm, because he winced in pain.

"It hurts, huh?" I took his book bag from him and slung it over my own shoulder, and we started walking slowly toward class.

"Yeah," he said. "Especially at night." When he reached for his backpack again, his fingertips grazed my shoulder. "Thanks, but I'm supposed to be carrying *your* books. Not the other way around."

"I think under the circumstances, it's OK," I said, pushing his hand away.

Our fingers kind of got tangled up for a moment, almost as if we were holding hands. He looked at me, and I looked at him, and that little flutter in my chest turned into a big flutter, and I forgot my name, where I was, where I was going, and everything else in my life that wasn't standing right next to me.

"M-my d-dad is letting some of the kids and me ride to my party in a limo on Saturday," I stammered as we reached the Blood Red Queen's classroom. "You want to go?"

"Sure," he said. Then Mrs. Hinckley swooped over to ask how he was and to tell him all about the work he'd missed.

That hazy, happy feeling that being around David gave me lasted right through the afternoon and until the end of the day. Of course, he sat next to me at lunch, too, and I was so happy I couldn't even eat. I guess Shanita and Courtney were up to their usual competition, but I didn't pay either one of them any attention. I floated through the afternoon. I could even face practicing "Maybe, Maybe," because I knew I'd have a phone call with David as my reward.

There are no buses at Gatewood; all of the kids in my school get picked up at the end of the day by someone. We wait for our rides in the main hallway. There aren't windows, but if you're looking at the front doors, you can see the parents coming in and be ready. As I've said, Tony, my dad's driver, usually comes in and walks me to the car, where my dad is waiting for me. But I wasn't thinking about Tony or dad or practice. I was watching David's mother walk him slowly up the hall, his backpack dangling awkwardly over her shoulder. I couldn't help thinking she really could use a makeover: she was wearing a pair of old capri pants that were at least three seasons ago and a blouse in a pale pink color that didn't do anything for her skin tone. If ever there was a woman whose complexion cried out for royal blue, she was the one.

I don't mean that in a mean way—I'm just telling you why I wasn't looking at the doors. I didn't see anything, but there was no way I could miss the noise and commotion from the hallway and then the sound of the entire school talking at once.

"Oh, my God!" Shanita said loudly. "Oh, my God! It's him!"

"Who?" I asked.

Dad strolled in, wearing a white T-shirt, sweatpants, sneakers, and sunglasses, a black Miami Heat ball cap covering the tattoos on his shaved head.

"Lullabye!" His name went up in a chorus of excited exclamations. "It's Kayla's father, Lullabye Jones!"

Everyone in the room—big kids, little kids, teachers, too—surged around him, trying to shake his hand, pat him on the back, ask a question, and introduce themselves.

Everyone, that is, except for me.

I stood back and watched. I felt really proud of him, but I was also worried. Dad never came inside the school—for this very reason. Why was he here?

"Hey, there. Hiya doin'?" Dad smiled and shook every hand that reached for him. He greeted every single person, nodding and smiling and offering high fives all around, but all the while, he was moving steadily toward me. I gathered my things and stood up, wading into the people as politely as possible, until I finally stood at his side.

"Nice to see everybody," Dad shouted, and the room quieted down as if the president was giving a speech about the state of the world. "We hope to see all y'all at the party this weekend. Kayla's turning thirteen, and she's gonna sing for y'all—her first performance ever. We gonna celebrate!"

*Great*, I thought, struggling to keep a calm smile on my face. *Now everyone knows.* Applause and a few cheers filled the room. Dad took my hand, and we started for the doors.

"'Bye, Kayla! 'Bye, Mr. Jones!" Voices rang out on every side. With his free hand, Dad offered more handshakes and high fives. But he kept his other hand clamped around my fingers as if I was still a very little girl.

That should have been my first clue.

Finally, we escaped the building and stepped into the warm March day, crossing the street quickly to where my dad's black and silver Maybach 62 sat at the curb.

We slid into the car. I buckled my seatbelt and grabbed some water from the refrigerator to hydrate before dance class, expecting the car to move forward as it always did. But nothing happened. The car sat parked, and my dad sat still beside me, staring at his hands and not saying anything.

*Uh-oh.*

"H-how come you came in?" I asked in a shaky voice. "You haven't done that in a long time."

He turned toward me. I couldn't see his eyes through the sunglasses, but I knew he was angry. "I went over to talk to your mother about some party stuff before coming for you today," he began. "And Anne was there."

All of the air in my lungs emptied out of me in a huge, defeated sigh. "Oh," I said softly. "I know I should have told you, Dad, but—"

"Told me? You shouldn't have done it at all, Kayla!" Dad's voice rose. "What are you *thinking*? Just refusing to take a test? That's not like you! And then lying about it? What's the matter with you, Kayla? You got a tutor to help you. You got advantages I never dreamed of having when I was your age. You crumple them up and throw them in the trash?" He shook his head in disgust.

Usually, when I'm getting yelled at, I just close my mouth and wait until it's over. But this time, I sort of snapped a little inside.

"You know why I did it, Dad?" My voice was shaking, and I wasn't sure if I was going to start crying or start shouting. "It was right after the Mickies. Right after Khrissy asked me to model and you just said no. Without even asking me if I wanted to."

"Of course, I said no! I know you like clothes and all that, and there will be time enough for endorsement deals and fashion lines after you have a career—"

"And what if I want *fashion* to be my career? What if I want to be a model? Or a designer?"

Dad's head wagged from side to side like a metronome. "You're not hearing what I'm saying, Kayla. I don't care if you do those things! Just do them after—"

"After I have a career in music. I heard you!" I snapped. "Did you hear me? I don't want a career in music, Dad. I'm no good at it. I hate it!"

My dad hit a button and raised the privacy shield between us and Tony.

"Don't you raise your voice to me, Kayla Jones," he said in a soft voice that was full of warning. "I'm your father, and

I'm not going to have that mess from you. I hear how some of these kids talk to their parents, and I'm telling you right now, I don't play that way."

I folded my lips, but his words just made me angrier. How would I ever get him to listen to me if the minute I started talking about the things that mattered to me, he told me I was "talking back"?

He waited a few seconds and then continued. "I know you feel like you're not good at music, but it's in there, I *know* it. That damn Aurora and her negativity—"

"Aurora was *right*, Dad!" He'd just told me not to yell at him, but I couldn't help it. "This is all . . . just torture for me! I'm not good at it. I hate it. I hate it all! But I'm good at fashion, Dad, and it's not just about playing dress-up and shopping, it's really not!" I reached for my backpack, pulled out my Look Book, and flipped to the hoodies I'd been working on.

"Every girl who sees this one wants it, Dad. And you can't buy it anywhere, because I just made it up." I flipped to the swimsuit. "I got the idea for this one from one of those old black-and-white movies. It's like retro but not. You put in the colors that are in this season and—"

Dad grimaced and pushed the book away. "Aw, come on, Kayla. This is just ridiculous. We got a serious issue here, and you're talking about a fashion show."

"Not a fashion show, Dad. It's way more than that!" My voice rose again, but this time with excitement. "Mary-Kate and Ashley Olsen were child actors. When they stopped acting, they started a fashion line that's now worth, like, like, a gajillion dollars! More money than they ever made as actors."

"But they were actors first!" Dad snapped. "People knew who they were. They had a platform, Kayla. You think you can just jump out with 'Hey, buy my clothes!'" He shook his head. "You don't get how this business works," he grumbled.

"But Dad—"

"No, Kayla. That's enough. I don't want to hear any more about it."

I should have stopped, I know that. I should have let it go and tried again another time. But I couldn't. Everything inside me—everything I'd been pressing down forever—just came bubbling up like lava. You can't shut up a volcano, and I couldn't shut up, either.

"You haven't heard anything I've said!" I spat. "Music isn't the only way to build a platform. Neither is being on TV." I grabbed the book and shook it at him. "This is *me*, Dad! This is what matters to me! Why can't you help me do what *I* want to do for once, instead of always making me do what *you* want me to do?"

My father's face—the part of it that I could see, since his shades still covered his eyes—closed down on me like Bergdorf on Christmas Eve.

"I'm s-sorry, Dad. I—" I backpedaled, but it was too late.

Without saying another word to me, Dad grabbed my Look Book. He took it between his two thick brown hands and pulled, ripping the book in half. Pages splintered away from its spiral binding with an awful wrenching sound.

"Nooo!" I wailed. "Dad!"

But he took the two halves and ripped them both again before throwing the pieces up in the air so that they floated around us like large, colorful squares of confetti.

I reached for them desperately, trying to gather up all of my hard work and salvage it if I could.

"Leave it, Kayla," my father said sharply.

I stopped, slumping back into my seat, with tears rolling down my face. On the seat, on the floor, everywhere around me, were fragments of my outfits. Like a cruel tease, the sketch of the cowl-neck hoodie lay right near my hand, still mostly intact, but I didn't dare touch it. Not after hearing the warning in my father's voice.

"I understand a whole lot better now." Dad spoke to the window, because he wouldn't look at me. "You've been going at this backward. You want to skip the hard work and go straight for the picture taking! But I'm telling you, that's not the way. Just because you're my daughter doesn't mean you get to skip the grind. I don't want anyone saying that you got anything the easy way, you understand? So that's that." He slid an envelope across the seat at me. "And if these pictures are your evidence, it's probably better for you to concentrate on music."

I wiped my tear-streaked face with my hands and took the envelope. Inside were the results of my photo shoot the week before.

I don't know what I was expecting. I knew while we were taking the pictures that everything was wrong. As I skimmed the dozens of photos in the package, the monumental awfulness of everything in my life settled on me like a backpack full of rocks.

The photos were horrible.

Terrible.

Bad.

Not one of them was good. I looked stiff, angry, and uncomfortable in every shot, my face frozen in the exact same stiff smile no matter what pose my body struck. With all the make-up on my face, I looked like a forty-year-old woman—wearing my four-year-old daughter's outfits. I hated them when I put them on, but I hated them even more now. I flipped through all of the shots twice and then crammed them all back into the envelope. If I could have thrown them out the window and let the traffic roll over them, I would have. Why couldn't my dad have ripped these up—and not my book?

"Now, can we forget this fashion business?" Dad said, still not looking at me as the car rolled to a stop. "Your energy goes to two things from now on: school and music. Do you understand, Kayla?"

I didn't answer. Who was he talking to? I felt so bad I wasn't even Kayla anymore. It was as if the "me" inside me was gone. His words were far away, as if they were coming at me from the top of the Grand Canyon and I was way, way down in the valley below.

"You hear me?" Dad repeated sternly, demanding an answer.

"Yes, Dad," I answered softly.

He opened the car door. "Good. You only have two days left before your party, so I want to see some changes in your attitude starting with this rehearsal. And if I don't, maybe this Look Book isn't the only privilege you need to lose."

# Chapter Fourteen

## PROMISE

"Promise?"

Deidre shook my shoulder, and that was when I first realized that I'd cried so hard I'd fallen asleep.

"Don't you want to go to your dad's show tonight?"

I sat up and looked around. The room was dark except for a little twilight coming through the open curtains.

"If you're going, it's time to go, honey," Deidre said softly. "But if you don't want to—"

"I want to," I muttered, swinging my legs off the bed. "I'll go get ready."

Deidre gave me a quick pat. "OK, but no need to get *glamorous.*" She rolled her eyes dramatically and laughed. "We're watching from the wings tonight."

As usual, there was a lot of activity backstage during the show. When you're in the audience, you just see the rappers and the musicians and the dancers and stuff. Most people don't have any clue how many more people there are behind the stage. It takes a lot of people to put on the kinds of concerts my dad does: people who handle the sound, people who move around the props and things you see on the stage, and the lighting and special-effects crews who help change the moods between songs. There are people who manage the travel and coordinate with the ticket sales in every city. There are people who keep track of every penny spent and of every person involved with the tour. There's even a nurse. And, of course, security. I know there's more, because there are people whose jobs I don't even understand.

And then, finally, there are people like me and Deidre and my dad's girlfriend, Serena.

Standing backstage at a concert means you're standing with a lot of people who work with the tour in some way or another. You have to be careful to stay out of the way of the people who have actual jobs to do during the performance — that's really important. You can get sent back to the hotel if you get in the way. Trust me, I know.

The other thing about standing on the wings of the stage is that you can't always see very well. In fact, sometimes you can't see anything at all. Sometimes that's because you're at a weird angle, and sometimes there are pieces of the set blocking your view. But other times, when it's pretty crowded back there and everyone is trying to see what's happening, it's just impossible to find a good enough spot.

Deidre had taken me to the green room for a little food, and I felt better. The whole conversation with Tia still stung, like when the flat iron gets too close to the back of your neck. I hoped that if I didn't think about it, it would go away.

Even though we got there a little late and the concert had begun, Deidre and I found a decent spot near the front edge of the stage. Dad had just gotten started, but the crowd was already on its feet.

Watching my dad perform is . . . well, it's a lot of things.

It's incredibly cool, because he's so good. I don't know all of his songs, but I know a lot of them, and I have a lot of fun singing along and just vibing on the whole thing. It's as if the energy of the audience does something to him and he gives it back to them with the power of his flow.

I always feel so proud to be his daughter, because he's just amazing.

But it's also weird, because that guy up there—that performer—I don't know him. The man I hug, the one who gives me lectures about doing my homework and watching my mouth and working hard, that guy is gone. The onstage guy isn't my dad, he's a superstar. He's IDK, Mickie-winning artist, and that's a whole other person.

"He's on fire tonight!" Deidre shouted above the sound. Oh, yeah, that's something I forgot to mention: how loud it is when you're standing in the wings. And you're standing if you want to see. There are sometimes chairs around, but they're too far away to be any good if you want to watch what's happening onstage. "I bet having you here helps, Promise. It's got to be nice for him to have his daughter with him."

I wasn't so sure. He'd probably seen the latest thing, the stuff about me being kicked out of school. That didn't seem like the kind of news to get a father particularly psyched up.

Deidre wasn't looking for an answer, anyway. She threw

her hands in the air, bobbing her head in time to the music, chanting lyrics with IDK with her eyes closed, as if she was dreaming *she* was the rock star.

On the next song, the lights on the stage changed from reds and yellows like a police siren to a gentle blue, signaling that one of Dad's slower songs was about to begin. I tried to guess which one it might be, but there wasn't any backbeat starting. In fact, there wasn't any sound at all—except for the cheers and whoops and yells of twenty thousand people.

"I'ma do something special for y'all tonight," IDK told the audience. "Got us one very, very special guest."

The crowd roared in anticipation. I looked around, wondering who was here. Had I fallen asleep and missed the chance to hang out with someone whose music I totally loved? Because usually, when Dad/IDK said something like that, the "other artist" was someone amazing whom the crowd would flip out to see perform a number onstage with him. Maybe Large Marge, one of the hottest female rappers on the label? I looked all around, but either it was too dark, or she was on the other side of the stage.

Or it could be Rick Denty, an old-school rapper who had just signed. Or even Alter Ego. My mind reeled with possibilities, and I was as excited as the rest of the audience. I inched closer to the stage, standing on tiptoes, hoping to peer into the darkness of the other wing and get a glimpse of this special mystery guest.

"This is a young artist—a very young artist—who is just starting out in her career. She's someone I'm very, very proud of, and I hope she'll sing us a little song we wrote together when she was just seven years old."

*What? He's writing songs with seven-year-olds?* It took me a few seconds to realize that the seven-year-old girl IDK was talking about was *me*.

The crowd broke into a burst of applause and cheering. "Promise! Promise!"

"That's right," IDK said, grinning and stretching his lean, muscled, tattoo-covered arm toward the wings of the stage. "My daughter, Promise Walker."

"YAY!" Deidre squealed, clapping her hands. "You'd better get out there, girl," she said into my ear, giving me a nudge. "Go!"

I hesitated. I won't lie: it's one thing to dream about performing in front of tens of thousands of people . . . and something else altogether actually to do it. I'd performed with the LOL Girls a dozen times or so, but I don't think our audience had ever been any more than a thousand people.

IDK's arm was still stretched out. He was looking from one side of the stage to the other. "Where are you, baby? Come on out and sing for Dallas!"

Another loud roar went up. It sounded like a giant monster ready to eat me alive if I didn't live up to its expectations. For the first time in a long time, I completely agreed with my dad: I wasn't ready for this.

"Go ahead!" Deidre hissed. This time, instead of a nudge, she shoved me hard enough to send me out of the shadows and onto the edge of the stage.

Immediately, a bright spotlight found me, and I was almost blinded. If Dad hadn't stretched out a hand and led me to the center of the stage, I'm not sure I would have ever found it. The giant monster—the crowd—was close and hungry, but I couldn't see anything, not a single face. My dad parked me on a stool someone had set in the center of the stage.

"You remember it?" he whispered, putting a microphone in my hand.

Of course, I remembered it. Until I got too old for good-night stories and bedtime songs, he'd sung it to me anytime we were together. I remembered it. I just wondered if I was too scared and too unprepared to sing it in front of all these people.

"Yeah," I said, as the opening chords began from some-where behind us.

I don't know why, but hearing the music calmed me down a bit. I put the microphone up close to my mouth, the way I'd learned practicing with the LOL Girls. I closed my eyes and sang.

> *Momma is here, and it's all right,*
> *Daddy is near, and it's all right,*
> *Nothing to fear, it's all right,*
> *It's all right, all right.*
>
> *The night is dark, but it's all right,*
> *The road is long, but it's all right,*
> *Soon we'll be home, and it's all right,*
> *It's all right, all right.*
>
> *Close your eyes and sleep.*
> *Close your eyes and dream.*
> *Close your eyes and reach*
> *For moonbeams, moonbeams.*

*Momma is here, and it's all right,*
*Daddy is near, and it's all right,*
*Nothing to fear, it's all right,*
*It's all right, all right.*

Look, I'll be the first to admit, it started out kind of shaky. My first few notes weren't all that, but I wasn't warmed up at all. And it's weird hearing your own voice sailing out over the crowd. It took me most of the first verse to find myself, but after that? Well, I'm not saying I was Rihanna or anything, but it wasn't bad. I could hear the monster yelling and clapping its love and approval, and that made me want to sing out for them that much more. I could almost imagine myself one day being as big as my dad.

When I got to the part about dreams and moonbeams, my dad started rapping words I'd never heard before, as if they belonged in the song. I heard rhymes about how I was growing up, about how I was going to follow in his footsteps, about the music dynasty that is our family. And there was something about not believing what you read and a warning to the haters. I wish I could have heard it all — I prayed that by tomorrow, someone would have posted the whole thing on YouTube — but I couldn't really listen. I had to sing.

Too soon, Dad and the music wound down. I was sweating from the heat of the lights and from the excitement of it all, but I didn't care. I felt good. Happy. Alive with energy. The applause swept toward me, and I wished more than anything that there was a way to gather it up and save it for those days when I felt like the biggest screw-up God ever made. I turned to give my dad a hug, but he had stepped away from me and was applauding, too.

"Good job, Promise," he said, taking my hand and helping my off the stool. "Good job, kid." He planted a kiss on my cheek, and then, with a last wave at the audience, I skipped off the stage.

Deidre grabbed me in a massive squeeze. "That was awesome, honey! Just awesome! And the fans loved it!" She wiped a tear from the corner of her eye. "I don't know why they pulled you from the LOL Girls. You're ready, honey. I think you really are."

I could barely hear her. I grabbed her hand and pulled her away from the stage, then ducked out a door that dumped us into the hallway.

"Did you know he was going to do that?" I asked, leaning against the cool white cinderblock. "He's never let me onstage before!"

Deidre shook her head, but a proud grin stayed plastered on her face. "I had no idea. I haven't seen him all day."

"Then maybe Mom talked him into it."

Deirdre shrugged. "Maybe." But she didn't sound as if she thought that was likely.

"But you don't think so."

"Well, I think your mom's just a little too busy with her own stuff, don't you?"

Something about the way she said it made it sound as if my mom didn't care about me. Or maybe I just took it that way.

"She talked to Dad today. She knew how bad I was feeling about school and the blogs and telling Tia that we won't be friends anymore. She might have told Dad!" I insisted defensively. "And she would be here if she could. You know she would, Deidre!"

Deidre sighed. "I'm sorry, Promise. I didn't mean to sound like that. It's just . . ." She shrugged her shoulders. "Your mom has a lot of changes happening in her life right now. Big changes. Including some that affect you and me."

I didn't have any idea what she was talking about, and I said so.

"I guess they haven't had time to tell you," Deidre said. "I hope they won't be upset with me for beating them to it, but you deserve to know."

"Know what?"

"I don't exactly work for your mother anymore. She's going to be hiring a new assistant to work with her."

I frowned. "She's getting a new assistant? Why? When?"

"Your mom doesn't think I'm the right person for 'this point in her career,'" Deidre said sadly. I knew she was using Mom's exact words—and that in saying them, Mom had hurt Deidre's feelings. "She wants someone who's more of a Los Angeles/ New York type. Someone who's got more experience with the Hollywood lifestyle." Deidre gestured at her blue jeans and T-shirt and tried to laugh. "And I think we can all agree that I'm not that! So I won't be involved with her career stuff anymore. Instead, I'm going to stick close and look after you while she's making movies and stuff. And I'm so glad, Promise. I wouldn't have missed tonight for anything in the whole world!"

Deidre squeezed my shoulder and smiled, but something about what she had said made me feel really angry with my mom, both for firing Deidre and for not being there to see me perform.

"Are you mad at her, Deidre? For letting you go?"

Deidre hugged me. "No, of course not. I love your mother. And I'm happy for her. She's dreamed of being an actress since I've known her, and now her dreams are coming true. Only . . ." She paused again to try to figure out how to explain herself. "I had gotten used to being a part of everything in your family, you know. I was used to helping you *and* your mother and it being just the three of us. I guess I thought I was a part of the family. Now there's going to be another assistant, and at some point when you go home from the tour, there will be another bodyguard. I guess I feel a little . . . left out." She patted me on the shoulder. "But let's look at the bright side. At least that awful Charley is gone!"

"He wasn't so bad."

Deidre rolled her eyes. "Oh, yes, he was, too. You know he wanted your mom to fire me? Apparently, I didn't pass his crazy background test!" She harrumphed indignantly. "I mean, who does he think he is, the CIA?"

"Yes," I replied, and we both laughed.

"We're better off without him, Promise," Deidre insisted when we could be serious again. "Forget him." She wrapped me tightly in one of those soft Deidre hugs that I've loved since I was four years old. "It's going to be just you and me now. Just you and me, no matter what!"

I hugged her, breathing in the smell of comfort, wondering what I would do if Deidre ever disappeared from my life. How could Mom just discard her like that? What was she thinking, just leaving her behind? And if Deidre didn't fit with her new Hollywood lifestyle, what about me? Did she plan to leave me behind, too?

She hadn't been calling as much; today had been the first time I'd talked to her since I'd joined my dad's entourage. I'd just figured she was busy filming, but now I wondered. Mom was reaching for her dreams, but even I understand that when you're reaching for something new, sometimes you have to let go of old things.

"You want to go back and see the rest of the concert?" Deidre asked.

"Yeah." I nodded, but it wasn't the same. I'd left the stage twenty minutes ago feeling loved and valued by thousands of people. I was returning to the wings now wondering if the one person I loved more than anyone in the whole world had decided to move on without me.

# Chapter Fifteen

## KAYLA

"**I** thought you should see this."

Mom set her iPad down on the kitchen table beside my bowl of Cheerios with her "serious" face on. There was a frown line showing in the center of her forehead, and her lips were pressed so tightly together they were almost invisible.

I glanced at the screen and saw "YouTube" in the upper left corner and immediately let my eyes stray back to the view out the window of the breakfast nook: a strip of quiet private beach and the Atlantic Ocean rolling in the distance in grayish-blue waves. I'd already seen what she was going to show me, but I didn't say it. I didn't want to have to explain that my friends had been texting me all night, ever since someone posted the video, to make sure I knew about it. So I just stared at the ocean and waited until she pressed play.

It wasn't a very good video; whoever had taken it hadn't had a very good seat. The figures onstage were tiny, and the light hovered around them like a weird halo. The audio wasn't all that good, either; you could hear a lot of crowd noise and people screaming so loud it sometimes drowned out the performers. But at other moments, the voice sailed out over the crowd, clear and strong, powerful and confident.

It was Promise, singing alone while her dad rapped in the background. Promise performing in front of thousands of people at IDK's sold-out show somewhere in Texas, looking a little scared but sounding as if she was doing what she was born to do. Even though you couldn't really see IDK/Terry, you could tell from the sound of his voice how very proud he was. He was proud like my dad wanted to be of me after the party tonight.

*Gee, thanks, Promise. Thanks for doing what you always do, making everything worse.*

"She did pretty good, huh?" Mom said gently.

I shrugged.

"Kayla," she began, and then stopped. I tried to keep eating as if I didn't care, but the cereal felt like metal pellets in my mouth. I pushed the bowl away and just sat there waiting for her to say what she was going to say.

She sighed. "I know your dad has been pretty hard on you about performing. And I know how you feel about it, too. It's not that he doesn't want you to have the chance to explore fashion—"

I stood up. "I know, I know. After I'm a Mickie-winning artist. Which I'm never going to be, so it's kind of the same, isn't it, Mom?"

"Don't say that, honey," Mom said gently, taking my hand. "And don't let *this* bug you," she continued, nodding her head at the video. "Everyone grows at her own pace. It's not a competition."

"Of course it is, Mom!" I pulled away from her angrily. "All I wanted was a party, something fun to do with my friends. But it's ruined now. Dad's turned it into this big musical event to show everyone that his daughter is this—this—superstar, and we all know I'm not." I pointed to the iPad. "I could never do that, Mom. Never. If I get through tonight without making a fool of myself, without all my friends laughing and talking about me behind my back and all the blogs calling Dad out for trying to push his kid into the spotlight—"

"Aw, honey. It's not like that. Your dad just wants you to do your best."

"Dad doesn't care what I'm the best at, Mom. If he did, he wouldn't have ripped up . . . my . . ." I couldn't say it. Tears were already prickling behind my eyes, and I didn't want to cry about the Look Book anymore. I took a deep breath and made myself as hard and angry as I knew how to be.

Mom put her arms around me. "He shouldn't have done that, baby. He just doesn't understand."

I didn't want to hear it. I didn't want to hear anything about what my dad wanted or how he felt or how he loved me and was doing what he thought was best. Just hearing my mom start to talk about him made me want to dive into the coldest part of the ocean and let the water fill my ears with silence. I closed my eyes, trying to block out her words, but all I could see was my Look Book in shreds on the black carpeting of the Maybach's floor. All I could hear was Dad telling me that what I loved doing more than anything was worthless. And now Promise had stepped out onstage and set a standard that I knew I wouldn't be able to meet, even if I had a hundred more years to practice.

I stepped out of my mom's arms. I could tell she was both surprised and hurt—I was basically rejecting her—but I just couldn't talk about it. I couldn't.

"I'd better go get ready," I said, without looking at her. "We have to meet Susan."

Mom nodded. "I'm glad you're getting to practice at the club, honey. I'm sure that will make you less nervous tonight."

I gave her another half-hearted shrug. The truth was, I wasn't nervous at all. I'd already resigned myself to failure; I'd already seen the disappointment in my dad's face. I saw it at the end of yesterday's rehearsal. It wouldn't be good, but I'd go through with it tonight. I'd do it, and my dad would get exactly what he deserved. All of that went through my head, but all I said to my mom was, "Susan said to bring my outfit. I'm going to go get it."

Mom nodded. "Kayla?" she called when I was about two steps from being out of her sight. "Happy birthday."

*Yeah, right.*

Club Flamingo is pretty small, and you could miss it if you weren't looking for it. The entrance is on the corner of a strip that has a bunch of restaurants and one of those tiny old hotels with old-style decorations all over it on the other corner. Late at night, the club is open to adults only, but for my friends and me, from seven until ten P.M., the owners had taken out the alcohol and set the place up especially for kids.

When I walked in, the first things I saw were all these cute little tables, covered with festive tablecloths and beads and

Mardi Gras-themed stuff. Each table had six chairs, except for one long table at the top of the room, just in front of the dance floor. That was the head table, where my close friends and I would sit.

But the float sitting right in the center of the dance floor was the real stunner.

It was huge: a life-size float of me made entirely of flowers. OK, I didn't think it looked that much like me, but it's got to be pretty hard to make flowers look like someone's face, so I wasn't mad about it. The designer had mounted it on a rotating platform, so it looked as if I was swirling around the room, greeting my guests. Even as upset as I was, I thought it was pretty cool.

Past the dance floor was a narrow strip of a stage and a little staircase that led to a small balcony. The seats up there would be the VIP section, where my dad and mom, Bella and Terry, and any of their guests would hang out. It wasn't done yet, but they would make some kind of pavilion up there with thick pieces of white fabric, so the VIPs could enjoy the party without having people gawk at them.

There were a few workmen there with ladders, hanging life-size photos of me all over the walls. They were old; none of the ones from that awful shoot with Willis made the cut. In one corner of the room, a tattoo artist was setting up a stand of temporary inks—getting ready early, I guessed. The DJ my dad hired was there, too—a dude named Diggity who was really popular in the local dance scene—completing his preparations on a riser behind the dance floor. He looked up at us as we walked in, his eyes saggy as if he had just finished Friday night's gig and hadn't been to bed yet.

Susan hurried down the stairs from the balcony. I knew she had classes today, so she was dressed as usual, in bicycle shorts and leotard; she had pulled a hot-pink sweatshirt over the top, probably so she wouldn't look so naked, but the color was way too strong for her pale skin and dark hair.

She gave me a quick hug, but her eyes went straight to my mom's. Susan was worried, too.

"Go get your clothes on, honey," she said to me. "We'll run it a couple of times, and that'll have to be enough. The DJ needs to get home, and I have a bunch of makeup classes today." She pointed to a hallway just past the long counter of the bar. "The bathroom's down there. On the left."

The bathroom was really cool, all pink and girly and really very pretty, with three small stalls and a black marble sink. It was the sort of room that I might have snapped a picture of and used in my Look Book. But there wasn't any point in that, not now. I slipped on the outfit I'd picked for the party but didn't bother to look at myself in the mirror. I headed back out into the club feeling as if someone had a gun pointed at my back.

"Cue it from the intro, eight bars in," Susan told the DJ after I took the stage. She flashed an encouraging smile at me. "I'll count you through the first time. The next time, you're on your own, OK? Now, here we go," she said as the music rose around me. "Five, six, seven, eight!"

I started to move without even thinking about it. The steps had been drilled into my head, just like the words to the song. I said the words to myself as I danced and spun and bounced and teased.

"Good, Kayla! Good!" Susan called. "Keep your energy up! You've got this!"

I tried. I really tried. And this time, I didn't miss a step. I finished on one knee with my hand stretched out to my "audience." When the music died, I heard applause from Susan and my mom and a few hoots of approval from the workmen.

"That was really, really good, Kayla!" Susan rushed onto the stage and gave me a hug. "I gotta tell you, I was worried. But you're going to do great!"

"Only we couldn't hear you singing," Mom said. She had taken a seat at one of the tables near the stage. She was wearing that maxi-dress, the black Marc Jacobs one she'd dressed up for the Mickies, with flat sandals with rhinestones set into the thong. I love her in that dress. It's really just a sundress, but she looked like a celebrity in it when she crossed her legs and leaned forward to talk to Diggity. "Do you have a microphone set up yet?"

"Yes, ma'am," the tired DJ said. He didn't look like a Diggity; he was a Hispanic guy with a lot of hair curling around his shoulders and a thick mustache. If I were naming him, I'd have called him Armando or something. He fiddled around a bit and then tapped on a thick black microphone with a silver head. "Testing," he said into it, and the room filled with the sound of his voice. "There you go, miss."

"Th-thank you," I said, and heard my voice amplified all around the room. I didn't like the sound of it. It sort of freaked me out to hear myself, loud in the quiet of the mostly empty club. And the thing was heavier than I thought it would be.

"OK, Kayla." Susan pulled a couple of bottles of water out of her big black dance bag. She handed one to me and offered the other to Mom. "Hydrate, and then let's try it again."

I took a long slug from the bottle—I was starting to get a

little sweaty—and wiped my forehead with the back of my hand before taking my place on the stage with the microphone again.

Susan nodded to Diggity. "Same spot." She looked at me as the music rose around me. She didn't say it out loud this time, but I could read her lips. "Five, six, seven, eight."

I started moving . . . but I forgot to sing. Then, when I did start singing and I heard my voice, shaky and uncertain, moving out over the empty room, I stopped doing either and just stood there.

"Stop the music!" Susan cried, waving her hands. "It's OK, Kayla. This is a different space, but you've done this with the karaoke mike in the studio. It's the same thing, only your voice sounds a bit louder. Take a breath and try it again."

I did. This time, I started singing at the right place, and I was moving OK, but then, when I hit the chorus, I lost the tune of the song and couldn't find it again no matter what I did. Once again, Susan stopped the music. This time, though, she didn't say anything to me. She crossed the room and bent over, talking to my mom in a low voice, while I stood there feeling like a fool. I noticed that the workmen wouldn't look at me; suddenly, they only had eyes for those pictures of me, steadily lining the walls of Club Flamingo. Diggity the DJ wouldn't look at me, either. He put on his headphones and started fiddling with the dials of his board as if I wasn't even there.

"Mr. DJ!" Susan called out at last. "Do you have the version with Kasha singing?"

"Yep," he replied, slipping off his headphones.

"Cue it up, please." She walked toward the edge of the

stage. "Kayla, let's try it with Kasha—down low, of course. I know you can do it, but, well, your mom and I think it will help you."

*Nothing can help me. I'm screwed.*

I thought it but didn't say it. Just thinking it almost made me smile, though, because those were the exact words David had used when I told him the whole story about the performance and the Look Book and what my dad expected me to do: "Man, you're screwed."

He was the only person I'd told about the whole scene with my dad. For a minute, I'd almost called Promise, but then I'd thought better of it. I couldn't forget what she'd said to me: "You're nothing, that's what you are, Kayla! If you didn't have a dad who could buy you a career, buy you some talent, buy you some friends, everyone would see you for the pathetic loser you really are!"

I'd told David and no one else.

"You're screwed," he had muttered dejectedly after hearing the story, and for some dumb reason, I'd burst out laughing. I needed to, I guess. I'd cried so hard through telling the story I didn't have any tears left. And I guess I laughed because it wasn't what I'd expected him to say. Most people would have tried to make me feel better. Or tried to explain my dad's reasons, as my mom had done. Or tried to help me figure out a solution.

Not David. He'd just stated the situation exactly as it was—and I loved him for it.

Well, not *loved* him loved him. But I did love him . . . sort of. I know I'm not old enough to have a boyfriend or date or anything like that, but it was nice to have a special friend who happened to be a boy. Seeing him and finding out what this mystery gift he was bringing me was were just about the only things I was looking forward to in the whole party.

"Five, six, seven, eight!" Susan forgot herself and counted out loud, yelling the numbers above the music.

You could still hear Kasha, but mostly, I could hear my own voice over the music. I didn't like the way it sounded at all, but I kept going, kept doing the choreography, kept concentrating. I never once looked out at Mom or Susan or anything else. If I could have closed my eyes, I would have. The whole time, I was thinking, *Just finish, Kayla. Just finish, so we can go.*

"Maybe, maybe!" I sang, mostly on key, then sank to my knee and stretched my hand out. It was over.

This time, there was no applause and no hoots of appreciation. When I looked at the faces in the room, the only thing I was sure of was that Mom and Susan looked relieved.

Diggity looked at his watch. "Will you need me much longer?" he asked wearily.

Susan looked at my mother, waiting for an answer.

Mom stood up. She studied me for a moment and then shook her head, her long dark hair swinging from side to side on her shoulders. "That's enough." Her voice was so decisive; if you didn't know better, you might have thought she was the music industry legend, not Dad. "Use that cut, with Kasha singing it, not the instrumental version. And Kayla, you do it just that way."

"Are you sure, Mara?" Susan looked nervous. "Lullabye said—"

"I'll deal with Lullabye," Mom said firmly. She clapped her hands. "That's enough, Kayla. You have a hair appointment."

Hours later, after a lot of running around and getting ready, I stepped away from my mirror and studied myself. My hair hung in a straight dark curtain down my back, held off my face by a silver hairband that looked a little like a tiara without announcing to the world, "Hey, I think I'm a princess!" I wore the white jeans that I'd worn to the Mickies, with a white tank top and a tailored white jacket that we'd had custom-made to fit me. For shoes, I wore the same pink high-tops studded with sequins and rhinestones that I'd been practicing with for the past week. I grabbed a pair of Gucci sunglasses and settled them on my face.

If only I could have brought myself to smile, I would have looked like a total rock star.

Dad had chartered a sweet limo to take my friends and me to the party. I've been in plenty of nice limos, but this one was blinged out in every way: an H2 Hummer with four banks of curved butter-colored seats, each with its own bar area stocked with ice-cold sodas of every imaginable kind. There were three television sets, each one playing a different music-video channel, a starlight rooftop, and the most amazing sound system I had ever heard in a car, except the Maybach, of course.

Shanita and Chemine were already inside, because they lived the farthest away, and it had made sense to get them before the others. I could tell they'd made themselves completely comfortable from the open sodas already on the little tables and IDK's latest single, "It Oughta Be," blasting my eardrums as if Terry was standing next to me.

"Oh, my gosh. This is amazing!" Shanita said as I slid in beside her. Her face lit up with happiness. "I've never been inside a limo before. It's unbelievable."

It was—and even though Tony was up front, it almost felt as if we were out without chaperones. As if we were really growing up, allowed to be out on our own.

"Let's open up the moon roof," Darryl said when he joined us. "Let's let Miami know Kayla has arrived!"

One by one, the kids from the lunch table joined us. A real party was starting in the car, and even I was starting to relax a bit. The happy mood lasted until we got to Courtney's house.

When I saw the huge box in her hands, I knew there was going to be a problem.

See, everyone else we had picked up was a scholarship kid. There hadn't been any presents—just as the invitation said. But Courtney wasn't a scholarship kid . . . and apparently, Courtney couldn't read.

She sat down beside me with that big pink box with its great big purple bow and cut her eyes at Shanita with that "Ha! See who's a real friend" look on her face. I was just done with her, right then and there.

"You look amazing, Kayla!" she cooed. "Where did you get that jacket?"

I was about to tell her how mad I was. I was about to tell her to take the box back into her house—that we'd wait—but I didn't get the chance. She made a big show of settling the present on the seat between herself and Shanita and said in an "I'm much too nice to be up to something" voice, "Oh, hi, Shanita. Be careful with the box. It's fragile!"

Shanita answered Courtney by pulling back her hand and smacking Courtney in the mouth.

The next thing I knew, they were rolling around the floor of the limo, pounding on each other and pulling each other's hair. The present crashed to the floor, and I heard the sound of breaking glass.

"Stop!" I yelled. "Both of you! Stop!"

Shanita's cute little skirt was up around her waist, and everyone—including all the boys—could see her "Hello Kitty" underwear. But Shanita didn't seem to care. She was much too focused on trying to stay on top of Courtney, and that was a struggle, because Courtney may be white, and she may look weak, but cheerleaders are athletes, too. She is stronger than she looks, and I happened to know for sure that she's had classes in martial arts.

"You bitch!" Shanita kept screaming the B word over and over.

"Get off me, cow!" Courtney roared, flipping over and grabbing Shanita by the hair.

The boys just stood there gawking and hooting and whooping as if they were at a boxing match. Chemine and Daria looked too terrified to do more than scream and scoot as far away from the fight as they could, as if it was contagious or something. It was up to me, and I did the only thing I knew to do.

"Tony!" I hit the intercom for the front seat. "Tony! Help!"

The car jerked to a stop. A moment later, the car door jerked open, and Tony loomed into the opening. He grabbed Shanita first and hoisted her out of the car.

She was a mess.

They were *both* a mess.

Courtney's bottom lip was all purple and bruised, and she had a scratch along the side of her face. One of Shanita's eyes was half-closed, and the skin beneath it was changing colors by the second. I noticed her braids looked funny, almost lopsided. It wasn't until I saw the clump of black rope in Courtney's hand that I understood why: Courtney had pulled out a track.

"What's this about?" Tony demanded. "You girls want to go home?"

"No, sir," Shanita said tearfully. "Please don't send me home. It's just she—"

"I don't care what she did!" We could all tell how annoyed he was. He looked ready to shake them. "You girls got a problem with each other, fine. But I gotta drive this car safely to Club Flamingo, and I'm not getting into an accident because of silly girl-drama, you understand?" He took Shanita by the arm. "You sit up front with me."

"But she started it," Shanita protested, until the look on Tony's face made her press her lips together.

The limo stopped in front of a small, neat house with a lot of flowers growing in pots all over its wide front porch. It reminded me of a picture I'd seen somewhere, the way the plants made vines around the railings. As I said, the house was small, but the location was killer. I suspected that David could walk to South Beach from there. He probably could have walked to Club Flamingo, too, but I guess he'd accepted the ride just to hang with the rest of us, if only for a few blocks.

Or he'd accepted the ride just to hang out with me.

The car door opened with a pop, and David slid in with a big, happy grin on his face.

"Hi, everyone!" He beamed. "Happy birthday, Kayla!"

I saw a little box wrapped in silver tucked into the sleeve of the blue sling holding his messed-up arm, but he didn't say anything about it. Instead, he settled into the now-open seat beside me. When no one was looking, he slipped the fingers of his good hand around mine. His hand was warm and soft and not the least bit sweaty.

When the car stopped again, I knew we were there.

*Hello, firing squad. Let's get this over with.*

One by one, the other kids got out, until David and I were the only ones left.

"Well," I said to David. "Now, do I finally get to hear the story about what happened to your arm?"

"Just a second," David said, pulling my gift from his sling. "Open it first. Then the story."

"OK, OK." I laughed. I pulled at the bow and gently loosened the paper. With the paper gone, I could see the writing on the box.

"Buck's Sporting Goods? What did you get me? A workout tape?"

David blushed. "That's just a dumb old box. It was the only one I could find that it would fit in."

"It's fine," I said, pulling at the tape on the cardboard.

I pulled out a lot of tissue paper. I mean *a lot* of tissue paper, considering how small the box was. I was beginning to think my present *was* tissue when I finally felt the tiny round snow globe under the wrappings.

It was New Orleans, but not the version re-created by the party trappings. There was no Mardi Gras, no Bourbon Street, no St. Andrew's Cathedral, and no Saints football. Instead, it was just the image of a little yellow house, half-covered with dirty water, with a red X signifying that someone inside had lost their lives to Hurricane Katrina.

It wasn't exactly pretty, but there was something about it that was so . . . special. I held it with the beginnings of tears in the corners of my eyes.

"I hope it isn't the wrong thing," David said quickly. He looked worried that he might have offended me. After all, it was supposed to be a good luck charm, and death and disaster aren't exactly lucky. "But I remembered what you said, about how Katrina reminded you that your family was the most important thing. That you love your dad. And maybe that's the charm—the luck—you know? Remembering who you love and who loves you, even when things look really bad?"

I didn't say anything. I couldn't.

David took a deep breath. "You said to pick something I liked, and this was the only thing I got when I visited New Orleans with my family a couple of years ago. The artist donates the money from the sales to help people who are still displaced from the hurricane, and I thought . . ."

"It's perfect," I said at last. "It's . . . it's just perfect. Really, David." I tried to smile. "But I don't understand what this has to do with your arm."

"We've moved . . ." He paused, nodding as he counted in his head. "Four, no, five times since then. It ended up in one of the boxes in my closet that I never unpacked. There are a bunch of them, at least a dozen or so. When I couldn't think of anything I could buy you, I remembered the snow globe, and I started looking for it. I was trying to reach what I thought was the right box by stacking some boxes on top of each other and standing on them—"

"And you fell."

"Yeah," he admitted with a dumb-looking smile of embarrassment. "But the globe didn't break. That's the important thing."

"You're such a dork," I said, laughing. "But thanks. I really love it. Really." I slipped the tiny globe into my pocket. "When I take the stage and you see my hand in my pocket . . ."

He smiled. "I'll cross my fingers for luck—or at least, I will on this hand!"

I meant to give him a hug, but when he turned toward me and I turned toward him and we looked at each other, there was this long, excruciating second, and then I knew what was going to happen next and closed my eyes.

It wasn't like in the movies, where the guy and the girl move their heads all around and grab each other and stuff. His lips just brushed mine, soft and gentle. It didn't last more than two seconds, and no other body parts but our lips touched. But for those wonderful two seconds, I felt as if my heart was going to pound out of my chest.

The car door swung open, and we practically jumped apart.

"Is that everybody?" Tony asked before he saw David. He eyed him suspiciously, but all he said was, "Come on out, young man."

David gave me a last smile. "Good luck," he said, saluting me with the fingertips of his good hand.

For the first time, I felt that maybe, just maybe, it would all come out fine.

# Chapter Sixteen

## PROMISE

**W**hen I heard that Kayla and some of her friends from school were getting to take a limo ride to the party, I was a little jealous, but it couldn't be helped. I was flying in with my dad and Deidre from "the road" (I love saying that!), and with my dad's security guys, of course. I hadn't heard a word from Charley yet; I was starting to wonder if I ever would. That didn't feel so good.

"It doesn't make any sense for us to go all the way to Kayla's house just so you can ride in a limo with her!"

That's what my dad said when I begged him to let me do it.

"No, Promise!" he repeated. I could tell he was getting annoyed and it was time to stop pleading. "You've ridden in plenty of limos! You'll see Kayla at the party, and that's that."

So there I was, at Club Flamingo with all the regular kids, waiting for an entourage I should have been a part of.

Club Flamingo is pretty small, but it's really funky-looking. Most of the place is pink—like a pink flamingo—but they didn't carry the concept too far and stick flamingoes all over everything, which was good. I guess they had set it up especially for kids, because I didn't see a single bottle of anything that wasn't water or soda anywhere on the long wooden bar that snaked across the left edge of the room.

Whoever decorated had done an amazing job. I mean, there was a giant float of Kayla turning in the middle of the room! There were these life-size photos of Kayla all over the walls. I didn't recognize any of them from the shoot we did together, but Kayla looked fierce in every pose, and every outfit was something I wished I'd thought to put together. There was a DJ set up just below a little strip of stage at the back, a champagne fountain spilled chocolate milk in another corner, and I saw two candy "bars" set up where the kids could eat their fill of just about any kind of candy ever made. I could even smell something wonderful coming from the kitchen.

I was so distracted by all the goodies that I almost didn't notice there was a second level to the place. My dad led us up a few stairs to a section hung with white privacy curtains. Behind the curtains were several plush pink sofas set around for conversations.

My mom was sitting there.

"Mom!"

At first, I was so happy to see her that I forgot all about what she'd done to Deidre. She looked so pretty in a fringed vest, black leggings, and heels and so glad to see me that I flew into her arms, hugging her. She rocked me from side to side in a huge embrace, then kissed both of my cheeks the way they do in Europe.

"Hi, baby!" she cried, looking me over. "I hear you're the next big musical sensation."

But that reminded me. "It would have been even better if you'd been there to see it." I pouted, pulling away from her.

Mom hesitated, and I could tell by her expression that she was thrown off balance by what I'd said. "If I'd known your dad was going to do that, I would have done my best to get there, Promise," she said, sounding a little hurt. "You know that, right?"

I believed her, but for Deidre's sake, I wasn't quite ready to let it go. "Well, at least Deidre was there," I huffed.

"Hello, Deidre." Mom leaned forward to give Deidre a hug. "How is everything?"

It was a little awkward for a second, and I thought Deidre hesitated before answering. Or maybe I imagined it, because when I blinked, Deidre and my mom were hugging, and everything seemed normal.

"Everything's great!" Deidre was saying cheerfully. "You should have seen her, Bella. She was just amazing. Amazing!"

"I'm so sorry I missed it." Mom sounded as if she meant it. "If only I could have."

"Is the movie over yet?" I demanded. My voice sounded bossy and obnoxious in my own ears, but I couldn't help it. Seeing Mom and Deidre together reminded me of all the things I wanted to talk to her about. It reminded me that I wanted things the way they'd always been, just the three of us.

Mom shook her head. "They've had to extend filming for two more weeks. There have been some weather problems, and one of the leads got sick, so —"

"So maybe Deidre and I can come up to New York and watch?" I said, taking Deidre's hand. "How 'bout it, Mom?

Now that I'm working with the tutor, it really doesn't matter where I am. I can still go to school, so—"

Mom blinked at me in surprise. "I don't know, Promise. Don't you like touring with your dad?"

Maybe I was hearing that wrong, but it almost sounded as if she didn't want to be bothered with me.

"Let's not get into that now," Dad said. "They should be here any minute. Why don't you go on downstairs and meet some of Kayla's friends? We'll be right in here."

"Yes, go ahead, Promise," Mom said. "We'll talk more later."

"But—"

"Go!" Dad said sternly.

I may not be the smartest kid on the planet, but I knew what that meant: it meant they wanted to talk—probably about what was going to happen to me next—without me around.

I clomped down the stairs, making as much noise as possible so they'd know that I didn't appreciate being sent away, and headed back to the tables. There was one long empty table right at the edge of the dance floor, and I found my name on a little card there. I put my bag on my chair and looked around the room for that girl Courtney whom I'd met on my last visit. But of course, she wasn't there.

She was in the limo.

"They're here!" The words went around the room as fast as fire, and kids—me included—jumped out of their seats, pressing toward the door to see Kayla arrive.

I didn't even see the Louisiana jazz band until they started playing. The limo door opened, and one by one, kids tumbled out. When Kayla's friend Courtney got out, she didn't hang back like the other kids to watch Kayla get out; she hurried inside the club with her hand over her mouth. The last kid to get out was the boy from the mall, but his arm was all messed up.

"Kayla! Kayla!" I was chanting it, too. This was going to be great, and I wanted to see it.

Kayla stepped out, dressed in white from head to toe. Even though it wasn't a ball gown, she managed to look like some kind of princess in her white jeans and jacket. She waved at everyone like a queen, and everyone was yelling and clapping and cheering as if we were the crowd at a red-carpet event.

And if that wasn't enough, a small float puttered around to the front of the club from a roped-off section near the curb. It was about the size of a golf cart and covered in pink flowers, with an arch of rhinestone-studded metal in the shape of a jeweled crown in the center. Below the arch was a wide plush chair in a tone of deep burgundy that looked just like every throne I've ever seen in the movies.

"Oh, man," I heard myself saying. "That is sweet!"

But it got even better.

Kayla climbed up onto the float, and as it started to move toward the entrance to Club Flamingo, she threw beads into the crowd, the way they do in New Orleans during the real Mardi Gras.

Kids were diving everywhere, trying to get beads. It was insane! I even jumped for one, and when I looked at it, I could see that every third bead had been stamped with the outline of Kayla's profile—just like George Washington on the quarter. That's who's on the quarter, right?

Anyway, whoever is on the quarter doesn't matter. What

matters is that Kayla's face was stamped on every third bead, and the other ones were stamped with either the date or the number 13.

It was wild!

The woman driving the float—she was dressed like a court jester—circled a few times so that Kayla could throw as many beads as possible. Then, from out of nowhere, other costumed performers arrived. A woman dressed like an angel and a man dressed like a Native American chief held open the club doors so that Kayla's float could drive right inside, all while the jazz band kept playing "When the Saints Go Marching In" over and over again.

Everyone crushed inside all at once, not wanting to miss a single minute. Kayla's golf-cart throne circled the room a few times and then came to rest in front of the huge Kayla float in the middle of the room.

"Thank you all for coming," Miss Fairy Princess said in a soft voice as the band wound down. "I hope you have fun!"

It was awesome. Waiters in elaborate costumes started bringing food to the tables, as everyone took their seats. I took a little slider from a woman dressed like a Vegas show-girl in one of those big headpieces and a sequined body suit. I grabbed a drink off the tray of a dude dressed like the pirate in that movie where they sail to the end of the world. The DJ started playing some hot music, and a few kids jumped up and ran to the dance floor. I headed to my seat and found Courtney sitting across from my spot. She looked a little better, except for a fat lip. She waved at me, but she was so busy talking to a brown-skinned girl with lopsided braids that we didn't really talk.

I felt a little left out. I didn't know any of Kayla's friends, and they were all so busy talking to each other there wasn't a chance for me to break in and introduce myself. I contented myself with a plate of sliders while I watched Kayla work the room, moving from friend to friend and table to table, group to group, talking and dancing.

I was starting to get bored.

"Hey, y'all." Parran had the microphone, and the DJ immediately killed the music. I turned and saw him standing on that little stage, just above the dance floor. "We got something special for you guys tonight. A special guest performance from one of Kayla's favorite artists . . ." He let the room buzz a bit about who that might be before continuing, "And then one from the birthday girl herself."

"It's Eugene," I said, catching Courtney's eye.

"Don't you mean Nu Gee?" she said, laughing. The girl beside her gasped.

"Oh, my God! You're Promise Walker!" she squealed. "Oh, my God!"

OK, so I loved that. Is that so wrong?

"I won't keep y'all waiting," Parran joked. "Come on out, Nu Gee."

Eugene came pimp-strolling out from a corner of the room just as Kayla finally made her way over to our table.

I stood up to hug her. We hadn't been on the best of terms lately, but I really didn't want it to go like that today. I mean, it was her birthday! I hoped she'd be able to forgive and forget, today of all days. And the party was the bomb! How could she stay mad with all this cool stuff happening in her honor?

But Kayla gave me the stiffest hug in the world, and when

she pulled away from me, it looked as if she wanted to crawl under the float in the middle of the room and hide there until the party was over.

"What's the matter?" I whispered. "Look, I'm sorry. I didn't do it, but I'm still sorry. I just don't want you to be mad at me anymore. At least, not today."

Kayla frowned as if she didn't have any idea what I was talking about. "I saw you on YouTube, Promise," she said in a sad voice. "You did really well. I wish—"

Eugene interrupted her. "I'd like to dedicate this song to Kayla," he said in his sexiest lover-boy voice. "I've known her for a long time, and so tonight I'd like to sing—"

"I just hope he doesn't sing . . ." Kayla began.

"'Special to Me,'" I finished for her, just as the DJ cued up the music.

"Oh, crap," Kayla hissed. It's the closest I've ever heard her come to cussing. "This is the worst day of my life. The worst."

"Come on up here, Kayla," Eugene said, gesturing to her. "Come on, girl."

People started applauding. Even Parran was clapping and smiling, waiting for her to cross the room and stand next to Nu Gee for his serenade.

"Do I have to?" Kayla looked as if she'd rather eat bugs.

"Looks like it," I muttered, giving her a little shove in the right direction. "Good luck."

It was awful.

Not Eugene—he has a great voice. And not Kayla, because I'll say one thing for her, she knows how to stand still and look pretty and hold her face as if she's not thinking what I knew she was thinking. But it was awful to sit there and watch her, knowing how fake it all was, as he made a big show out of singing his love song to her as if he meant it. I don't know how Kayla did it. I wouldn't have been able to.

"Now, I know what y'all are all waiting for," Eugene said into the mike when the excruciating song was finally over. "And here it comes."

The front doors swung open, and the lights in the club dimmed almost to darkness. There were a few long seconds when no one was sure what was going on, and then I saw the blazing lights of candles as the biggest, most beautiful cake was wheeled into the room. It looked like presents stacked into a tower, each adorned with the initials KJ and iced in the most beautiful colors of pink, purple, and baby blue I've ever seen.

"Happy birthday to you," Eugene sang, and everyone — friends and family, the jazz band, the servers and costumed dancers — joined in, filling the room with the words, "Happy birthday, dear Kayla! Happy birthday to you!"

Eugene escorted Kayla right up to the cake as if he was the royal consort or something. "Make a wish!" he said.

I took one look at Kayla's face and thought she might have wished that Eugene would just go away. But then I noticed that her hand had slipped into the pocket of that bad white jacket she was wearing, as if she was holding on to something in there. Her face sort of changed, getting really focused and determined. If you'd asked me at that moment, I would have guessed that she had made a decision about something — something much more important than Eugene.

Then she blew out the candles, and the room erupted into more cheers.

Parran hugged her. "I've got something special for Kayla," he shouted, pulling an envelope from his pocket and handing it to Kayla. "Go on, open it."

I couldn't see Parran's eyes under his sunglasses, but I know his voice, and whatever was in that envelope was something so amazing I knew I was going to have to start nagging my parents *right now* if I wanted anything like it for my own thirteenth birthday.

Kayla ripped at the envelope, and a small black card dropped into her hand. She looked at it in confusion, and at first, I thought it was a business card or something, until it hit me.

"Oh, my God," I said. I didn't meant to talk so loudly, but that's how quiet it had gotten and how excited I was. "Kayla! Don't tell me you got a black American Express card! Do you know how much money you have to have to get one of those?" I was talking too loudly, but I couldn't stop myself. "Most of y'all need to take a good look, because this is as close as you're going to get to money like that."

"Shush, Promise." I couldn't see my mom—I guessed she was still in the VIP area upstairs—but I could tell by her voice that she was annoyed with me.

"Oops, sorry," I muttered. "Just sayin'."

"I—I—I don't know what to say," Kayla said, sliding the card into her pocket. "Thank you, Dad."

"Be smart with it," Parran said in a soft, no-big-deal-voice. "Now, sit down, everyone! Get back to your seats!" He handed the microphone back to Eugene and followed his own advice by jogging back up the stairs to the balcony.

Eugene took Kayla's hand and led her back to the stage.

All of a sudden, a camera crew appeared, and I saw a bright spotlight go up on Kayla's face.

"Ladies and gentlemen, it's an honor for me to get to introduce you to the newest artist on the Big Dollar label. In addition to the party of the century, y'all are witness to the birth of the next big thing: Miss Kayla Jones!"

Everyone started cheering and screaming and hooting. I looked around a little in surprise. I guess I was the only one who didn't know this was going to happen. I turned back to the stage in time to see Kayla, holding the microphone with one hand while the other one was jammed into her pocket—what on earth was in there?—with that same determined look on her face.

On cue, the DJ started Kasha's "Maybe, Maybe."

Kayla just stood there. She didn't move or step to the center of the stage or start singing or anything. The music played and played, and Kayla stood there, not even looking at the crowd but more like at a spot somewhere on the back wall. Everyone started talking, looking at one another, looking at the DJ, looking up to the balcony, where Kayla's dad was, and you could hear the murmuring of a hundred confused voices over the music.

"What's going on?"

"Is she supposed to be singing?'

"Is it the wrong music?"

Parran hopped down from the balcony just as the DJ stopped the music. He hurried across the stage to Kayla and said something to her. She answered him, but she was holding the microphone too far away from her mouth for me to hear the words.

Parran must not have liked what she said. His voice rose just enough for the words ". . . do this to me!" to float back over the crowd.

It got kind of quiet then.

"I tried to tell you. I'm sorry." Kayla's voice was loud and clear as she stepped away from Parran with her head held high. She handed the DJ his microphone and strode off the stage like a model on the catwalk, back straight, as fierce as anything I've ever seen.

It wasn't until she descended the three steps that you could see that she was crying. She covered her face with her hands and disappeared into the corridor that led to the kitchen.

I jumped up and ran after her. I don't know why, exactly — I wasn't sure she would talk to me — but there was something about the look of guilt and fear on her face that made me start moving. I guess I know the feeling. I hoped she'd talk to me. I hoped I could help.

But she'd locked the bathroom door and wouldn't open it, no matter how much I knocked.

"Kayla!" Aunt Titi was right behind me. So was my mother. And my dad. And Parran. Titi pounded on the door. "Let me in!"

Parran sort of nudged the rest of us out of the way.

"Kayla!" he called. "It's OK, Queen. You were right not to do it if it didn't feel right. That's the mark of a true artist —"

"Be quiet, Lullabye," Aunt Titi snapped. "I really don't think that's what she wants to hear right now." She addressed the pink door again. "Won't you come out and talk to us about it? All your friends are still here, waiting to celebrate your birthday with you, and —"

"I don't think she wants to hear that, either," I muttered under my breath, but everyone heard me, anyway.

"Hush," Mom said.

"Well, it's true. If I had a bad performance in front of everyone in my entire school . . ." I shook my head. "I wouldn't come out until everyone had gone home."

I watched the adults look at one another as if they'd never thought of that.

"Do you think we should end the party?" Aunt Titi had that frown line in her forehead again. "The kids were just starting to have a good time. We haven't even cut the cake."

"Maybe y'all should just leave her alone for a while," my dad said. His voice was soft, but he sounded absolutely certain. "Give her a chance to cry it out." He shrugged. "After she gets her feelings out, she might come out on her own, you know?"

"Yeah," Parran agreed, sounding reluctant. "Maybe so." He stepped up to the door. "We're gonna leave you alone for a bit, Queen. Let you get yourself together, OK?" He paused a little, and the way his face changed, I got the feeling there was something else he wanted to say, just not with all of us standing there looking at him. "We're gonna go, OK?"

No answer on the other side of the door, but by then, I don't think any of us expected one.

"Come on, Mara." Parran dropped his arm around Aunt Titi's shoulder.

"I'd rather stay. What if—?"

"I'll stay," I volunteered. They all looked at me doubtfully—everyone knows how much Kayla and I fight—but I lifted my chin and kept talking. "Hey, I think she'll talk to *me* before she'll talk to you."

Mom laughed. "She's got a point."

Aunt Titi didn't look any happier about leaving than she had before, but with one last look over her shoulder, she let Parran lead her back to the party. To cover the drama, the DJ had thrown on some of his best jams, and the little corner of the dance floor I could see was packed with jumping, dancing kids.

I leaned against the wall and waited, watching the party from the shadows. I didn't pound on the door anymore, and I didn't call Kayla's name. I just stood there and waited. I knew she'd come out eventually. Kayla's tough. Not only that, but she doesn't like for people to know she's upset. She'd come out before the party was over, make the rounds of her guests, and act as if nothing had ever happened. I've seen her do things like that a hundred times.

I was just standing there, minding my business, when the boy with the sling loped up the hallway. At first, I thought he was looking for the men's room, and I pointed to a purple door on the other side of the hall. But he wasn't.

"Is she in there?" he asked. "Kayla?"

I nodded.

He knocked on the door, very gently, as if he was afraid she was asleep in there or something. "Kayla? It's me, David." He pressed his forehead against the door as if he was trying to hug it. "I think that was really brave," he said. "For what it's worth, I think that was the best debut performance I've ever seen."

If I were Kayla, I probably would have opened the door after hearing that. I mean, it was really nice what he said, something only a real friend would say. But the door didn't open.

"I'm going home now. It's . . ." He cut his eyes at me, and I felt like the third wheel on a date. "It's not the same out there without you," he muttered. "I'll text you later."

Then he trudged away with his head down.

He hadn't been gone three minutes when I heard the lock tumble and the door open just a crack. Kayla's tear-streaked face appeared in the opening, leaning out just enough to see me there. I thought she'd be disappointed—that she would have rather seen her boyfriend or boy-who's-a-friend or whatever he was—but to my surprise, she looked relieved.

"I hoped you'd be here," she said in a low voice, grabbing my hand and pulling me into the bathroom and locking the door behind us again. "You're just the person I need to talk to."

The bathroom was really pretty: pink and fuchsia walls, black granite sinks, and black leather stall doors studded with those brass ornamental balls that made it look really elegant. Except, of course, for the used tissues all over the floor. I guess when you're having a full-on meltdown, you don't always feel like throwing them in the trash. The room smelled like lemons or oranges or something like that. Really fresh and light and not bathroomy at all.

Kayla was a mess. I don't think I've ever seen her when every hair wasn't perfect, when her clothes weren't hanging on her as if she was a store mannequin. But now her hair was standing up in raggedy spikes, as if she'd been pulling it, and that pretty white jacket was stained at the elbows as if she'd been lying on the floor. Her nose was red and swollen, and there were puffy dark shadows under her eyes.

She blew her nose with a bit of toilet paper. I guess the tissues were all gone.

"Are you OK, Kayla?" I asked. "Everyone's really worried about you."

She waved my concern away with an impatient hand. "Promise," she said. "I need you to help me with something."

"Sure. Anything." I dropped my arm over her shoulder and squeezed, glad for once to be needed and useful. It was funny, but at that moment, I realized how much I'd missed Kayla. Even though the circumstances weren't exactly anything to post on your Twitter feed ("Locked in pink bathroom at Club Flamingo with @KaylaJones, missing #PartyofCentury," I wrote in my head, just for the fun of it), it just felt good to be friends again. "Name it."

Kayla fixed her sad eyes on my face. "Help me run away."

# Chapter Seventeen

## KAYLA

"Are you serious?" Promise's voice dropped to nearly a whisper, and she looked at me as if she'd never seen me before.

I nodded. "I've never been so serious about anything in my whole life." I felt more tears rising from the pit of my stomach. "I—I—I can't go back out there. I can never go to school again, Promise. Never!" I covered my face with my hands. "I—I—I can't go home, either! Do you have any idea how mad my dad is? He said I was making a fool out of myself and him and—"

"Parran?" Promise laughed. "He's not upset. He's a little worried, I guess, but he's not mad!"

I stared at her as if she'd sprouted bunny ears and a furry tail. "You don't know, Promise. I told him over and over again that I couldn't do it. That I didn't *want* to do it. But he wouldn't listen. JJ's off the hook because he's so good at basketball. But me? I have to be the next generation of Big Dollar. He says just because I'm his daughter, I have to have his talent. And then you go out there with your dad and do so great, and I go out and—"

"You got scared, that's all. You just need more practice."

"No. I could practice until my vocal cords are sore, and it wouldn't be any better. And even if I got better, I'd still hate it. I don't want to sing, Kayla! I don't want to dance! I hate it!"

"But you're a good dancer. I saw you with the cheerleaders last year, and you always looked fierce!"

"That's different," I muttered. "That was something I could do with my friends. It was just fun, you know? There wasn't all this . . ." I raked my fingers through my hair, trying to find a word that explained what I was feeling. "Pressure, you know? I mean, do you feel like that when you sing? Did you feel like that when you were with the LOL Girls? Or when you went onstage with your dad?"

Promise laughed. "Are you kidding? I love singing. I'd run onstage every show if my dad would let me."

I sighed. Promise liked singing, and she was good at it. Dad would probably have been happier if I was more like her—but I wasn't. No matter how hard I tried, I wasn't. She loved to be onstage, and I would have been just as happy to live my life behind it.

"I'm not like you," I muttered, and saying it made me feel as if I'd lost a battle I hadn't even known I was fighting. "I wish I were, but I'm not. Dad wants a superstar, and he's got *me* instead." I thought about the look on my father's face when he jumped onto the stage and hissed, "Are you gonna just stand there? You're not even going to *try*?" He sounded angry, but when I looked into his eyes, I only saw how hurt and disappointed he was. He probably would have been OK with failure. What he couldn't understand was giving up. When I thought of it that way, I felt like the worst daughter ever.

"I bet he never wants to look at me again," I said sadly, and I knew I was going to start crying again, even though I really, really didn't want to. I wanted to find that girl who just a few minutes ago had been so sure she was doing the right thing that she'd said no in front of everybody. But she was gone. All that was left was me, a girl who knew she'd made a bad situation worse. I fingered David's snow globe, still in the pocket of my jacket. Maybe its magic was kind of like the spell the Fairy Godmother used on Cinderella, good only for a limited time.

"I need to go," I told Promise firmly, blinking hard to keep the tears back. "I need to go and never come back."

"But running away is crazy, Kayla!" Promise kept shaking her head from side to side, making her hair—styled in bouncing curls—sway with every turn. As rotten as I felt, I couldn't help notice her black leggings and black-and-white cropped jacket. Cute, but it needed something. Normally, I know exactly what accessory will make an outfit pop, but today I couldn't figure it out, probably because my head hurt from crying. Either that, or after less than a week without fashion magazines, I was seriously slipping.

"And where would you go, anyway?" Promise continued. "You're still a kid. You can't just rent an apartment and move out. Your dad might be disappointed, but he'll get over it. So what if you can't sing? You're good at so many other things! You're smart, you get good grades." Promise reached toward the black granite countertop and grabbed a wad of paper towels and handed them to me. "And girl, nobody, but *nobody*, puts clothes together like you do."

"None of that matters," I said bitterly. Then I told her everything that had happened since the Mickies—and I used every one of the paper towels and a few more, because I couldn't stop crying, no matter how hard I tried. When I got to the part where Dad ripped up my Look Book, Promise gasped.

"He tore it up!" she exclaimed in horror. "Why would Parran do something like that? You had *amazing* stuff in there."

I shook my head. "Dad said it's backward. He said I needed a platform first, and then I could do fashion later. He said no one would buy clothes from me if they didn't know who I was already—not unless I was a real designer, that is. And since our family is known for rap and music, he said that's what I should be concentrating on. And you know what the worst part is, Promise?"

Promise's eyes were wide with pure shock as she shook her head.

"The worst part is, he might be right. And if he is, not even this . . . *disaster* will get him to let me quit music. There will be more coaches, more gurus, and more performances—until I get it right, just like David said."

Promise's eyebrows shot up, making a question mark in her forehead. "That's the kid from the mall, right?"

Even after crying as much and as hard as I had been, I had to try hard not to smile, but I'm not sure I succeeded, because Promise's eyebrow stayed quirked over her eye as if it was stuck there.

"OMG, Kayla!" she said in a hushed voice. "You've got a boyfriend! Does Parran know?"

My face seesawed between a happy smile and another round of tears. "He's not—I mean, he's my friend, and he's a boy, and I guess I like him." I thought about how it felt holding his hand and the gentle touch of his lips when they brushed mine. "*Really* like him. But no, Dad doesn't know. If he did . . ." I didn't need to finish that sentence; I could tell by Promise's face that she had a good idea of how he'd react to *that* news. I mean, I'm only thirteen. You tell your parents you like a boy, and they act as if you said you were pregnant or something. Trust me, "pregnant" is the last thing on my mind.

"Well," she said at last, "*I'm* not going to tell him. You can count on that. But he's probably going to find out one day, and then—"

I stood up and paced the small bathroom, looking up toward the ceiling.

"What are you doing?"

"Looking for a window. You know, like in the movies, there's always some tiny window in the bathroom just when the actor needs to escape."

I studied the walls, but I didn't see anything that looked as if it was or ever had been a window.

"That means I'm going to have to go out through the door. And if I'm going to do that, it'll have to be soon, while the party is still going on." I stared at the bathroom door as though I could see through it. I'd been ignoring it while I was talking to Promise, but I could hear the thumping beat of the music and the sounds of voices, squeals, and laughter. Clearly, some people were having a great time at my birthday party . . . too bad I wasn't one of them.

"Come on, Kayla! This is ridiculous."

I ignored her protest. I know Promise really well, and I know she loves two things. The first is attention, but by now, almost everyone knew that. But the second thing Promise loves is a challenge. It was probably wrong of me to be so manipulative, but I was desperate. I was determined not to face my dad—or anyone else—and I think Promise could tell by my face how serious I was.

"Please, Promise. I need you," I begged, my eyes filling with tears again. "How do I do it? How would *you* do it?"

"I'd do it like the Jenner girls," she said without hesitation, and before she could stop it, her brown eyes lit up with ideas. "Remember when Kendall and Kylie ran away to Vegas? Well, they didn't 'run away,' exactly. They went to their brother's party, but they weren't supposed to go on their own. They just booked a flight and hopped on it, and boom! Gone. And they're only a couple of years older than us."

"They ran away to family," I said, thinking, *Whom could I run to? Where could I go?* "My cousins still live in New Orleans."

"Oh, then that's really simple, especially now." Promise won't turn thirteen until November, but sometimes she thinks as if she's a decade older than me. "I mean, your dad gave you a credit card, didn't he?"

I nodded.

"And you still have it?"

I reached into my pocket to pull out the little black square of plastic. The snow globe came out with the credit card. I balled it into my fist—I didn't want to share it with Promise, it was too special—but she had eyes like an eagle.

"What's that?" she asked, reaching for it.

"Nothing. Just a snow globe." I showed it to her quickly, hoping that maybe she wouldn't be interested.

"Wow," she said softly, staring at it. "It's pretty and sad

and . . ." She stopped, seeming to struggle for the right words. "It makes me remember all kinds of things."

I nodded. "It's supposed to be a reminder about what's really important. Life and the people you love."

Promise nodded. "Yeah. I get that. Where'd you get it?"

I didn't want to tell that story just yet—I wanted to hold that moment with David as my very own for as long as I could—so I just said, "One of the kids from school," and I handed her the black card.

Promise forgot all about the globe. She was much, much, *much* more psyched by the credit card.

"Cool," Promise murmured. She kept turning the card over and over in her hands, admiring it from every angle. "OK, so grab your iPhone and book a ticket to New Orleans."

"But how would I get to the airport?"

"The same way you always do: call a car service to take you, though I wouldn't have them come here. Maybe have them meet you somewhere. At the hotel on the corner, maybe." Promise didn't say "duh," but her expression made me feel pretty dumb. "Then, when you get to New Orleans, check yourself into a hotel room." Promise grinned. "With this little baby right here." She traced my name on the card with a perfectly polished purple fingernail—and suddenly, I knew what her outfit was missing: a deep purple scarf, maybe with a few threads of silver in the fringe, wrapped in a coil around her neck.

Promise was still fixated on my birthday present. "This is *power*, Kayla. As long as you've got this, you can pretty much do what you want, when you want."

"So I just pick an airline—"

"Southeast. We always fly to New Orleans on Southeast. Their VIP lounge is really nice, too. They bake chocolate chip cookies."

"So I just call Southeast and get a ticket—"

"And then call a car service to get you there."

"A car service," I repeated. I still wanted to do it—my feelings about seeing my parents or rejoining the party hadn't changed—but now that Promise was laying out the steps, I wasn't sure. I couldn't get past the idea of myself, alone on an airplane, alone in a hotel. The truth is, I've never been anywhere completely alone. Some adult—my mom or my dad or Anne or Tony or *somebody*—was always with me. I wanted to run away, but the thought of being all alone was almost as scary as facing my dad's disappointment.

"Come with me, Promise." I didn't know I was going to say it until the words flew out of my mouth. "Come with me."

Promise likes to talk tough, but the expression on her face when I suggested action was priceless. Her mouth dropped open, and her eyes went wide. She tried to hide it, but she looked a little scared. "Wh-what?"

"Come with me. Please. I don't want to do this by myself."

Promise hesitated, and I knew what she was going to say before she shook her head. "I can't, Kayla. I really . . . I really can't."

"Why not?"

"Do you know how much trouble I'm already in?" Promise exclaimed. "I just narrowly avoided getting sent to Atlanta Prep! It's a *girls'* school, Kayla. No way." She shook her head. "No way. I've reformed. I'm walking the straight and narrow from here on out."

"Please. For me." I grabbed her hands and stared hard into her eyes. "Please. Please! It won't be forever, just a few days, maybe. Until I can figure out a way to face my dad and everyone." Tears rolled down my face again. "Please, Promise. Please."

Promise looked at everything in the little pink bathroom but my eyes. She studied the granite, the ceiling, even the door to an open stall. "Oh, Kayla . . . I just don't know. I mean, how would we even get out of here? You can't just go marching out the front door!"

"I was thinking that maybe we could go through the back," I offered. "Through the kitchen. Maybe if you went first to see if anyone's there."

"I don't think that's going to work, either. First of all, there are probably people working back there, the caterers and servers coming back and forth through the hallway. Someone's bound to see us, and the second *that* happens?" Promise rolled her eyes. "You're busted. They're not going to let the guest of honor and her friend just walk out of this place without any adult supervision. It's a crazy plan, Kayla. I was just talking—you know I like to talk. No, the only way this would even have a shot of working is—"

She stopped. The look on her face told me she'd figured it out and that she wished she hadn't.

"Tell me," I said.

Promise couldn't meet my eyes. "Never mind."

"Tell me!"

"It probably still won't work."

"Tell me, Promise! I'm asking you for help! Why doesn't anyone ever want to do what I want to do? Why do I always have to go along with everyone else's plans for me? *Why?* All my life, I've done everything I could to make everyone happy: my parents, my friends, you." Suddenly, all the tears were gone, and I was just angry, at Promise, at my dad, at myself. I kicked at the door to the bathroom stall, over and over and over, slamming it hard against the metal frame of the interior. "What. About. ME?" I shouted with every kick. "What. About. Me?" I bellowed. "Can't I do what I really want to do? Just ONCE?"

For a moment, Promise stared at me as if I'd completely lost my mind, and then, to my surprise, she laughed. "All right, calm down, already!" She rolled her eyes. "Geez, I never thought you'd be the one coming up with the crazy ideas and I'd be the one trying to talk you out of it."

"So you're going to tell me your idea?"

"It's not really an idea." Promise sighed. "It's just something Deidre said. She said the next time I needed to get away for any reason to tell her, and she'd help me figure out a way to do it so I'd be safe and my parents wouldn't be mad. And it just occurred to me that if we left through the kitchen with an adult—"

I snatched my credit card out of her hand and hurried to the bathroom door and unlocked it. "Go get her. Get her right *now!* I'm going to book us for the very next flight."

"But Kayla, Deidre's up in the VIP section with our parents!" Promise protested. "What am I supposed to say to get her to come down without all of them coming?"

"You'll think of something." I grabbed her by the shoulder and half-pushed, half-dragged her to the door.

"But what do you want me to tell your parents?"

"Tell them anything you want," I said, and the anger sputtered back to life again. "Tell them you talked to me and I'll be out in just a few more minutes. Whatever. Just get Deidre down here, and by the time they come looking for me, I'll be gone."

Promise pulled on the leather-studded exit door. "All right, Kayla." She sighed. "Just make sure the tickets are first-class. I've never flown coach, and I don't intend to start."

As soon as she was gone, I looked up the number, cleared my throat, and found my calmest, most adult voice.

"Yes," I said when the representative answered. "I'd like to book three first-class tickets on your next flight from Miami to New Orleans."

# Chapter Eighteen

## PROMISE

*I* couldn't believe any of this was happening.

First of all, level-headed, calm, and easygoing Kayla freaks out, disobeys Parran, and wants to run away from home—and I try to talk her out of it? I needed to drop to my knees and talk to Jesus, because the world was coming to an end.

*Where are you, Charley?* I thought as I moved through the crowd of kids on the dance floor toward the stairs to the VIP area. I missed him. If he were around, this whole plan would have been completely impossible. I don't think Kayla would have seriously considered something this crazy knowing we had Charley to contend with.

But it was pretty clear that Charley was through with me. It had been a week, and I hadn't heard from him. Dad said he'd asked for some time to think about whether he was coming back, but if he hadn't decided after seven whole days—after I'd sent him a present and everything—I knew the answer. He'd decided the answer was no.

Deidre was sitting with my parents and godparents, smiling as Mom told a story about something that happened on the movie set. She was stretching her face and mimicking people's voices, really putting on a show. Maybe she was just trying to keep everyone's mind off Kayla, but seeing the "actress" side of her annoyed me so much I was glad to interrupt her.

"Deidre?"

Mom stopped talking and looked at me. "What's the matter, sweetheart? Is Kayla OK?"

I nodded. "She said to tell you she'd be out in a minute," I lied. "But she asked me to check and see if Deidre had any face wash in her big bag."

"Face wash?" Aunt Titi frowned.

It was all I could think of, and if Deidre actually had some, I'd have to come up with something else, really quick.

"She's been crying and . . . well, you know Kayla. She likes to look perfect. I told her Deidre carries some of everything in her purse and that I'd ask."

Deidre's head had already disappeared into the huge folds of her gigantic black tote.

"I . . . I don't think . . ." She shook her head. "I'm sorry, honey."

I sighed heavily, as if I was disappointed, but inside I was happy-dancing around the room. *This might just work.*

"Oh. Well, do you think you could walk with me over to the drugstore to get her something? I thought I saw a Drug-World around the corner."

"Can't she just splash her face with some cold water?" Aunt Titi asked, sounding a little annoyed. "That girl—"

"It's OK, Aunt Titi. As I said, she's ready to come out. If

face wash will make it easier for her, I'll go get it," I said, trying hard to sound loving and self-sacrificing. "I know how I'd feel if I were her."

That got them. They all got quiet.

Finally, Aunt Titi hugged me. "Kayla's lucky to have a sister like you, Promise." She stood up. "I'll go with you."

"No!" I exclaimed so loudly and so quickly that all of the adults in the VIP section looked alarmed. "I—I just meant you should stay here," I said, thinking quickly. "She might change her mind and come out without it. I wouldn't want her to come out and you're not here. Deidre can come. The rest of you are too famous for the drugstore," I finished, fixing my eyes on my mom.

If she got what I was saying, I couldn't tell from her face. Her eyes swung from Aunt Titi to Deidre, waiting for an answer.

Deidre stood up. "Sure, baby. Let's get something to help Kayla pretty up."

"What on earth is this about?" Deidre asked, when instead of leading her out the front door, I hustled her down to the bathroom and Kayla opened the door to let us inside. "Just what are you two up to?"

I looked at Kayla. This was her moment of crazy; I was just along for the ride. I stood there and listened while she poured out the whole story about running away and why.

"But we can only get out of here with an adult. And we can only fly with an adult, so . . ." Kayla finished, raising her puffy eyes in tearful appeal.

I really thought Deidre would try to talk her out of it. I mean, this kind of thing couldn't have been good for her to be involved with. She wasn't Mom's assistant anymore, but would they ever trust her again if she ran off with Kayla and me to New Orleans without telling them?

No way.

I was sure Deidre would turn her down flat. I was sure she'd tell Kayla she'd been joking or something. But to my surprise, Deidre burst out laughing. For the longest time, she kept laughing and laughing and laughing, and while she laughed, I realized that Deidre was probably going to help us, even if it meant losing her job.

"This is great! Just great! The best story ever!"

"Story?" I repeated. "This isn't a story. This is for real, Deidre."

"I just meant that if you two ever decided to write a book, that would be the very best part. That's all," Deidre said, shaking out the last few chuckles. "In fact, that's a good idea, the two of you writing a book. It'd probably sell a million copies."

"Please, Deidre," Kayla pleaded. "Please say you'll help us. I've always felt you understood how hard it is to be a celebrity kid. That time you let me talk to Eugene by myself? No one's ever trusted me like that before. Please say you'll go with us. Please?"

Deidre stared hard into Kayla's face. There was still a smile dancing at the corners of her lips. "OK," she said at last, flashing us her big, gap-toothed smile. "Let's do it." She took a deep breath and stood up. "But good Lord! No wonder you two always get caught!" Her earrings—big silver coins strung together like beads—scraped her shoulder. "And that's exactly what will happen if we do this the way you girls have planned. I'm going to have to talk to your parents, Kayla. I'm going to have to persuade them to let you come to the hotel with Promise and me tonight. And you might have to come out of here first. Let them see you. Convince them you're OK."

"No," Kayla said. "I can't do that. I won't do that."

Deidre hesitated. She stared at Kayla with her eyes nearly squinted shut, she was thinking so hard.

*Good move, Deidre,* I thought, taking a deep breath of relief. Deidre was going to tell Kayla that if she wouldn't see her family, she couldn't help her. Deidre probably figured that if she could get Kayla to talk to her parents, she'd realize how silly this whole plan was.

Still staring seriously at Kayla, Deidre slowly pulled her phone out of her bag. She hunted through her contacts, then dialed. "Hello, Joel? It's Deidre Shaw, personal assistant to Bella and Promise Walker. I'm fine! How are you?" She listened for a few seconds and then laughed. "I know *that's* right," she said into the phone. "Listen. I was calling because I need a favor. I need one of your planes. Tonight. As soon as possible, like forty-five minutes. And I need your complete discretion, Joel. No one can know who's on this flight." She paused again. "Oh, no! Nothing illegal. Just a big publicity stunt. I need to take Promise and one of her little friends to New Orleans, then on to LA." Another pause. "No, no. We've already made arrangements for that. Just to New Orleans. We've booked a commercial flight to LA."

She chatted a few seconds more, then, with a girlish giggle about Joel being a "lifesaver," hung up. She pressed another contact and, as she waited to be connected, quirked an eyebrow at Kayla.

"Cancel that other flight to New Orleans," she said firmly. "Book something from Miami to Los Angeles instead."

"But I don't want to go to LA—" Kayla began, but Deidre interrupted her with a wave of her hand.

"We're not going to LA. What we're doing is throwing your parents off our trail. Every purchase you make with that thing is traceable, little girl. Immediately after you make it. So what we're going to do is send them on a goose chase. Yes," she said into the phone. "I need a cab at the corner of Twenty-second and South Beach Boulevard. I'm wearing a red T-shirt, and I'll have two girls with me. Ten minutes? Perfect."

She hung up and sighed with satisfaction.

"OK, girls. Let's do this."

Kayla threw herself into Deidre's arms. "Thank you!" she said. "Thank you so much!"

I tried to smile as if I was grateful, too, but I didn't feel grateful. This was just wrong. There was a part of me that wanted to run straight to Parran and tattle on all of us, except that I was up to my neck in this scheme. I'd lied to them, and my father's warning about what would happen to me if I slipped up just one more time rang in my memory. I wasn't sure the excuse of trying to help Kayla would get me anywhere, and I wasn't sure that I'd be in any less trouble if I stopped Kayla instead of going with her.

*Should I stay or go?* I thought as Kayla gathered herself to execute Deidre's plan. *Why is Deidre going along with this? Isn't she worried about what will happen to her job? It doesn't make any sense.*

"Something wrong, Promise?" Deidre asked with a wide, warm smile of concern fixed on her face.

"I just . . . I don't even have a change of clothes."

"We'll get some once we're on the ground in New Orleans," Deidre said cheerfully. "Now, give me your phones."

"What?" My head swiveled toward her so fast my neck hurt.

"Your phones have GPS tracking in them," Deidre explained. "The only way to disable it is to take out the battery." She stretched out her hand and stared at me with her eyebrows raised. "You don't want Kayla to get caught before she even leaves, do you?"

I didn't like it. Me without my phone is like peanut butter without jelly or cheese without crackers. It's abnormal. It's a crime against humanity.

"Give it to her, Promise," Kayla said dully, placing her own device in Deidre's outstretched hand.

I sighed and did the same.

Deidre's grin brightened to a thousand kilowatts as she dropped the phones and their batteries deep into her black bag. "Now, let's get out of here. It's getting late, and this party will be ending soon. They're sure to come looking for us if we wait too long." She turned the handle on the bathroom door, opened it, and peered outside. "OK, through the kitchen." She grabbed the last of the paper towels from the dispenser beside the sink. "Hold these over your face, Kayla, and pretend you're crying. Be loud about it. Make some 'boo-hoo' noises. Promise, you put your arm around her . . . that's it." She nodded her approval as I draped an arm over Kayla's shoulder. "Good, that'll work. And if anyone says anything, let me do the talking, OK?" She took a deep breath, then yanked the door open wide. "Let's go."

It was only about five steps from the ladies' room to the swinging doors of the kitchen, and we were under its bright lights in a matter of seconds. The food service must have been winding down, because there didn't seem to be much cooking happening now. Instead, it looked as if an all-hands-on-deck clean-up was going on.

"Boo-hoo-hooo!" Kayla wailed. "Boo-hoo!"

"It's OK, honey," Deidre said soothingly. She looked up at a harried-looking woman in chef's whites who must have been the caterer. "Teen girls! Nothing but drama!" she told the woman, taking Kayla's arm. "Come on. Let's just get you some air."

"Does she want a glass of water or something?" A young woman in a pair of black slacks and a pink polo shirt whom I recognized as one of the party planner's assistants stopped us.

"Maybe in a little bit," Deidre said, lowering her voice conspiratorially as she continued. "First, we're just gonna remove ourselves form the situation, if you know what I mean. Will you do me a favor, though? Will you go up and tell the birthday girl's parents that Deidre has the situation under control and that their little darling will be up in ten minutes?"

The girl nodded and sprinted off on her errand, while the three us moved the last few feet toward the club's rear doors.

It was later than I thought. The sky was dark, and now that the sun had gone down, the breeze from the ocean made the air feel chilly. I was wearing a little jacket, but it wasn't exactly warm. I hurried along with Deidre and Kayla, hugging myself against the cold. Deidre rushed us along the three blocks to Twenty-second Street as if the cops were after us. Every twenty seconds or so, she'd say, "Hurry up, girls!" and glance over her shoulder as though she expected pursuit.

Me, I was *hoping* we'd get caught, but I didn't see anyone behind us. The bad feeling I had about this whole idea hadn't gone away. If anything, it had gotten stronger with every hour. If it hadn't been for Kayla and not wanting to leave her alone, I think I would have broken away from Deidre and run back to Club Flamingo. I didn't do it, though. And that's how I ended up in the rear seat of a dirty taxicab at nine-thirty at night, headed for one of Miami's private airfields.

I'd never been to this one before. It felt far away, because we drove and drove, getting farther and farther from the lights of the city, until it seemed we were driving along the dark swamp roads into deeper and deeper darkness.

"Where is it?" I asked Deidre at least three times.

"Not too much farther," she answered every time, smiling reassuringly.

I glanced at Kayla, but if she was concerned, she wasn't showing it. She sat still between Deidre and me, with her hands folded in her lap, staring straight ahead. Now that her plan was under way, she'd shut down.

At last, we turned down a bumpy, rutted stretch of road. I could see what looked like a small air-traffic control tower with lights blinking at the top ahead of us.

"This is it!" Deidre said happily as the cab rolled to a stop in front of a low, flat concrete building that didn't look like any airport terminal I had ever been in. "Come on, girls."

She paid the driver as Kayla and I slid out. There was something grimy smeared on the shoulders of Kayla's cute white jacket, but I didn't say anything to her about it. I was afraid of what she'd tell me was on my own clothes.

As Deidre pulled open the door to the little building, a bell jangled, announcing our presence.

The building was part office, part waiting area, and part hangar. There was a long wooden counter in front of us, but beyond it, we could see wide glass windows looking out at the darkened runway. Through an open door to the left, I could see a tiny two-seater plane resting on the concrete floor. The whole place smelled like gasoline and oil and the fumes from engines.

A man appeared through the hangar doorway, a short, stocky black man wearing a baseball cap set far off his head and an undershirt that was probably only white the day he first took it out of its plastic bag.

He grinned, showing a mouthful of stained teeth. "Deidre!" he said, opening his arms wide and stepping around the counter to give her a hug. "Look at you, girl!"

"Hey, Joel." Deidre hugged him back. "Thanks for doing this."

"No problem, no problem," Joel said, scratching his armpit. "Wish you'd given me a bit more notice, though. I don't have anything fancy right now. The only thing big enough on the field right now is a Columbia 350. She won't do much altitude, but she's got four seats, and I should be able to get you there in five or six hours."

"Five or six hours!" I exclaimed. "But it only takes two!"

Joel laughed. "It takes two on a commercial jet, little lady. Little plane like this"—he shrugged—"only does about 190 knots under the best of circumstances. And night flying isn't the best of circumstances. If we get to about 150 knots—that's about 200 miles an hour—we'll be making good time, especially if we don't have to refuel."

"Refuel!" I rolled my eyes at Deidre with an expression that said, "Are you serious?" Then I turned to Kayla. "This is crazy. I don't want to spend five or six hours on some rinky-dink airplane, Kayla. The party is over. They're already missing us. You've made your point, so let's just go *home*."

"No," Kayla said firmly. She lifted a pair of determined brown eyes to Joel's face. "Are you ready? Do I have to sign something to pay you? Or—"

"I'll handle that, Kayla," Deidre said quickly. "Joel does a lot of . . . uh, private business. It'll be like we were never here. You girls should go use the bathroom." She pointed to an ugly brown door that someone had stuck a gold-lettered "Restroom" sign on. "There's none on this plane."

It was The. Worst. Flight. *Ever.*

The plane was clean enough, but it was tiny, just two seats in the front and two seats in the back. The seats had seatbelts, but that was just about the only thing they had in common with the kind of airplane seats I'm used to. And it was loud; I couldn't talk to Kayla over the constant thrumming of the engine. I wanted to ask her why she thought Deidre was doing this, sticking her neck out so far. I wanted her to tell me that I didn't need to be worried and that it was fine. But I *was* worried. I was worried, and I didn't know why I had this uneasy feeling in the pit of my stomach. A feeling as if there was even more wrong with this trip than the fact that I'd broken my promises to my parents and I'd most certainly be going to a girls' school when I got home.

All of that was going on in my mind on that awful plane ride, but the worst part by far was the bouncing. Every pocket of air or gust of wind sent the little plane jerking and wobbling through sky as if it was about to crash. Some of the bumps were relatively minor, just enough to keep you from going to sleep, and others were terrifying jolts that bounced me so high that I wasn't sure my seatbelt would withstand the strain, or they pulled us so close to the ground I expected to open my eyes and see heaven.

"Eeee!" I screamed every time. I couldn't stop myself, even though Joel and Deidre kept laughing at me. Kayla didn't laugh, though. She grabbed my hand and squeezed so hard the pain almost distracted me.

OMG. Can you imagine being on a six-hour roller coaster? That's what this trip was like. And it was pitch-black outside. And I was exhausted from having traveled from Houston to be with Kayla for her party. By the time we finally saw the lights of New Orleans from the plane's windows, I felt as if every nerve in my body was on the outside, not the inside. I climbed slowly out of the plane with stiff and shaking legs. I was so happy to be off that I could have fallen onto the ground and kissed it, no lie.

"Thanks, Joel," Deidre said wearily, giving her friend another hug. "Take care."

"You need a lift into town?" he asked.

Deidre shook her head. "I called for a ride. Come on, girls. It should be here by now."

We moved off the tarmac and into another small terminal. There was a big black clock hanging on the wall above a line of chairs facing the runway. It read 3:15 A.M.

We dragged ourselves through the waiting area and out the front door. To my relief, a black stretch limo sat waiting.

"Oh, thank you, God," I muttered, tumbling inside after Deidre opened the door. "Please tell me we're going to the Plaza. After that plane ride, I don't think I could deal with any cut-rate motel. How about you, Kayla?"

Kayla didn't say anything. I could tell by looking into her eyes that she was beyond exhausted in the way that crying too hard can make you feel, just washed-out and sick and empty. I felt awful for her. She needed a good night's sleep. Maybe under the morning sun, she'd feel better, and we could turn around and take a plane—a real one—home.

"I didn't want to go all the way downtown," Deidre began. "I was thinking we could just—"

"Please, please, please, Deidre? You deserve a comfortable night. And look at Kayla. She needs some sleep, on a decent bed," I couldn't stop myself from saying.

Deidre twirled her earrings while she thought. "Yeah, why not?" she said at last. "One last night."

*One last night? What does she mean by that?* I was about to ask her when she suddenly opened the limo's door.

"I've got some stuff to take care of, so I think I'll sit up front with the driver. You two can stretch out. I'll wake you up when we get there," she said, closing the door firmly. A few seconds later, I heard a pop. We were locked inside.

I should have felt safer. It was after three in the morning, and I was in a strange part of New Orleans, after all. But instead, that funny uneasy feeling stirred in the pit of my stomach.

"Kayla?" I whispered. "Don't you think —"

Kayla had already leaned her head on my shoulder and closed her eyes. "It's OK, Promise," she murmured. "Go to sleep." Her hair was warm against my cheek. "It's OK," she said again.

I hoped that was true, that it really *was* OK, but I couldn't shake the feeling that this whole trip was a mistake. I couldn't shake the feeling that all three of us were going to be in more trouble than we'd ever knew existed when we got caught.

I guess I fell asleep, because the next thing I knew, the limo was parked outside the Grande Plaza, and Deidre was leaning into the backseat, shaking us awake.

"We're all checked in," she murmured, waving a card key. "The lobby is empty, and I've told them we don't need the butler service. If we hurry, no one will see you. No one will ever know you were here."

She was right; the lobby was empty. Our footsteps echoed

on the marble floors as we hurried to the elevators. I didn't see anyone in any of those gilt-edged old chairs and padded sofas they have all around the room. Thirty seconds later, we were gliding quickly up to the penthouse.

Girl, when I saw my reflection in the elevator doors, I was *glad* no one had seen us. I looked as bad as I've ever looked, even when I wake up in the morning. Even sick. My clothes were wrinkled, my hair was wild, and my eyes looked as if I hadn't slept in two weeks. Kayla looked even worse . . . but Deidre had a relaxed and happy smile on her face. She almost looked as if she'd just come back from a nice vacation.

I was too tired to be jealous.

When the elevator deposited us on the top floor and I knew the whole ordeal of Kayla's escape from Miami was over, I surrendered. I didn't notice anything about the penthouse, except that my bed was fluffy, with all sorts of little pillows and a heavy burgundy-colored comforter with golden tassels. I stripped out of my dirty clothes, dropped them into a pile on the floor beside the bed, and even though I could hear Kayla running the shower in the bedroom next to mine, I laid my sweaty self down in my underwear and fell fast asleep.

* * *

When I woke up, there was sun streaming in through the drapes, and the digital clock on the nightstand read 11:00 A.M.

I stretched and looked around. I'd been to the Grande Plaza many times, and I'd even stayed in this very room before. Like in the rest of the hotel, the décor is very French, lots of gold curlicued furniture and dark fabrics, but it looks super luxe.

Kayla was next door in a room that was as elaborate as mine, and as much as I wanted to go in and see her, one whiff of my armpits told me there was only one place I needed to go: under a stream of hot water.

As soon as I stepped into the shower, my mind started going. I replayed everything that had happened the night before, and even under the bright light of day, it all still felt really weird and wrong. I was eager to see if Kayla was awake—and to find out if she still thought this was such a great idea. And as I scrubbed away the memory of our strange travel together, I'd just about decided that even if Kayla wanted to remain a runaway, I'd had enough. I was going to call my parents and turn myself in.

*My phone!*

Deidre still had it, somewhere in the bottom of her big black tote. I shut off the water, dried myself with a soft white towel, wrapped myself in a huge hotel bathrobe, and stepped out of my room.

The penthouse had a huge common area that was as big as most people's living rooms and certainly nicer. There were several antique-looking sofas and chairs and a gold-toned coffee table. All of the lamps had these little beaded shades, giving the whole place the feeling of a museum of another time—except, of course, for the sixty-inch TV sitting in a huge gilt chest against the wall. There was a kitchen and a dining room, too, but I didn't pay much attention to them. Deidre's room was on the other side of the suite, and that's where I was headed.

"Promise?"

Kayla was standing in the doorway to her room. She was

wearing a bathrobe, too, and I knew by the look in her eyes what she was going to say.

"This was a really dumb idea," she said softly, staring down at her bare toes. "I'm so sorry I got you and Deidre involved in this."

I crossed the room and hugged her. "It's OK. Let's ask Deidre to take us back on the very next plane. I just hope she doesn't get fired for this."

"She won't," Kayla said, determination in her voice. "It was my fault."

*But you're a child; she's an adult.* That's what my mom had said when Deidre left me in the dark at the storage unit. I could only imagine what she'd say about all *this*. I didn't want to make Kayla feel bad, though, so I didn't say anything.

"Deidre?" I called, heading toward her room.

Deidre wasn't there. The door was wide open, but her bed didn't even look slept in. The only evidence that she'd even been there was her big black tote bag, tossed onto an ornate blue chair near the window.

"Deidre?" I called, stepping into the room. "Where are you?"

"She's not in the bathroom, either," Kayla said after peering into that corner of the room.

I grabbed her bag and reached inside. "Well, at least we can use our phones. Call our parents."

"Yeah," Kayla said with a sigh. "Well, it was nice seeing you, Promise. I don't guess we'll be hanging out much until we're off punishment."

"Which will probably be when we're twenty-one," I muttered, pulling out first one phone and then the other, then reaching back inside for the batteries. "Here we go," I said at last, handing Kayla the little black rectangle that would make her iPhone come alive. "Ready?"

Kayla nodded. "One, two, three . . ."

We popped our batteries in simultaneously, and while the phones powered up, we eased them back into their covers. Kayla's was pink and studded with rhinestones. Mine was silver with the image of a crown imprinted on the back.

A dozen phone calls, most from my mom. I swallowed hard as I began reading the twenty or so text messages she'd sent.

"Where r u?" and then "Please answer, baby. I'm so scared."

The weight of her worry settled around my neck like a rock.

"Oh, boy." I sighed. "I need to—"

A sound from the doorway distracted me.

"What are you two doing?" Deidre demanded angrily, her eyes darting between us. She was carrying a dark backpack I'd never seen before but wearing the same clothes from yesterday. Her eyes narrowed on the phone in my hand. "Who are you calling?" Deidre lunged across the room and snatched the phone away from me. "You called your parents?" she screamed.

At first, I was too stunned to be scared. I'd never seen Deidre act like that. I'd never even seen her angry before. I thought she was acting, being dramatic, since she'd gone to so much trouble to help us.

"Not yet, but—" I began.

"You rat!" she squealed. Her palm flashed out, and I felt her fingers slam into my cheek as she slapped me so hard my head rocked on my neck. The sting of the blow brought tears to my eyes.

"Gimme your phone!" Deidre shouted at Kayla, her hand raised to strike again. "Where is it? Give it to me, or I'll give you some, too!"

Deidre pried Kayla's phone out of her hands and then, her fingers shaking with fury, pulled the battery out of first one device and then the other.

"Stupid little girls!" she hollered, hurling the phones across the room. They slammed into the wall and crashed to the floor in pieces. "Stupid, spoiled . . ." She whirled on us, breathing hard and angry like something wild. "What did you do that for? I knew I should have taken care of you two last night."

And then, all of a sudden, I understood. I knew what that funny feeling in my stomach was, that uneasiness that had been churning in the base of my stomach ever since Deidre agreed to come with us on this ridiculous trip. My brain started arranging memories, details, events, lining them up like the squares of a Rubik's Cube. Deidre was with me when I was robbed. Deidre was with Kayla when she met with Eugene. Deidre knew I wasn't at Riverside anymore. Deidre, Deidre, Deidre.

"It was you, wasn't it?" I demanded. "You're the leak! You told the gossip magazine all those things about us and our families."

Deidre burst into sudden, crazy laughter. "Yeah, I did it!" She leaned toward Kayla, breathing fury into her face. "I even stole your pretty pink shoes and laughed my butt off when you blamed Promise! So?"

Kayla's eyes widened with horror. "But why? Did someone make you . . . ?"

Deidre's laughter was hard and cruel. "Oh, please. No one makes me do anything. I've been doing it for years—sometimes your mother even knew it!" She exulted, glaring at me. "There was a time when Miss Bella didn't mind a little story about her in the papers. But now that she's so famous, now that she needs a bodyguard to watch over things and she's doing movies in New York and talking about moving to LA and leaving me to mind her little brat, things have changed."

*Brat?* True, I bring the drama, but that doesn't make me a brat!

"I know you are not talking about me," I said with as much attitude as I could muster. I was getting more and more scared with every second, but I couldn't let Deidre know that.

"Who else? What, you don't think so? Denial, party of one!" Deidre said, and then cackled like a witch at her own little joke.

"Then why?" Kayla asked. Her voice quavered. "Wh-why would you do that? What did I ever do to you?"

"You two don't get it, do you? You live in this perfect world where there's always enough money, and all you have to do is ask and your dreams come true. You don't know what it's like to work or to worry that you won't have enough." She grimaced. "A woman my age needs security. And security means money. The details of your silly little lives are worth money." She shook her head. "You know what I made on that last little bit, the story about you getting kicked out of school? Twenty thousand dollars! Twenty thousand dollars, Promise! Do you know how much crap I'd have to put up with to earn that working for you and your mommy? And the video I took of Kayla telling her daddy she don't want to be a singer is in a bidding war right now. Last time I checked, it was up to fifty thousand dollars. Fifty!" she concluded jubilantly. "Well, inquiring minds got to know!" She glared at them. "Do you know how much this little stunt you guys wanted to pull is going to net? And when you just disappear and I'm the only one who has any inside information about where you went and where you were last seen?" Her eyes glowed with the prospect. "I'll be famous. I'll sell my story for millions. Maybe even movie rights. Oprah will interview me. Me!" She showed her teeth, and her smile made her look even scarier.

Only one word in the whole long tirade really caught my attention

"Wh-what do you mean, 'disappear'?" I stammered.

Deidre laughed. "Well, you didn't think I would tell you all of this and then let you go home back *home*, did you, Promise? I know you're not too smart, but I didn't think you were stupid! No, it's very sad, but Kayla's little headstrong teenage excursion is going to end in tragedy." She sighed dramatically. "You see, poor Kayla was so upset about breaking her promise to Daddy that she ran away to New Orleans. She decided to go back their old house, the one that they abandoned just as Katrina hit." She shook her head. "Very dangerous place now. All boarded up. Condemned. Should have been torn down years ago. I did my best to stop you, and when I couldn't, I raced out here to try to stop you, but it was too late. By the time I got there . . . it was too late. Or at least, that's my version of the story. You two won't be around to contradict me, either."

Her phone beeped, and Deidre's personality flipped back to the familiar cheerfulness that I had thought of as the real Deidre my whole life.

"Oh, good," she said, looking at the message. "Our ride is here. Let's go."

"I'm not going anywhere with you," I said. I knew she'd probably hit me again, but I lifted my face in defiance.

"Yeah." Kayla looked as scared as I felt, but her voice was steady and determined. "We're not just going to jump because you say so. There's two of us and one of you, and we're going to fight you. I don't know who you think we are, Deidre, but we're not that weak. We're not getting in any car."

Deidre sighed. "You're right, of course, Kayla. I forgot I was dealing with Lullabye Jones's daughter. I guess you think you're an original gangster, huh? OK, then." She pulled a shiny black pistol from her backpack and aimed it right at Kayla's chest. "Does this change your mind any?"

Neither of us moved a muscle. I don't know about Kayla, but I was too scared to do anything. I kept hearing the awful sound of the gun in the robbery at the storage unit. Deidre's gun looked just like it. Too much like it, in fact . . .

"Oh, my God! You set up the robbery!" I said, blinking at her in surprise. "It was all on purpose! Leaving me in the car and going into the unit and shooting out the windows!"

"Yay!" Deidre said sarcastically. "A gold star for Promise! And—"

She reached out in a flash and grabbed Kayla by her long black hair, making Kayla scream in pain. "Nice try, you two, but no more chatting. It's time to go. We've got an accident to stage, and your ride is waiting."

She jerked Kayla to her feet and turned her weapon on me. "Get your clothes on. We'll take the stairs, and if either of you makes a single sound . . ." Deidre showed the gap between her teeth. "I'll blow the other one's head off. Got it?"

# Chapter Nineteen

## KAYLA

Because we were staying in the penthouse, we had to walk down about two dozen flights of stairs. And of course, we didn't meet a single soul. No one takes the stairs anymore, unless the elevator's broken or something. Even if we'd screamed, I don't think it would have mattered. No one would have heard us through those heavy fire doors that separate the ugly concrete emergency staircases from the pretty parts of the hotel.

Deidre kept jerking my hair, which hurt so bad I could almost forget how scared I was.

"Shut up!" she hissed at me when I cried out. She yanked my hair so hard it felt as if my scalp was being ripped away from my skull, and I whimpered again, but one look into Deidre's eyes was enough to keep me from crying out at the pain.

She looked . . . crazy.

It was weird, because she looked the way she always had. Only now there was this weird light behind her eyes that either I had never noticed or had never been there before. And that weird light said that she wasn't kidding: she *would* kill us. The thought made my heart pound as if it was going to jump out of my chest and try to make a run for it all by itself. I kept trying to think of a way to escape, but my brain couldn't think of anything but that weird look in Deidre's eyes, the ugly black gun, and the endless stairs that Deidre yanked and pulled us down on our way to whatever terrible end she had planned for us.

I glanced at Promise. The spot on her face where Deidre had slapped her was a pink stain on her brown skin. There were big tears rolling down her face, and I could tell by her eyes that she was scared, too.

My legs were hurting when we finally reached the last step, but Deidre wasn't about to let anyone rest. She pushed us through the fire doors onto the street.

After all that time on the stuffy, damp staircase, the after-noon sun was blinding. The air was heavy with humidity, even though it was only March, but that's New Orleans. In the summer, it can feel as if you're living in the swamp, because, well, I guess you are. At that moment, though, as hot as I was from all the stairs, with my heart pounding like a trapped animal in my chest, the humidity was like a punch in the gut. I felt as if all the air had been sucked out of me as Deidre shoved us out onto the street and started marching us along, glancing nervously all around her. She lowered the gun a bit, holding it closer to her body, but she didn't put it away.

"Move!" she muttered. "MOVE!"

She twisted her arm and yanked my hair again, this time so

hard I stumbled and almost fell onto the dirty asphalt. Promise reached out and grabbed my hand, and that was the only thing that saved me. Her hand was sweaty, but I didn't let go. It felt better to have something to hold on to, even if Promise's hand was slick and clammy with nervous sweat.

We stumbled along in some kind of alley behind the hotel. On my right side, I could see the brick walls of the Plaza, but there weren't any windows on this end, not until high above my head. At both ends of the alley, I could see the wide streets of downtown, but there didn't seem to be anyone walking on those streets, and there were very few cars. Then I remembered that it was Sunday and most people weren't at their jobs today. That was the reason everything looked so deserted.

With every step, glass and gravel crunched beneath the soles of my Balenciaga sneakers. That was all I could hear: glass, gravel, the our footsteps, and the sounds of our breath as we dragged ourselves through the humid air toward whatever awful fate Deidre had planned for us.

"This way!" Deidre growled, jerking her gun to steer us off to the left.

I smelled the dumpsters before I saw them, about six of them on a street that was probably just wide enough for a garbage truck to get into and out of. The smell of rotting food was strong enough to make me want to throw up, even though I hadn't had any breakfast. My nose burned, it was so bad. I could hear flies buzzing around the garbage bins, too.

I looked around, desperately hoping for a maid, a garbage man, another guest, anyone. But all I saw was an old tan Honda sitting in the alley by the fire doors with its engine running. The windows were tinted dark, and the driver inside was impossible to see.

"Get in the car," Deidre ordered.

Reluctantly, I reached for the door handle, my hand shaking like leaves in the wind. Deidre slapped it away.

"Oh, *no*, Miss Jones. You're not sitting there. You've had your last limo ride," Deidre said, laughing. "The cargo goes in the back." And as if she'd said the secret password, the trunk popped open wide.

*What?*

As scared as I was, the idea of climbing into that hot, dark, dirty trunk seemed even worse than getting shot on the street. I looked first at Deidre and then at Promise. Promise's face glistened with tears and sweat, but she shook her head a little, saying what I was thinking without using any words.

*No.*

We'd told her we'd fight her, and this was probably our last chance. In my mind, I said good-bye to my parents, to JJ and Anne, to David and all my friends from school. All of the embarrassment that I'd been so afraid of when I'd decided to run away seemed unimportant now. I wished for just one last chance to be with them all again. I knew Deidre would probably kill us, but there was no way either of us was going to get into that trunk. I might die in this dirty, smelly old alley behind one of the nicest hotels in New Orleans, but I knew I'd rather make my stand here than climb into that tiny, hot trunk even for one second. I wished I had David's snow globe—it had given me courage once before—but it was locked safely in my suitcase, way up in the lush penthouse, far above my head.

"Maybe that's the charm—the luck—you know? Remembering who you love and who loves you even when things look really bad?"

That's what David had said. I turned just a little, looking into Promise's terrified eyes, and I knew my face was a mirror of hers. I closed my eyes, asked God for strength, and stepped toward the dark hole of the trunk. I lifted my knee and bent my head as if I was going to dive inside, but I didn't. Instead, I jumped up and flicked out my foot the way I'd learned to do when you make a jump in cheerleading, bouncing up on my toes and sending my right leg out toward Deidre and my left toward the driver's side of the car, as if I was doing the splits in midair.

My foot struck Deidre higher than I meant to—I was aiming for her gun hand but ended up hitting her in the chin. She stumbled backward, grabbing at her face in stunned surprise.

I was trying to think of what to do next, before whoever was driving the car got out and we lost our advantage, when Promise rushed past me in a blur of sound and motion.

"AAAAAARRGGG!" she screamed as she rushed at Deidre and drove her shoulder into the woman's chest as hard as she could. Deidre stumbled backward another step. This time, as if in slow motion, the gun slipped from her fingers. It clattered to the ground in the space between Deidre and me. For a long, slow-motion second, Deidre glared at us both with fresh hatred. Then she lunged toward the ground while I dove for that ugly thing like an action-movie hero.

"No—you—don't!" I heard Promise scream. She jumped onto Deidre's back and started pounding on her, scratching at her eyes and her face, pulling her hair, anything and everything she could do, all the while riding her back as if Deidre was some kind of animal. "No—you—don't!"

I reached for the gun again, and I almost had it, but then Deidre's foot slid as she struggled to shake Promise off of her, and she kicked the gun, sending it skittering toward the dumpsters.

I was about to run to get it when Promise screamed, "Kayla! Look out!"

Deidre had broken free of Promise and was coming toward me, as slowly and steadily as a zombie in a movie. Her face looked like one of those ugly tribal masks I've seen pictures of in my social studies book. She was as scary as the god of death or war or human sacrifice or some other terrible thing. I couldn't believe that I'd once thought she was pretty or that I had ever wanted that *thing* to come and live with my family.

I turned around and ran for the gun, scooping it up off the filthy ground with sweaty, shaking fingers, breathing through my mouth against the horrible smell of the nearby dumpster. It was heavier than I thought it would be, and as I lifted it, my fingers curled around the trigger and—

BAM!

The gun exploded, shattering the atmosphere, jerking my hand up and down, and making me deaf for what felt like the longest time. Terrified, I dropped the weapon again, and this time, it landed right in a dripping puddle of something nasty. I'd never held a gun before, and I didn't want to do it again. I didn't even realize I'd pulled the trigger. The sound was so much louder, so much more frightening than it seemed on TV, and there was a funny burning smell in the air that mixed with the smell of garbage and made me want to throw up.

I knew I couldn't have hit either one of them—I'd been pointing the gun in the wrong direction—but I whirled around, looking first at Deidre and Promise, then down at myself. There was a part of me that was praying that somehow, by accident, I had hit Deidre, and it would be like one of those movies where at first the villain doesn't realize that he's bleeding . . . until he looks down and sees the wound. But I was just as scared that I might have accidentally hurt Promise, and to be honest, I really didn't want to see anyone's blood. Not even Deidre's.

The bullet must have lodged in the hotel building or one of the dumpsters or something, because no one seemed to be hurt.

"Get it, Kayla!" Promise screamed, running to try to attack Deidre again. "Get it before she does!"

This time, Deidre was ready for her. She whirled around and punched Promise in the gut as hard as she could. Promise crumpled to the ground, grabbing her stomach, gasping with pain, tears running down her sweaty cheeks.

That was all the motivation I needed. I pushed aside my disgust and jammed my hand under the dumpster, ignoring the squishy feel of the puddle and the sickly-sweet, rancid smell. The gun was slick, but I held it with both hands and pointed it straight at Deidre as if I meant business.

"Gimme that before you shoot yourself, you dumb little girl!" Deidre hissed.

"Shoot . . . her . . ." Promise gasped. "Shoot . . . her . . ." Then her head dropped, and she lay flat and still on the ground.

gun went off, but this time, the bullet echoed inside the metal of the dumpster, shaking it so loudly that I covered my ears and ducked flat against the ground. Then I heard it land softly on whatever mess was inside the garbage can.

"Damn it!" Deidre shrieked. She looked as if she was about to dive inside the can herself. "Damn—"

A window opened from one of the hotel rooms. "What was that? What's going on down there?"

Another window opened, and we could hear other voices.

"That sounded like a gunshot!"

"Somebody call the police!"

"H-help!" I heard Promise murmur from the ground. "S-somebody . . . Help . . ."

"Call the police!" I yelled. "I'm Kayla Jones, and that's Promise Walker, and this lady is trying to kidnap us!"

Deidre glanced around her, looking panic-stricken, then reached out as if she was going to make one last grab to throw me into that waiting car and drive away.

"Hey! Hey!" someone yelled from over our heads. "What are you doing with those girls?"

"The police are on the way!"

"Was someone shot? Do you need an ambulance?"

Deidre looked up and around her. Several people were on their balconies, looking down at us. I thought some of the windows might be open, or at least, I saw faces peering out from the white privacy curtains. I even saw someone with an iPad stretched toward us, recording.

Deidre saw it, too. She smiled a cruel smile. "This is isn't over," she hissed at me, and then sprinted like a wildcat toward the car. She threw herself into the backseat of the car, and a dead? *If Dad wants me to sing, I'll sing. I'll try my hardest,* I vowed. At that moment, I just wanted to go home. More than anything else in the world.

There were people coming toward us: hotel security in dark blue uniforms and a few others who looked as if they worked in the hotel's administrative offices, with walkie-talkies in their hands and concerned looks on their faces. The wail of sirens, faint at first, then louder, surrounded us.

"It's OK, Promise," I said, and this time, my voice was stronger, because this time, I was finally starting to believe it was the truth. "She's gone. We're gonna be OK."

Promise lifted her head. Her face was puffy and tear-streaked, and her mouth was twisted into an ugly slash of pain. "You—you don't understand . . ." she said in the softest, most heartbreaking voice I'd ever heard. "I—I—I thought she loved me," and then she started to cry all over again, big hic-cupping sobs that sounded as if they were tearing out pieces of her heart.

I knew I smelled like sweat and garbage—so did Prom-ise—but at that moment, I didn't care. I put my arms around my sister and hugged her as hard as I could. I've said a million times that Promise goes too far and that she gets what she deserves. But it isn't true. No one deserves to be betrayed like that. And for the first time, I really under-stood how alike we are. We both just want to be loved for ourselves, not for who our parents are or what other people want us to be.

"I love you, Promise," I said, the words tumbling out of me in a hurried, breathless rush of emotion. "I love you for all the wonderful, crazy, amazing things you are. And I understand how you feel, because I feel the same way. I just want to be loved, too."

Promise wrapped her arms tightly around me and sobbed harder.

"It's OK. I love you, Promise." I said the words over and over again, rocking and hugging, ignoring all the questions and noise going on around us as the police arrived and people started telling them what they'd seen. "It's OK, Promise," I kept saying. "You're my sister, and I'm always going to love you. It's going to be OK. It's all going to be OK."

# Chapter Twenty

## PROMISE

"Hi, Tia," I said when I finally got the chance to make the call I knew I needed to make.

For a little while, things were crazy. We spent hours at the police station—first just me and Kayla and then with our parents and lawyers and stuff—telling every detail of our story over and over again. They put out a search for Deidre and her driver friend and that ugly tan car, but they hadn't caught her by the time we left New Orleans. It turned out that her buddy Joel was someone the police suspected of being involved with trafficking drugs. But when the authorities raided the airfield, they didn't find anything, and he wouldn't say a single word about Deidre, even though they told him he might go to jail.

They still hadn't caught her, and that really scared me. Even though I was back home in Atlanta, in my own room, with my mom and some of my dad's security guys and even a couple of police cars out front, I would go to sleep at night and see the crazy way she looked at me, feel the sting of her hand when she slapped me, and hear her calling me "brat." I would wake up and feel as if I was back in that alley and be terrified all over again. I don't usually have bad dreams—everyone says I could snore through a nuclear bomb—but I started having them every night. I started to wonder if I'd ever feel safe again, you know?

My parents didn't know what to do with me. My mom had taken such a long break from her movie that I was worried they might replace her. And even though my dad had only canceled two shows on the tour, he was calling three and four times a day to check on me. Normally, I like that kind of attention, and I'll confess that at first, all of their hovering made me feel safe and loved. But after a while, I started to feel bad. I liked that my parents were doing exciting things, and I didn't want them to put their careers in jeopardy because of me.

And it was worse because I felt so guilty, knowing how mad I'd been at my mom because of the things Deidre had said. I'd been scared that she was going to leave me behind for her career, and now here she was, risking losing her part in her very first movie—because of me.

Everything Deidre had ever said to me was a lie. Everything. And that made me feel angry and sad and scared to death, all at the same time.

My parents were talking to each other every single day, which wasn't something that happened unless something was wrong. It would have been nice if I'd had any reason to hope they might get back together. But that's not what they were talking about. They were trying to figure out what to do about me.

"Maybe she should go back to Riverside."

"Or back to the tour."

"Or maybe it's time to leave Atlanta. Move to New York. Or Los Angeles. Or somewhere else."

"What do you want to do, Promise?" they kept asking me. But for the first time in my life, I didn't have much to say about my future. After what happened with Deidre, I just wasn't sure anymore. I mean, when you trust someone like that, when you love her and confide in her and treat her like family, only to have her lie and steal and cause trouble between you and your friends and family and then try to kill you—

It sort of makes you wonder if you really know anything about anyone. That was a weird feeling for me. I've always loved people. I've never liked to be alone, and I've always been happy to have a friend—any friend. But now I wondered if maybe I needed to be more careful. I wasn't even sure how I would go about it; I just knew that I would never trust as easily ever again.

I didn't really want to go back to Riverside. I didn't really want to go back to the tour. I wasn't sure about moving, although I like New York, and I've always dreamed of living there. I have this image in my mind of myself on the Broadway stage, belting out a song. Only now, I wasn't sure about it. New York would be a big change, and right now, I didn't want to do anything besides stay in the house, watching TV and texting Kayla.

Kayla was the only one who understood.

I didn't want to talk to my other friends, but I knew I owed Tia an apology. So one afternoon about three days after that horrible trip to New Orleans, I screwed up my courage and called her.

"Promise," she said when she heard my voice. She sounded pretty mad, and I guess she had reason to be.

I took a deep breath. "I called to tell you how sorry I am," I said. "There was a big part of me that never believed you would do anything like that, but then things kept coming up that only you knew, and . . . well, I never suspected Deidre would do anything like that to us. She was like . . ." My voice got a little shaky, the way it always did when I talked about Deidre. "She was like my second *mom*, you know? I just never thought—"

"It's OK, Promise," Tia said. "I forgive you. And I miss you! Are you coming back to school?"

"I don't know," I said. "They haven't decided yet. My mom has to go back to New York, and we've been talking about me going with her, at least for a while. She's going to be doing some auditions and stuff up there, so if I do that, I probably won't come back to Riverside until next year."

"Oh," Tia said sadly. "But if you leave . . ." She sighed.

For a few long seconds, neither one of us said anything. I started thinking about how much I had loved being the queen bee of Riverside, but I was kind of ready to move on. So many things had happened to me over the past few weeks that I didn't even feel like the same person. Going back to Riverside would have been like trying to squeeze my almost-teenage feet into baby shoes.

Tia interrupted my thoughts with a sudden sharp squeal. "I just had the best idea!"

"What?"

"Maybe I could go, too!"

"Go?" I swear I didn't have a clue what she was talking about. "Go where?"

"To New York, silly. With you! They can't expect you to go without any friends, can they?"

She got me that time. I truly wasn't expecting that. I made a noise like Scooby-Doo, a cross between a "huh" and a "what" that probably sounded really stupid. "Uhrhat? But what about your family?"

"Oh, they'd think it was great. They really like the idea of me hanging out with you, meeting famous people, doing cool things. Anything I do with you is going to be fine with them as long as . . ." She hesitated just a bit before continuing in the same bright, happy voice. "Well, you know my folks don't have anywhere close to the money you have. But that's OK, because you have more money than you know what to do with!" She laughed. "So how about it? Ask your mom and dad, and—"

"No."

Even I was surprised at how final and hard the word came out. I mean, I could have explained to her that it wasn't for sure that we were moving there. Or that I might go back on tour. But I didn't. I just said no, even knowing that she'd tell everyone at school.

And for once, I didn't even care. I mean, after nearly getting killed by the woman who had practically raised me, school gossip didn't seem like a big deal. Neither did trying to keep Tia as a friend.

"What's the matter? Don't you want me to come?" Tia asked. "Think of how much fun it will be. We can be like sisters! We can share everything. It'll be great! Besides, Promise," Tia continued, "it's not like your family can't afford to have me come along. You have the money! What you *don't* have is anyone to share it with. That's where I come in. I'm doing you a favor!" She laughed.

"No, Tia. I'm sorry," I said sadly. I was sad, but not for the reasons she probably thought. "Look, I gotta go," I lied. The truth was, I just didn't want to talk to her anymore. She wasn't who I thought she was, either . . . and there was only one other person I knew who would understand exactly how I felt about it.

*Promise to Kayla:* "U won't believe what Tia just said."

*Kayla to Promise:* "????"

*Promise to Kayla:* "If we go, she wants to move to NYC with us!!!"

*Kayla to Promise:* "That girl is tripping."

I started laughing. OK, I was alone in my room, and that probably looked and sounded crazy if you couldn't see what was on my phone, but that's what I was doing. I got that warm, happy feeling in my heart when Kayla texted things like that. She got it. She got *me*. I was sorry I'd ever fought with her or been mean or tried to hurt her feelings. After everything we went through at the Grande Plaza, I didn't think I could ever be truly mad at her again.

That's what I was thinking when I heard my mom shout, "They caught her! Promise, come quick! They caught Deidre!"

I dropped the phone and ran down the stairs toward the living room. Mom had her phone against her ear and the TV tuned to the twenty-four-hour news station. On the screen, a woman of about Deidre's size and shape shuffled through an airport terminal in handcuffs, with uniformed officers on either side. I couldn't see her face—her jacket was over her head—but I recognized the T-shirt and tight jeans the woman wore. I even thought I saw an earring swing out from under the hoodie. I don't think I've ever been so relieved to see anything in my whole life as I was to see Deidre in police custody . . . but seeing her also made me feel sad all over again. The memories of the good times we'd had got mixed up with the way things had ended. I felt Deidre hugging me after I sang with my dad, and I heard her telling me she was proud of me one second, then felt her slap my face and call me a brat the next. I almost wished for a broken bone; at least, you can get a painkiller when it hurts. What Deidre had done was a different kind of hurt, and I sometimes wondered if it would ever go away.

"She was trying to get on a plane to the Cayman Islands," Mom said. "Can you believe that? Yes, it's a relief," she said into the phone, sinking onto the sofa beside me and patting my knee. "Now maybe we can get back to normal, whatever *that* is!" she finished with a laugh. "Yeah, I'm going to tell her about it now, and we can discuss it later."

She hung up.

"Well, that's that. You may have to testify, but we'll see. Dad's lawyers seem to think she might plead guilty. There's so much evidence she really doesn't have a defense."

"Did they get the other one? The person driving the car?"

"Not yet, but I'm sure once the police have the chance to talk to Deidre, it'll come out."

*Yeah, right.* I had the sick feeling that Deidre would lock that information somewhere deep inside her messed-up, crazy brain and never, ever tell. "This isn't over"—that was the last thing she had said to Kayla. I shuddered.

"What's the matter?" Mom asked.

I shook my head. Mom was already so worried about me that I didn't have the heart to tell her all the things I was feeling anymore. "Nothing."

Mom was smart enough to know I was lying, so I quickly told her about my conversation with Tia. She hugged me. "I know this has been awful, but at least we have each other, right? And we have your dad."

"And we have Kayla and her family." I added.

"I hope you'll always have Kayla. No matter what else happens, you'll always know she won't do things like that. She doesn't need to. And that's worth something."

I nodded. "I know."

"And we have one other person," Mom said, giving me a sly smile.

The doorbell rang as if Mom's words were a signal.

Her smile widened. "I guess you'd better get that."

I hesitated. "You want me to get the door?" I asked, and to be honest, the thought brought back that little quivery feeling of fear that I'd been fighting with since Deidre slapped me in the hotel room. "But—"

"It's OK," Mom said. "I know who it is, and you'll be perfectly safe."

I can't tell you how hard it was to get to that door. I really thought my mom would come with me, but she stayed on the sofa, watching me with an encouraging smile on her face. When I finally reached it and peered through the little window, though, I understood.

"Charley!" I cried, yanking open the door to let him inside. "You came back!"

For the first time ever, he wasn't wearing the black T-shirt and pants. Instead, he wore the white TRUKFIT T-shirt I had bought him in Houston when I was touring with my dad. That felt like years ago, but it had been only about ten days.

I threw myself into his arms as if he was my long-lost brother. I hate to say it, but I even cried a little, tears of gratitude and joy.

"You're wearing it!" I said when I'd calmed down enough to compliment him. "It looks good on you!"

Charley grinned. He did a little turn in the doorway like an oversized male model before stepping inside. "Thanks. My stylist picked it. Hi, Bella," he said to Mom.

"Thanks for coming over, Charley. It looks like someone is very glad to see you. This is the most animated she's been in days."

"Well, I think she'll have fun." He looked at me. "Are you ready to go?"

"Go?" Once again, there was a nervous moment when I didn't think I could go anywhere. I looked at them both as if they had to be kidding me. "Where? Do I have to go?"

"Charley thought it would be fun for you to go to the gym with him," Mom explained. "Learn some self-defense moves."

"Though it sounds like you did pretty well without any training whatsoever." Charley laughed. "Still, it wouldn't hurt for you to learn a few tricks. That way, even if I'm not with you, you know how to take care of yourself."

"Oh," I said as my happiness dipped. A second ago, I'd been super happy, but listening to Charley talk, it seemed pretty clear that this was just a visit because he felt sorry for me after all the stuff I'd been through. I'd tried to apologize over and over again, but it hadn't done me any good. I swallowed hard, feeling the weight of the fact that sometimes if you treat someone badly enough, "sorry" isn't enough. I'd done it to Charley, and now Deidre had done it to me.

"What's the matter?" he asked. "I'll go easy on you, recruit. You'll still be able to walk when we get done."

"Look, Charley," I said slowly. "I know it's not going to change anything. I know you think I'm too difficult and a real"—my throat caught on the word—"brat . . . but I really am sorry for running from you like that in the mall. And I'm sorry for all the mean things I said to you and about you. I realize now that you were just trying to help me."

Charley lifted his eyebrows at my mother, but she just smiled.

"I think you two have things to talk about," she said. "I've got some calls to make, so . . ." She turned and jogged up the stairs to her room.

Charley sat down beside me on the sofa. "Promise, I'd love to come back. But . . ." He shook his head. "I can't come back if I can't protect you. I know you don't mean half the things you say—that doesn't even matter. What matters is that we were at war with each other, and that kept me from doing my job. See, if you hate me that much—"

"But I don't! At least, not anymore," I told him. "The problem was all that covert-affairs stuff. Sneaking around the school, hiding in closets, running my life like the military. 'Affirmative' this and 'negative' that." I rolled my eyes. "And the way you treated Tia that day. Come on, now. Was that really necessary? Do you know how embarrassing all that secret-service stuff is for me? I already know I'm different from other kids. I already know that because of who my parents are, they expect me to be a snob. And then you act like that?" I shook my head. "Dude, I don't need that kind of help!"

Charley laughed. "Well, your mother *did* tell me to ease off you a little. But I don't exactly know how to do that. I've never guarded a girl your age." He frowned. "In fact, I don't know anything about girls. I have a couple of nephews I spend time with. My brother's sons. I guess I'm like a dad to them, since my brother . . ." He paused, then finished quickly, as if he didn't want to talk about the details. "He's had some struggles. I don't have any sisters. My unit in the military didn't have any female soldiers." He laughed. "I don't even have a girlfriend right now. So what I know about girls is next to nothing."

Girlfriend? Charley had had a girlfriend? That was something I couldn't picture. I looked him over again from his shaved head to the toes of his trainers, and I still couldn't picture it. I wanted to ask a million questions about that whole situation, but then I decided maybe that wasn't the best idea. I mean, I was trying to convince him that I had changed. That I had grown up a little. A little voice in my head told me that prying into his personal business wasn't the way to go . . . and this time, I listened to it.

"I wish you'd talked to me like this from the beginning," I said instead. "I think things might have gone better."

Charley considered that. "Well, I guess we both learned a lesson, then." He stood up. "So get some shoes, and let's go. Nothing like a good workout to get you motivated. And we'll grab some dinner afterward."

"And then I guess you'll have to go. Do you have another client already?"

Charley grinned. "Well, I was kinda hoping you'd give me another chance, Promise. What do you say?"

I couldn't stop myself from throwing my arms around his massive neck.

"Affirmative!" I cried, and for the first time since the whole mess with Deidre, the world made sense again. I was with someone I loved and trusted in the same way that I loved and trusted my family. Deidre was in jail, and Kayla and I were closer than ever. I took a deep breath, then bounded up off the sofa. "Just let me get my sneakers," I called over my shoulder. "Get ready to get your butt kicked, Charley!"

I could hear him laughing all the way up the stairs to my room. Suddenly, I could imagine the three of us—Mom and Charley and me—conquering the Big Apple. The image was so clear and real I could barely wait to run and tell my mom. It was time to leave Atlanta. It was time for a new house, new faces, and new memories. It was time for a fresh start, and maybe, after all the love and friendship, the trust and betrayal, maybe it was time for a more grown-up version of me. Maybe I don't have to try so hard to get people's attention. Maybe I don't have to say yes to everything just to have friends or worry so much about what everyone else will think. And maybe, if I try really hard, I can share the spotlight with the people around me . . . sometimes.

# Chapter Twenty-one

## KAYLA

"Here's one for you and one for you . . ." I handed each of my friends a tiny black scrap of plastic as they took their seats at lunch under the gazebo. "And here's yours, Shanita, and yours, Courtney. I waited until David had set his tray down, then put his piece in his open palm.

He stared at it in confusion and then asked the question I saw in all their faces. "What is it, Kayla?"

"It's all that's left of my black card," I said proudly. "Consider it the ultimate party souvenir. My mom cut it up less than twenty-four hours after my dad gave it to me. That's all that's left."

"I don't get it," Shanita said. "Why did your parents cut up the card? What did *you* do? It wasn't your fault that crazy lady kidnapped you."

I scooted into a spot next to her. "Well, actually, it kinda was. Now for the story you *won't* see on the news—but if I read this on any blog, I'll know it was one of you." I glared at each of them. "And I know where you live!"

So I told them everything, including how my dad wanted me to be a singer and that's why I'd had to quit cheerleading, because of the voice lessons with Ms. Aurora.

I told them about all of the stupid things I'd done and what my parents said and how I'd decided to try to run away. Even though a lot of the story was scary, I was happy to tell it. The only thing that would have made it better would have been for Promise to be there.

"I bet those kids at school all think you're Little Miss Perfect, too," Promise had said last night when we talked on the phone. We'd been talking and texting a lot since the whole ordeal. The experience was horrible, but the silver lining was Promise. I felt connected to her in a way I hadn't felt since before middle school, a long time ago, when we were little kids and we didn't know or understand all the stuff I did now. "They'd never believe you had anything to do with what happened. I'm not saying you have to screw up as much as I do, but people like you better when they know you make mistakes, too."

Promise says a lot of crazy things, but she can also make a lot of sense if you take the time to listen to her.

"You didn't!" Shanita's eyes got wide when I got to the part about using the credit card. "Oh, my God! You used the card to buy the airplane tickets!"

The kids barely ate their lunches. I tried to "bring the drama"—the way Promise would have done—and at the part where Deidre pulled a gun on us, Courtney grabbed Shanita's arm in terror.

"Wow," David said when I was done. "You guys were brave."

"I'd have been terrified," Courtney said.

"Me, too," Shanita agreed.

I was going to tell them how scared I'd been, but the bell rang signaling the end of lunch, and it was time to get to class.

"You know something," Shanita said as the other kids dispersed. "I've always been a little jealous of you, Kayla. I mean, you're pretty, and you're smart, and you're rich and even famous. Seems like you've got everything a girl could want. But I never thought about all the ugly sides to your life. About the pressure to be successful like your dad or about people wanting to hurt you and all that." She shook her head. "I guess everybody's life is hard, it's just hard in different ways." She wrapped her arms around me. "I'm glad you're OK."

"Hey, Shanita! Come on! We'll be late!" Courtney called from across the quad.

What? Courtney waiting up for Shanita? I looked around, half expecting to see snow falling on this warm Miami afternoon.

"What's the matter?" Shanita asked.

"Since when are you two friends? Have I been gone that long?"

Shanita grinned. "We made up at your party. After what happened in the limo, we both felt pretty bad. So we just sat down and tried to talk it out. You probably missed it because, well, you know, having to go on the stage and all that," she said tactfully. "But she's not so bad. She's convinced me I should try out for cheerleading next year. See ya!"

Shanita darted away from me, and David stepped into her spot. His cast wasn't bright white anymore; in fact, it was starting to look kind of old and dingy compared with all the different colors of marker that covered it. Other than that, though, he looked exactly the same as the last time I'd seen him, which, if you didn't count English class, was in the limo when we kissed.

"You seem different," he said at last. "In a good way."

"I feel different," I said, and I meant it. "There's nothing like escaping from a maniac to help you build your confidence!"

David laughed until he saw the way I was looking at him. "What?" he asked.

"There's something I want you to do for me after school," I told him in the most serious and grown-up voice.

"Sure. Anything."

"You might not say that when you hear what it is."

David's grin slipped a bit. "What is it?"

"I want you to meet my father."

David blinked a little. I mean, he's seen my dad before, but he's never really said hello or anything. And I know some people find my dad's looks a little scary—something about those tattoos and the platinum teeth and all that.

"OK," he said at last. "But why?"

I shrugged. "It's something we decided after the whole thing with Deidre: to be honest with each other. Really honest. He said he would try to listen to me better and to appreciate what was important to me. And . . ." I felt my cheeks getting a little warm, but I pressed through it. "And you're important to me."

David still looked kind of as if he was being asked to eat bugs, but he took a deep breath and nodded. "OK. When?"

"After school. Today."

When Tony came for me after school, David trudged along behind me to the car. I wanted to reassure him, but to be honest, I couldn't. I really wasn't sure how this was going to go.

The car door swung open, and Dad was slumped in the back with his shades on, the stereo blasting a tune I knew he'd been working on in the studio for the past couple of weeks. He'd told me once that he'd imagined me singing it and even showed me the latest version of the lyrics. And if it meant that much to him, I would try. I remembered the promise I'd made to myself when I thought I was going to die, and I would honor it. Music's not my thing, but my dad is. I would try, and this time, I would give it my all.

Dad smiled when he saw me, but the smile quickly faded as David leaned in behind me.

"Dad, I want you to meet my friend David Levine. You saw him at my party the other night . . . but I wanted you to actually meet him."

"H-hello, sir," David stammered. He looked as if he was sweating, and that wasn't just because of the warmth of the Miami afternoon. He stretched out his hand as if he thought it was the right thing to do, and for a while, it hung there while my dad looked first at me and then at him. He took off his sunglasses and wiped his eyes with his hand, as if there might be something wrong with them, then looked at us both again.

"Hi there," Dad said at last. He took David's hand and gave it a quick shake.

"It's very nice to meet you," David said nervously, and then the three of us just looked at one another for a few weird seconds, until David said, "My mom's going to be looking for me. I gotta go. Nice to meet you, Mr. Jones. See you tomorrow, Kayla."

"Nice to meet you, too, David," Dad muttered, but his eyes were eating a new hole into the side of my face.

"'Bye, David," I said, and climbed into the car. I watched him dart across toward a silver minivan and toss his backpack in the rear before climbing into the passenger seat.

"OK . . ." Dad said with a long exhale. "Who's that?"

"David," I repeated, trying not to smile too big. "He's my friend."

"I see . . ." He sighed and didn't say anything for a long time. Then he settled his sunglasses back on his face. "Kayla, I know it's normal for girls your age to get interested in boys. I just don't want you to get sidetracked. I have big plans for you, Kayla Jones. Big, big plans."

I sighed. I wished I could be more enthusiastic, but I pushed that halfhearted feeling down deep inside and tried to smile. "I know, Dad. But maybe I should just forget the singing. Maybe I'd be better at rapping or—"

Dad stopped me with a wave of his hand. "No, Kayla," he said in his soft, not-much-going-on voice. "Not music. I'm gonna move on from that. We're gonna let that go."

My head swung toward him in surprise. I'm pretty sure my mouth was open so wide I could have swallowed one of JJ's basketballs. I was too shocked to say anything, so I just sat there with my eyes wide and my mouth open and waited for him to tell me what he was talking about.

But Dad didn't say anything for a long time. He kept staring at me as if he was waiting for *me* to say something first. Finally, though, he swept his ball cap off his head, showing the faint outlines of his tattoos. "You know something, you really are growing up," he said at last. He put his cap back on and rubbed his hands together. "OK, Kayla," he began with a sigh. "This is hard for me to say, but . . . we're trying to play it straight up, so here it is. I think part of this whole thing is my fault."

I was getting ready to point out that it was my bright idea to run away and that he hadn't had anything to do with that, but he stopped me.

"If I hadn't pushed you so hard on the music stuff . . ." His voice got even softer. "Well, that stuff with Deidre probably wouldn't have happened. If you hadn't felt like I wasn't listening . . ." He shook his head and turned toward the window for a long time. When he spoke again, I understood he was trying hard not to cry. "I almost lost you because I was being so hard-headed about what I wanted for you and what I thought you needed to do that . . ." He couldn't finish but instead took my hand and squeezed it hard.

I squeezed back, feeling tears rising in my eyes. I was about to tell him again how much I loved him and how sorry I was, when he cleared his throat. "If I had a dollar for every time someone told me I wouldn't make it. That I was doing it wrong. That I didn't have the right stuff to make it. Wait, I *do* have a dollar for every time someone said that, and people are still saying it, even though Big Dollar is making bank now. The point is, people will always want to tell you your vision is wrong. Part of being successful is knowing when to listen to 'em and change your game . . . and when to tell 'em to kick rocks and stick to your guns. You had the good sense to fight for your own dream and to stand up for it, even when everyone else—especially me—was trying to get you do something else. And that's why I'm giving you this back."

He reached behind him and pulled out a plain black notebook. It wasn't anything special at all on the outside, and at first I didn't understand. I just sort of stared at him until he said, "Open it."

I turned the cover. I recognized first one image and then another: girls from magazines, drawings of my own, plans for outfits I hoped I'd wear someday, all carefully and lovingly glued back together on the pages inside.

"It's my Look Book!" I exclaimed. "But I thought—"

"Tony collected up the pieces, and he was gonna throw them away, like I told him to do. But then he said one of the drawings caught his eye. This one." Dad thumbed through the book to one of my hoodies. "Seems his daughter's been looking for something like this, and he wanted to find out where to get it. But he knew it was kind of a sensitive subject, so he didn't ask me. He asked your mom. She said you designed it and that it he couldn't buy it anywhere and asked for the rest of the pieces. She's smart; she knew how much time you'd spent on it, and I guess she figured one day I'd regret ripping it up like that."

He rubbed his face as if the memory of that awful day bugged him as much as it bugged me.

"She didn't tell me that story until we thought you were . . ." He stopped, avoiding another painful subject. "So, anyway, I started thinking about it. And I realized how many times people want what you're wearing. Like Khrissy. And at your birthday party, Bella asked about one of the outfits in your pictures, and your mom said you'd designed that one, too. Somehow they got to talking, and it came out that the girls and the mothers are always asking where you get stuff, and . . ." Dad tapped the side of his head. "Well, I didn't think I was paying attention, but after all that Deidre mess, I remembered it, and I started to think differently about you and this whole modeling and fashion thing."

I couldn't believe my ears. My heart started to pound harder than the bass line in some of my dad's music. I leaned so far toward him in my excitement that the seatbelt stretched nearly to its limit. "Oh, my God . . . oh, my God!" I exclaimed, bouncing up and down in my excitement. "You mean you'll let me model for Khrissy's line after all? You're going to let me do it?"

Dad shook his head. "Nah. That's too small for you. Why model for someone else when you can model your own stuff? Khrissy isn't the only one who can have a fashion line, Kayla. You could have your *own* line."

I sat there, looking at him as if he'd just said I should find a sewing machine and make tiny costumes for Santa's elves or something.

"B-but—but," I stammered, trying to sort through the millions of thoughts that were zooming around in my head. On the one hand, I was so psyched I could hardly see straight. Outfits started rotating in my head, outfits in all colors, with all kinds of fun accessories dancing along with them. But then there were all the things Dad had told me in the past, reasons it would never work—at least, not until I was better known.

"But—but—but I thought you said I needed the music first. To build a platform."

Dad waved that away. "*I* got a platform you can borrow.

Big Dollar Records is about to launch a clothing line, designed by my daughter, Kayla Jones."

My expression must have been pretty hilarious, because he started laughing.

I couldn't believe what I was hearing. It was my dream . . . but bigger and better than I could have imagined. Visions of girls my age strolling around in the looks I'd created filled my brain.

"My own clothing line! Like Mary-Kate and Ashley!"

"No, not like Mary-Kate and Ashley. We don't do nothing copycat. Like Kayla Jones—an original."

Happy doesn't begin to describe how I felt right then. I don't think there's a word for the feelings of joy, gratitude, and excitement that were building up in my heart. I threw my arms around my father's neck.

"You're the best dad ever," I told him, kissing his cheeks over and over and over. "I'm going to make you proud, you'll see!"

He grinned as if I'd just presented him with a Mickie, a million dollars, and a Miami Heat victory, all at the same time. "I'm already proud, Kayla. Win or lose, it's all the same to me. You're a star, and I'm always going to be your biggest fan." He nodded toward the Look Book. "Now, don't you have work to do?"

"Yeah," I said, grabbing my backpack for a pencil and my phone. "But there's somebody I need to call first."

"Who's that, Madam Executive?"

"Promise. When she hears this, she's going to *freak*! She's been dying to have one of those hoodies, too."

"She'll get the first one, then," Dad said. "Be your very first customer."

He slid back into his seat and opened his arm, making a spot for me right at his shoulder, and watched as I dialed.

"Promise!" I said into the phone. "You'll never guess what I'm going to get to do!"

We must have talked for the rest of the ride home, about our news, about school, about Deidre being arrested. I wanted to tell her that I'd introduced my dad to David, but that would have to wait until later, just before bed, when we could talk or text without POS—parent over shoulder. Before I knew it, Tony was pulling up in front of my mom's house.

"I gotta go do my homework," I told Promise.

"Me, too," she said with a sigh. "I'm not going back to Riverside, but I'm gonna be tutored until Mom finds me a school in New York. You want to come to Atlanta this weekend? I think I'm going to try to write a song, put some of the feelings and things I've been going through on paper, you know?"

"I think that's a great idea," I agreed. "I'll ask, but I probably can."

"Charley says he'll take us to the mall," she said, and we both burst out laughing, remembering the last time that had happened, until Promise added, "Just you and me, though."

I knew what she was saying. There was no need for a Tia or a Courtney anymore. We'd let a lot come between us, but looking back, none of it had been important. What was important was that we were two girls with a lot of the same privileges and challenges. We were girls who would always have to measure up to our famous parents. We were two girls who would always have to wonder whether the people in our lives liked us for ourselves or because of who we were related to. But we were also two girls with opportunities most girls only dream of—and together, we were going to build on what our dads started.

We're the daughters of celebrities, but at the end of the day, it's not the red carpets or the cameras that make Promise and me who we are. It's the love we share for our families and for each other.

I grabbed my pencil and made a quick note in my Look Book: "Paparazzi Princesses." Sounds like a good name for a fashion line to me.